10738975

Retreat

The Obscured Series
Book Four

C. M. Boers

Dedication

For one of my biggest fans,
who tells everyone he meets about his Momma that writes.
It's truly the biggest compliment. Your excitement for the
world is infectious.
I love you P.

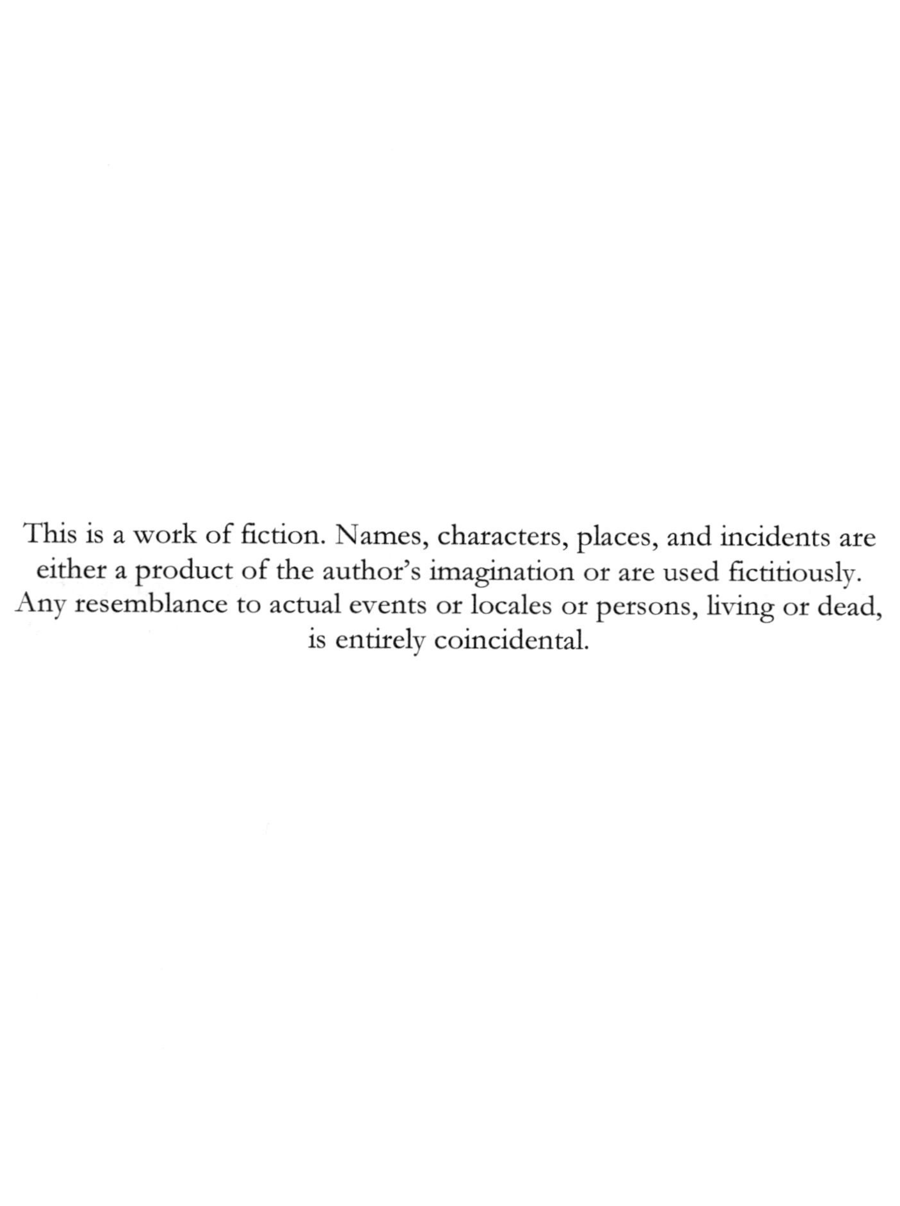

Table of Contents

CHAPTER ONE

My heart raced in the darkness. I felt cornered with no escape. I took a few steps. My footsteps echoed around me. The room sounded huge, yet still felt as if the walls were closing in on me. I held my arms out in front of me, testing the ground with my feet. Hard. Concrete.

I shook my head, trying to recall what led me here, but everything blurred in my mind.

This is wrong.

Disoriented . . .

Alone . . .

I need to get out. I shouldn't be here.

A door opened behind me. Light engulfed the other half of the room, revealing nothing but empty space and the furthest wall. I swiveled around on my heel to face the light. A figure stood in the doorway, looking in. I shrank away until my back slammed against a wall.

No.

Taking the only opportunity, I looked around using the only shred of light I had . . .

I sat up fast, breathing hard. Sweat dripped down my forehead. Throwing back the covers, I fanned my legs.

"Hot," I breathed to myself.

My newest reoccurring nightmare was beginning to take shape, and it was really getting under my skin.

Months had passed since the hearing with the elders, yet when I thought back to that day, I could still feel their penetrating gaze as they looked down on me. My mouth still went dry thinking about retelling all the events that led up to that moment. *"And then . . . he threw me from the train . . ."*

My words echoed in my head. I shuddered. Their ruling that day was exactly what I'd hoped for ever since he turned his back on me.

Guilty.

Eli had been stripped of his immortality, and all of his gifts. He was sentenced to working at the elders' compound, a place I hadn't even known existed. I think they mentioned something about cleaning. But I stopped listening after I heard "life sentence." All that mattered was that I never saw him again. Never again would I have to look at the face that deceived me, sent who-knows-how-many goons to follow me, and then tried to kill me.

I walked out that day feeling victorious. He was out of my life for good, and I couldn't be happier. The worry, however, that one of his goons might come out of hiding always tingled in the back of my mind.

I grabbed my bag and headed to the door. If only school could distract me from the nerves in the pit of my stomach. At eight o'clock tonight, I would meet with Lucian—who might be my one chance to fine-tune these nightmares. I could think of nothing else. I feared that my gift wouldn't work the same as his and he wouldn't be able to help me.

Of course, there were good thoughts mixed in there too. With his help, I might stop something bad from happening. Then my anxiety filled me all over again like some never-ending toilet flush of emotions.

Christmas was just weeks away, which also meant finals and study-cram sessions were in full swing. For the first two classes of the day, we studied, making it hard to think of anything except math, science, and my empty stomach. In third hour, Bailey and I were able to collaborate on a book report we were writing together, which really meant we chatted since the report was already done. The hour flew by.

"We need to go dress shopping! The dance is in two weeks! When can you go?" Bailey asked as we gathered our things and left the classroom.

"Ah . . . next weekend." Part of me knew I'd been putting off going shopping because I knew Casey couldn't attend—school rules since he wasn't a student. But I couldn't put it off any longer.

"*Yes!* Finally!" She arm pumped her excitement.

A few people looked our way.

"Shh!" I giggled.

Bailey covered her mouth. "Oops."

Alexis and Breanne joined us just outside the classroom.

"What's *oops?*" Alexis asked.

"Oh, we were just talking about the dance," Bailey said.

"Ooh, are you all going?" Alexis clapped her hands.

"Oh, I am," Bailey giggled. "I just have to make sure Ryan knows."

Listening to the girls talk about their dates made me feel somehow detached from them.

"If I can find a date," Breanne said next, her voice timid.

"You've still got time," I said, hoping to encourage her.

"Just a few weeks!" Alexis said. "I can't wait. I'm so not bothering with a date. Who wants to only dance with one guy the whole time? *Boring*."

We all giggled. *Boy-crazy Alexis.*

"I still can't believe it's already December," Breanne said. "Feels like the school year just started."

"I know what you mean." I ran a hand through my hair.

We walked together to lunch, and my phone rang. I checked the screen. *Casey.*

"I'll meet you in there," I said to them and waved at them to go ahead.

Bailey raised her eyebrows twice and flashed an amused smile.

"Ooooh, the boyfriend!" Alexis sang.

Breanne just giggled, blushing.

I shook my head and turned away. "Hello."

"Hey," Casey's smooth voice came through the phone. "You're at lunch, right?"

"Yep."

"Good. Come outside."

A smile formed on my lips. "What are you up to, mister?"

"Oh nothing . . ."

I burst through the front doors and saw Casey sitting on a blanket in the grass. A small cooler perched next to him.

"Casey! This is so sweet."

I knelt down, threw my arms around his neck, and gave him a kiss, pulling back slowly to stare into his eyes.

"It's nice to see you too." A smile tugged at his lips.

We sat up, and Casey started pulling things from the cooler. Two sodas, two salads, dressing, and cookies.

"I figured since you have the meeting with Lucian tonight, you might be nervous so I thought I'd bring you lunch and maybe help you forget for a while. Plus, I won't get to see you tonight, and I missed you."

"Aww . . . I missed you too. You're the best. Seriously." I picked up the salad he gave me and started eating. "So, what are you going to do tonight?"

"The guys are going to go fishing." He made a face. "Figure I'll tag along. I'm not much for fishing, but it's fun watching them try."

I giggled. "I don't see Ferdinand fishing."

Casey leaned over, "He's part of the reason it's so fun to watch."

I pictured Ferdinand in a fishing hat with lures hooked to it and laughed harder.

"Are we still on for dinner tomorrow night?" he asked, taking a bite.

"Planning on it."

"Good."

I'd finished a little over half of my salad when the warning bell rang.

"Shoot, I've got to go," I said.

"Here, take the cookies with you." He handed me the bag.

"This was the best school lunch I've ever had. Thank you." I gathered up all my things and stood.

Casey gave me a quick squeeze and kiss before he let go.

"Bye," I said.

The rest of the day, all I could think about was Casey and that lunch. The overly thoughtful gesture made my heart melt. Once in a while, thoughts of Lucian popped into my head, making my head a jumble of everything but school. It was hard to focus.

With my change of clothes packed in my trunk, I drove straight to the coffee house from school.

It wasn't long before I stood at the counter, mindlessly wiping it down over and over, the distant hum of Christmas music crooning overhead.

What will today bring?

This could turn out to be one of the best things to happen to me. I could gain control over the dreams or even some insight into how to unlock their mysteries. It would make my life that much easier.

I watched the clock throughout my shift, waiting for the time to come. The second the small hand struck eight, the door opened, and a man walked in. His black hair was slicked back, and the sides were shaved. He looked like he could have just stepped off the runway in his black shirt and designer jeans. He didn't have to introduce himself; I knew it was him right away. The power that emanated from him was familiar, something I'd come to recognize as distinctively Protector. I clocked out and made a beeline for him.

"Hi, you must be Lucian. I'm Abby." I extended my hand, but he embraced me in a big hug. My hands awkwardly pressed into my sides, and my face smashed against his solid chest.

"One thing you'll learn fast about me, Abby, I'm a hugger." He pulled away, grinning at me. "Shall we?"

I led the way out the door, then realized I didn't know where we were going. I turned back toward him to ask, but before I could formulate the question, he spoke.

"Why don't we go somewhere a little more private?" He held out a remote, and an all-black sports car with all-black wheels flashed its lights. My lips curled. It was him in car form.

He opened my door for me and waited until I slipped both feet inside before closing my door and strutting to the other side. The engine revved to life, and I could feel the rumble of the exhaust underneath me. We flew backward, then shot into drive. It didn't take a genius to figure out Lucian liked to go fast. Very fast.

"So, where *are* we going?" I asked, hoping to focus on something else. Anything to keep my stomach from lurching into my throat as we gained speed. I gripped the door handle.

"Somewhere private." He grinned.

It surprised me how comfortable he was making me squirm after meeting me just minutes earlier. I got the impression he was used to getting a rise out of people and enjoyed it.

"People just go wherever you want?" I asked in a teasing voice.

He raised an eyebrow, and a half grin appeared on his face. "Maybe . . ."

I sighed, rolling my eyes.

"What? You don't trust me?"

"What is it with you Protectors and blind trust?" I turned to face him. "I mean, seriously, do you know how many Protectors have said that to me?"

"Have any of them steered you wrong?" A cocky smile was still on his face.

I thought for a moment. "No," I said. "Well, yes."

He raised a brow. "Which is it?"

"It's complicated."

"Maybe it's time to uncomplicate things and give blind trust a chance."

I crossed my arms. "Eli tried to get me to trust him exactly as you're suggesting, and look how that turned out."

He stopped smiling. "I'm sorry."

Lucian drove another ten minutes before he turned off into a neighborhood that looked run down. He wound his way through the streets like he could do it with his eyes closed and stopped in front of a house on the end. A chain-link fence separated the neighborhood from an industrial park.

What an eyesore.

He pressed a few buttons on his phone, and the garage door began to lift, slowly at first, then quickly as if a weight had been lifted off of it. He swung the car into the garage and shut the door behind us. He cut the engine before the door closed all the way. The sudden quiet of the garage after the rumble of the exhaust triggered goosebumps on my arms.

I smacked my lips. "So . . . now what?"

"Now we go inside." He grinned. I could sense sarcasm in his voice.

He pressed the unlock button on both our seatbelts and climbed out. When I looked around at the garage, it seemed enormous, certainly not the two-car garage it appeared to be from the outside. I spun around, examining it all.

"This is impressive," I said.

"Eh, it's functional," he said, shrugging.

I shook my head and rolled my eyes. *Modesty.*

"You coming?" He stood in the doorway.

"Ah, yeah." I took one last look and followed him.

He held the door open, leaving a wide space for me to pass through. My jaw dropped the second I was inside. The living room boasted floor-to-ceiling windows, but that wasn't what caught my attention. The view outside the windows captivated me above all else. Waves crashed on the beach as the last of the sun's rays disappeared in the distance. The dull glow that remained in the sky highlighted the white-tipped waves, making the water look as if it were dancing.

Absently, I stumbled to the window, dropping my purse as I walked, gawking at the sandy beach.

"I take it you like the beach?" he said.

I nodded.

"Want anything to drink?"

"No, I'm okay. Is that real out there?"

The beach called to me like a long-lost friend.

He gave me a strange look. "Of course."

This was another amazing Protector endowment—not some smokescreen but a portal somewhere else. I couldn't believe it. Nothing would ever compare to this.

He leaned back against the counter with his arms crossed.

"Where are we?" I asked.

"Florida."

My hand fumbled for the latch to the door. I couldn't resist the urge to go outside. Leaving my flip flops on the deck, I sank my feet into the warm sand and let the cool ocean breeze wash over me. My eyes closed as I breathed in the salty air. *God, I missed this.*

My whole reason for being here was momentarily forgotten as the serenity of the beach relaxed me.

A few minutes later, Lucian sat down on the deck, his chin propped in his hand. He waited patiently with a smirk. My cheeks warmed.

I lifted myself up and pulled my feet from the sand, feeling strange for making myself so comfortable.

"Sorry." Blushing, I stepped back into my shoes.

"Don't let me stop you from your fun," he said.

I was beginning to wonder if his sly grin ever faded or if he just enjoyed teasing me too much.

"Should we get started?" I asked.

"Out here or inside?"

A sheepish smile formed as I turned toward the ocean.

"Guess that answers my question."

He leaned forward to pat the chair next to him. Leaving my flip flops where I stood, I made my way over and sat down.

"Why don't you start by telling me about yourself and your problem."

I fiddled with my hands.

"I'm from California, thus the obsession with the beach. I moved here a year ago when my parents got divorced—my mom's choice, not mine. My dreams started right before I moved here. Of course, I didn't think much of them at the time. My dreams continued through all the drama with Pete and Eli, if you know about that. Three of them have come true. The fourth and most recent started a few months ago."

"From what Edward says, these are bad dreams, is that right?"

"Yeah. Life-or-death moments, at least so far."

"Mine started like that as well. Over time, they evolved to include other important moments. For example, big moments for those around me. As I grew older, they included events that weren't in any way related to me. Those are especially hard because often I haven't met the individuals involved."

"So, what do you do?" I asked.

"Well, in those cases, there isn't a whole lot I can do, but I still try. Just like for the other dreams, I make a list of every detail I can recall when I wake. The lighting. The surroundings. Everything. Sometimes I can figure out the location from memory. Other times, nothing kicks in until right before it unfolds in real life."

"That's it?"

"Well, no. But the rest will take time and training."

"The places you've been are easy to spot in your dreams?" I asked.

"Sometimes." His face wrinkled. "That's not going to work in your favor since you haven't lived here very long."

"Great." I sighed.

"Hey, it may seem like there's a lot stacked against you right now, but you aren't alone. You've got a lot more help than I ever had."

"Really?" I asked.

He nodded. "It's going to take work, but eventually you'll get it."

I sighed and ran my hands through my hair.

"Relax. There isn't a sure-fire trick to get the job done. I'll help you the best I can. If my tricks don't work, I'll keep trying to find something that does."

"Why?"

"Why what?" His brows furrowed.

"Why would you try so hard to help me? You don't even know me." I glanced out at the crashing waves to avoid his stare.

"You say you've been around Protectors a lot, yet you still have to ask?"

I turned back to him, my expression flat. "You could say I have issues believing what people say."

He chuckled. "Edward said you'd been through a lot. I guess I should have known. So, what do you want to know?"

I scrunched up my face.

Lucian couldn't hold back his laughter. "What is *that* look for?"

"Why are you asking what I want to know?"

"How else would we build trust?"

I shrugged.

He looked out at the water. Seagulls squawked in the distance.

"Let's go for a walk." He rose to his feet.

We walked for a while without saying anything, taking in the beauty around us—or at least that's what I did.

"I've got to ask. What's with the secret oasis? I mean it's nothing short of amazing, but what gives?"

"What? You wouldn't want to hide your special place inside a dump?" he asked.

"Well, of course! Who wouldn't? But how?"

A half grin formed once again on his face, and a twinkle shone in his eye.

"That is a question that most Protectors outside of the elders don't even know." ""

"Is there a rule against people knowing?" I asked.

"No." He sighed. "Not really. It's just kind of known to be a secret. Imagine if everyone knew how. Everyone would want to have one. Of course, that wouldn't be such a problem if it didn't draw attention to us."

I walked silently, considering this.

"Maybe I'll tell you someday," he said. "Just give me some time on that one."

"Fair enough."

I strolled onward, trying to think of something else I wanted to know, but nothing came to mind.

A couple minutes later, Lucian broke the silence. "What, cat's got your tongue?"

I laughed. "No, I'm just not sure what to ask."

And I hate to be put on the spot.

"Fine. I'm thirty-one years old. I'm originally from Florida, obviously." He gestured around us. "Umm . . . I come from a long line of Protectors."

I tried to take it all in. Thirty-one? He looked to be twenty, but I'd assumed he was older because of how high in the ranks he was. Maybe he was an exception. Eventually, maybe I'd ask, but I was afraid it was another thing he couldn't answer, so I kept my mouth shut.

"I heard you had a pretty bad fight with Eli Jacobs," he said.

I choked. "Uh, yeah."

"Did I bring up a sore subject?"

"Sort of."

"Why?"

I stopped and looked at him nervously. My eyes flickered back and forth from his gaze to the sand.

"It's a long story," I said.

"It's a long beach."

I eyed him once more, biting my lip. "You've probably already heard it all. News seems to travel fast in your circles."

"Haven't heard it from you. For all I know, what I heard could all be rumors. I don't believe everything I hear." His eyes held mine.

I rolled my eyes and started walking again.

"Eli and I dated." I glanced at him out of the corner of my eye. I figured he probably knew that much. "When we first met, I was interested in Pete Denali."

He blew out a whistle, cutting me off. "There's a family you don't want to mess with."

I rolled my eyes. "Yeah, thanks."

"I take it you figured that out."

"You could say that. Pete's uncle murdered Eli's mother." I paused.

"Yeah . . ."

". . . and since I was the one who got involved with Pete, you can imagine who Eli blamed."

"That's ridiculous." Lucian shook his head.

"Not to Eli. After dropping me like a hot cake and ignoring me for weeks, Eli came back. He was amazing, so naturally I thought he had put it behind him. But then he would act distant—not all the time, just sometimes. Of course, I figured he was sorting through his feelings. The joke was on me. In reality, he was having me followed and making me think the threat was elsewhere. Just when I thought we were going to get to the bottom of who was following me, he turned on me. And that brings us to when he ambushed me and threw me off a moving train."

"Whoa, I thought *that* was just a rumor. He actually threw you off a train, and you survived?" Surprise emanated from his words.

My hands shook.

"Oh my gosh," I gasped, tapping my front, patting my arms, and looking over my body. Throwing in a little dramatic flair. "I think I did." I couldn't let the residual anxiety show. It still lingered and reared its head in moments of weakness.

"Ha ha, very funny," he said. "How *did* you survive? According to Edward, you aren't immortal."

"I had a little help."

Then I wondered if Protectors shared their gifts with each other. I figured some probably did, but I decided not to out Casey and his gift of air manipulation.

"So cryptic," he said, his expression amused.

I grinned. "I have to keep some things to myself."

"Fair enough." He shoved his hands into his pockets.

The last rays of sunlight disappeared, and the sky went dark. I thought of Casey, who was probably waiting for me to call, wondering how today went.

"Maybe we should turn back," I said. "It's getting late."

"Aww. Are we scared of the dark?" he teased.

"No." I crossed my arms.

"Come on. There's something I think you'll like. It's not much farther."

I hesitated only a step, then kept marching forward beside him.

"What is it?"

"You'll see."

Again, I could tell that he enjoyed keeping me in the dark. I remained silent and watched the waves as we walked.

Before long, the beach extended out into a peninsula, and my breath stopped when a magnificent lighthouse came into view. The beauty of it made me falter. I stopped, taking it all in.

It was dark enough that the light glowed off the night waters. Floodlights on the ground illuminated the whole building, showing off each and every curve and dip. In the shadows below, I could see planter boxes with flowers peeking out.

"You like?" he asked. I could feel his eyes on me.

"Like? I love. How did you know I love lighthouses?"

"Just a hunch." He shrugged. "Who loves the beach but doesn't have an affinity for lighthouses?"

"No idea." I smiled. "It's magnificent."

"This one is still functional, and the keeper lives there. Maybe one day he'll give us a tour."

"Oh no, I don't do tours."

Lucian's head jerked back to me. "What?"

I gave him a sheepish look, not wanting to elaborate.

"Oh, there's got to be a good story here." He turned his full body to face me, his hands on his hips. "Out with it."

I sighed. How did he drag so much out of me in such a short time? "I'm afraid of them."

"What?"

"I love to look at them . . . from afar. The inside . . . I'm afraid."

He looked at me and then back at the lighthouse.

"I don't get it." The stumped expression on his face made me want to bury my head in the sand. But even in his confusion, he couldn't make his faint smile disappear.

I closed my eyes. "There are ghosts in lighthouses."

A few moments passed in silence. My heart beat loudly in my ears. I opened one eye to peek at him. At that, he started laughing so hard he dropped down on his back in the sand and rolled around, holding his stomach, laughing uncontrollably.

I blew out a breath and stalked back in the direction of his secret hideaway, leaving him behind. I could hear him shuffling to his feet behind me.

"Wait, wait." He sounded breathless through bursts of laughter. "Stop." He grabbed my arm.

My body kicked into gear. Without thinking, I whirled around, pushed into him, twisted my arm, and yanked it free just as Casey had taught me, then side kicked him in the stomach. I took two steps backward before I realized what I'd done.

The dumbfounded look on Lucian's face as he doubled over holding his stomach, trying to catch the breath I'd knocked out of him, promptly morphed into a grin.

"Wow, I underestimated you. You've got some skills," he said.

I looked down at my arm and wondered how they had kicked in. I'd never even remotely had an instinct to fight, let alone someone who wasn't even a threat.

"I'm sorry . . . I didn't mean to . . ." I stammered. I wanted to crawl in a hole.

"Relax. It's no big deal. I'm sorry I laughed. Clearly that wasn't a good idea." He chuckled. "So, you think there are ghosts in lighthouses?"

"Lighthouses are old. It's only natural to have ghosts hanging around, don't you think?"

He considered this. "Well, I guess maybe in some, but not all."

"I'm just not interested in getting up close and personal with one."

Lucian held up his hands in surrender. "Noted. No lighthouse tours. Got it. Just don't beat me up."

I glared at him and his amused expression.

He strode beside me on the way back to his place, and I crossed my arms feeling self-conscious. I yawned and glanced at my watch. Almost 10 o'clock.

"Why is it that I feel you got to know me far more than I got to know you?" I asked.

For once, there was tenderness in his smile. "Because I think that's how today went. That's not a bad thing."

"No, I guess not."

"Maybe it just means you're beginning to trust me."

"Don't bet on it," I said.

He drove me back to work and left me to drive myself home.

As he left, he rolled down the window and called out, "Do me a favor. The next time you have a dream, write down every detail and text or call me if you need anything, even if it's the middle of the night. That's what I'm here for."

I nodded.

I doubted I'd ever call him in the middle of the night. That seemed strange. It's not like he could come over or even do anything for me. No, my problems would wait for the morning.

I dug through my purse for my keys when an unsettling feeling came over me. The hair on the back of my neck prickled. I felt like I was being watched. A chill spread through me.

My eyes roamed the dark parking lot before I caught sight of someone sitting in the chairs in front of the coffee house. I turned my full attention to the dark silhouette almost hidden in the shadows, watching as they stood.

My breath hitched in my throat.

They shoved their hands in the front pockets of a black jacket. The hood covering their head hid any glimpse of their face.

My hands closed around my keys, and I yanked them from my purse.

The dark figure took two steps toward me, and that's where they stopped, ten feet away, staring at me.

I fumbled with my keys, picking out the one I needed. Forgetting all about my remote, I unlocked my door and threw it open. My eyes never left the hooded figure as I threw all of my belongings in the car and dropped into my seat. I slammed my hand down on the lock when the door shut behind me.

From this angle, the light caught their face under the hoodie just enough for me to see a wicked smile creep up on their lips. And just like that, they walked away into the darkness behind the building.

My car roared to life with a flick of my wrist. I threw my car in reverse and sped out of the parking lot.

My arms shook as I held the steering wheel.

What was that?

I breathed deeply, trying to calm myself. In and out.

My first impulse was to call Casey, but then I changed my mind.

Am I reading too much into this?

Nothing had actually happened. The person didn't threaten me or hurt me. They didn't even speak to me. They looked at me, sure, but I was the only person around. Then they walked away. Surely if they meant me harm, nothing was there to stop them.

Maybe they thought I looked like a crazy person fumbling around like I did. Freaking out over what? That there was someone there?

I shook my head.

Nope. I wouldn't be telling Casey, or anyone else for that matter.

*   *   *   *

The next day, Casey and I picked up take-out and went back to his apartment. He wanted to know all about my meeting with Lucian. Though, I had no intention of letting him in on my ghost fears or my unnecessary martial arts. I already felt transparent enough with Lucian knowing.

"You should have seen his place, Casey. It was amazing. To have the beach right out your back door. Gosh, I'd love that."

We sat huddled around his coffee table, the fire unlit. The heat of summer made me not even want to think about turning it on, no matter how cozy it made his apartment feel.

"I know you would. It sounds amazing." He popped a piece of chicken into his mouth. "What did he say about your dreams?"

"Not a whole lot. He wants me to write down every detail when I wake up from one."

He nodded. "Sounds like a good idea."

"I guess."

"You don't sound so sure."

"I guess I'm not. I mean, I can see how it would be helpful. I was just hoping for more."

"You'll get there," Casey said. "Just give it time."

"I hope so."

CHAPTER TWO

Darkness surrounded me. My heart raced.

Cornered with no escape.

I took a few steps, and they echoed around me. It felt as if the walls were closing in on me. I held my arms out in front of me, testing my surroundings.

I shook my head, trying to recall what led me here, but everything was fuzzy. This was wrong. I needed to get out. I shouldn't be here. I spun around, trying to see something, anything.

A door opened behind me. Light flooded part of the room, revealing empty space. I swiveled around on my heel to face the light.

A figure stood in the doorway gazing in. I shrunk back into the shadows until I pressed against the wall.

Taking the only opportunity, I looked around for a way out, using the small amount of light . . .

I woke in a deep sweat, trembling. I sat up in bed and rubbed my eyes. It took a few moments for it to click that I needed to write down everything I remembered. I closed my eyes and pictured what I'd seen. Darkness. Light from the doorway. I could almost feel the wall against my back.

It had been two days since my meeting with Lucian. This was the first chance I had to follow his instructions and write down all the details I could remember.

I grabbed a pen and paper and started scribbling as it all came back.

-Looked like a warehouse

-Dark

-Someone opened a door, it wasn't dark on the other side

- Person looked more like a dark figure in the doorway. I couldn't see a face.

-I pressed myself into the wall to hide

It wasn't much to go on when I looked over the list. I sighed and tossed it on my nightstand. *There, I did it. Now what?*

I had to admit—it did feel good writing it out. It didn't seem as scary this way staring back at me from the page. Nothing more than a few words.

I fell back to sleep with little trouble and woke to sunlight in my eyes.

While I ate a bowl of cereal, I mulled over the notes. When I finished, I grabbed my phone. Ten o'clock in the morning. It was late enough, so I texted Lucian.

Had a dream last night . . .

Mom ventured in from the kitchen just as I hit *send*. Her long, curly brown hair was pulled back away from her face, except for a few shorter tendrils that hung around her cheeks.

"I'm headed into the office for a few hours," she said.

"Oh? On a Saturday?"

"My boss wants to get ahead on some projects."

"Okay."

"Need anything before I go?"

I shook my head.

"All right. George is upstairs if you need anything."

"I'll be fine. I have to work later anyway."

She was about to leave the room when she noticed the piece of paper on the table. Her eyes swept over it. I quickly covered it. Her brows rose.

"What's that?" she asked.

"Nothing."

My heart thumped in my chest. I couldn't explain to her what it was. I hoped she would drop it. I held my breath as I maintained eye contact.

She gave my hand one last glance and turned to leave.

It used to be that I never kept anything from her, but after I was thrown into this new realm, I hid more and more. The guilt of those lies kept mounting.

I closed my eyes and let out my breath when the garage door slammed shut.

Then I folded up the note and shoved it in my bra just in case George happened to come down.

My phone chimed, snapping my attention away from my food again. Lucian.

Can we meet today?

I typed out my response.

I have to work at three. I can meet before or after.

I finished eating, washed my bowl, and when I returned, a message was waiting.

I'll pick you up in twenty minutes.

I looked down at my pajamas and jogged upstairs. He hadn't given me much time. I typed a single '*K*' back. Then I called Casey.

He answered on the third ring, sounding breathless. "Hello?"

"Hey, change of plans . . ."

The phone crackled like he was shifting around. Then his voice got louder.

"Why? What's up?"

I held the phone with my shoulder and pulled on a pair of shorts.

"I had a dream. I'm meeting with Lucian."

Everything on his end of the line fell silent. I remembered back to the first time I dreamed this nightmare. I'd fallen asleep in Casey's apartment on accident. We woke in the middle of the night after sleeping through my curfew. In my haste to get home, I didn't tell him, and it never occurred to me to bring it up again. Until now.

"What was the dream about?"

"I don't have time to talk about it right now. He's picking me up in fifteen minutes."

"Okay." He sounded dejected. "Call me tonight?"

"Sure. I work until eight."

"All right, babe, I'll let you go. I'm just finishing up my workout."

"Talk to you tonight."

"Bye."

I set the phone down and checked my reflection in the mirror. *Good enough.* As I came out of the bathroom, I bumped into George.

"Oops. Sorry," I said.

"Headed out?"

"Yeah."

"Your mom know where you'll be?"

"I'll call her in a few."

The doorbell rang, ending our conversation and freeing me to leave.

"See ya!" I called behind me.

Stepdad mode—not my favorite when it came to George. Sometimes I fought the urge to tell him it wasn't his business, but deep down I knew this was his way of showing he cared. Or faking that he cared.

I flung the door open.

Lucian and his giant grin stood on the porch.

"Hey. Let's go."

"Good to see you too," he said.

I beat him to the car and climbed in without waiting for him to open the door.

When he got in, his smile had broadened. I don't know why I wanted to smack it off his face sometimes.

"You are far too chipper." I slumped to the side, leaning into the car door.

"And you are grumpy. Now that we've established our moods. You hungry?"

I shook my head.

"Well, I am. We can go to a place I know. Best tacos around."

He drove to a little building with a walk-up window and no dining room. I stood at the counter next to him and inspected the menu as he ordered. It was somewhat limited—tacos and only tacos. So many different combos I'd never dreamed of, from s'mores dessert tacos to pizza tacos.

Lucian ordered brisket tacos and cinnamon apple pie tacos but also added "his usual," and I couldn't help but wonder what that was. I watched the workers toss wrapped tacos into a bag and call his name. He grabbed the sack and still beat me to the car to open my door. He set the bag down on the center console as he started the car. The smell of savory beef and onion mixed with a hint of sweet cinnamon filled the enclosed space, making my mouth water.

I tried to hide my intense interest in the tantalizing smell. The longer he drove, the hungrier I became. I regretted not ordering anything. He pulled into his driveway, and once again, the garage door lifted, revealing the spacious garage.

I followed Lucian through the house to the deck in back. I stopped in the doorway, leaning on the frame, and breathed in the fresh, salty air. My whole body relaxed.

Lucian unpacked the bag of food. My stomach grumbled. *How much food did he order?* My eyebrows rose as he finished unloading the bag and tossed it to the side. The pile of food in the center of the table looked like it was big enough for four.

"Are you going to sit or just stand there wishing you'd ordered something?"

I frowned at him, but then I couldn't stop the happiness that spread through my aching stomach.

"Sit." He pointed at the chair across from him.

I plopped myself down.

"Happy?" I grinned.

"Yes. Now pick what you want."

"What?"

"Pick. Brisket, chicken, pork. Then, of course, you have the dessert tacos: strawberry chocolate, and cinnamon apple."

"I didn't order anything." I folded my hands in front of me.

He cocked his head. "Exactly. Nobody can resist these tacos, so I ordered extra. More than we both can eat, I'm sure."

I eyed the pile again.

"You can't go wrong with any of them," he added as he unwrapped one and sank his teeth into it.

I walked my fingers across the table and picked one. I didn't look at which one it was because it all smelled so good.

Chicken. I wasted no time taking a bite. The chicken was exceptionally moist, and there was a sauce I couldn't place, but it was creamy and packed a pretty good punch.

Three bites later, it was gone. My stomach growled.

I eyed the pile of tacos.

"Keep going," Lucian said through a mouthful of taco.

So, I grabbed a second. Then I reached in my shirt, pulled the note from my bra strap, and slid my notes across the table to him.

He raised his eyebrows but didn't comment. I blushed. Why hadn't I thought to put it in a less embarrassing place before he picked me up?

Lucian held the notes written in my sloppy handwriting. He closed his eyes and was quiet for a while. I fidgeted, and my hands fussed with the paper the taco had been wrapped in. I tried to focus on the waves crashing behind him.

"Have you been here before?" He pointed to the paper.

I shrugged. "I don't recognize it, and I don't know when I would have been to a warehouse, but it was so dark it's hard to say."

"So, it's new," he said to himself more than to me. His eyes seemed to light up a moment. "Are there any warehouses near anywhere you go often? Work? School? Maybe even ones you never gave a second thought about. Think back."

"No. Well, the ones over there," I said, pointing back toward the driveway. Then I dropped my finger, realizing they weren't actually there in Florida.

He turned and looked up the beach. Then it clicked, and he turned back to look me in the eyes.

"You're right. There are warehouses next door, aren't there?"

"Well, in Arizona, anyway."

"We have to go explore them," he said, again more to himself than me.

"How?" I asked.

"I'll make it happen."

I could almost see the wheels turning in his head.

"Do you really think that's a good idea?" I asked.

He thought for a moment. "Maybe not just yet. But soon."

I nodded, though I was sure he didn't see.

"Next time, I want you to try to see more. Move around the room."

"What do you mean?"

He looked at me, puzzled.

"How am I supposed to move around the room? It's a dream."

Lucian's eyebrows raised. "That's the trick. You have to make yourself aware *in* your dream."

"That's insane. How am I supposed to do that?"

He shrugged. "It's just a feeling, a feeling of bringing awareness to your mind. I don't think I can really teach it to you."

I sighed.

"Try drinking lots of water before you go to bed, and clear your mind of anything else."

I nodded. "Does any of this get easier?" I asked.

He raised his eyebrows, leaned forward, and rested his arms on the table, his ever-constant smirk present. "Of course."

*   *   *   *

Later that night, I arrived home and headed straight to the mailbox. The darkness around me sent a shiver up my spine. I clutched my phone so its light gleamed in my face.

I dialed Casey, and the phone rang until his chipper voicemail message began to play. I waited for the *beep.*

"He's insane! Seriously insane! Call me back."

Halfway to the mailbox, goosebumps rose on my arms. I ended the call, stopped, and lifted my gaze from my phone. Nothing stood out, yet a sinking feeling lurked in the pit of my stomach.

My mind raced back to the hooded man outside the coffee house, and my mouth went dry.

A strange shadow formed on the wall across the street. I stumbled, watching it move.

The bush in front of the shadow rustled. I froze. A cat darted out from the bush and ran across the street in front of me. I gasped, jumping back, grabbing at my chest. Then I groaned at my foolishness.

It's just a cat. What's wrong with you?

Rushing forward, I tripped on a crack in the sidewalk, making me heart rate spike even higher.

Still, I couldn't calm myself. The idea someone was watching me wouldn't go away. Adrenaline coursed through my veins. I shoved the key in the mailbox and turned it with a sharp twist of my wrist. Empty. *Ugh!*

I slammed it shut and power-walked back home as my eyes darted around me. *Just get home. Just get inside.* The uneasy feeling crescendoed, and for the last hundred yards, I sprinted in complete panic mode. I panted as I walked toward the stairs, my heart pounding.

I crossed paths with my mom, and she gave me a sideways glance.

"What have you been doing?" she asked.

"Uh . . . I decided to run back from the mailbox."

"Why?" Her suspicious gaze didn't falter.

I don't know. Why would your daughter, who hates to run, run of her own free will?

"I heard a noise . . . I got freaked out." I shrugged.

She shook her head. "You're so silly. It was probably just an animal."

"Probably." I nodded.

I jogged up the stairs to my room, shutting the door behind me. I took a deep breath as I leaned against the door. *I must be crazy. There was nothing there. What is my problem?*

My phone buzzed in my pocket.

"Hello," I sighed into the mouthpiece.

"I'm sorry. I take it things didn't go well today?"

"They went fine." I threw myself onto my bed.

"But he's insane?"

"Yes, he is."

"Why?"

"He wants me to try to move in my dream. How the heck am I supposed to do that?"

"I don't know."

"Exactly." I stood up and paced my room.

"Did he give you any tips?"

"Drink lots of water, and clear my mind before I fall asleep."

"Well, those sound easy enough."

"Yeah, maybe." I stopped in front of the window, looking out into the night.

"Just give yourself time."

"Yeah. I'll try. It's just overwhelming. I'm sorry, I guess I needed to vent. What have you been up to?" I asked.

I decided not to tell him about my mailbox trip. I didn't need any other witnesses to my crazy, overactive imagination.

"Don't apologize. You can always vent to me. The guys just left. We were watching football."

"I miss them."

"They were asking about you. I think they miss you too."

I sighed. "I'm going to go to bed. I'm exhausted."

"Okay. Goodnight."

"Night," I said to empty air.

CHAPTER THREE

The Christmas dance was only a week away, and with school and work this, was the first opportunity to shop. Bailey had been begging to go for weeks. Today, on a sunny Sunday afternoon, dresses were the only thing on our minds as we headed to the mall.

Bailey clutched my arm, her ponytail bouncing side to side as she pulled me along. We stopped in front of a window lined with mannequins in sparkly short and floor-length gowns.

"That one." She pointed to an all-black dress that glistened when the light hit it. It was knee length with a slit halfway up the thigh. "I've been eyeing it for weeks! It's gorgeous!"

"Go! Try it on," I said, ushering her into the store.

We lifted dress after dress from the racks and held them up, deciding if we liked them or not.

"Oh my gosh, Bailey, look at this one." I held up a dress that glittered rainbow all over, with enormous puffy sleeves, and flared out at the bottom.

Her mouth dropped. "Who would wear that? It's hideous!"

I shook my head. "No idea."

I set it back down and pulled out a few more. "Ooh, Bailey this one would look great on you!"

"Oooh," she gushed. "I *like* it!"

After filling our hands with dresses, we headed to the fitting rooms.

I heaved the load of dresses onto the hooks and started undressing when squealing erupted from Bailey's dressing room. "Oh my gosh! I think this is it!" Her door flung open.

I pulled on the first dress I could and stepped out.

She was beaming. Then her face scrunched. "That one is not you."

"Ah, I couldn't agree more." I gazed down at the over-the-top gown I wore, and I cringed at all of the gaudy gemstones. "It looked a lot nicer on the hanger."

Bailey nodded.

"But that one"—I pointed at her—"is stunning."

She bounced up and down, let out one more squeal, and headed back into the dressing room.

A dark plum one had really caught my eye when I plucked it from the rack, and after trying on the other dresses, I reached for it. Once it slid over my body, falling just above my knee, I knew it was the one. The silky, tight-fitting material shimmered in the light and hugged me in the right places, showing off all my curves.

I stepped out of the dressing room smiling from ear to ear.

Bailey gasped. "That's the one."

I nodded. "Hands down."

Then she made a face and pulled the dress she was wearing out to the sides. "This one makes me look frumpy."

I made a sour face and nodded. "I think that first one is the one."

"I think so too." She leaned back into her dressing room. "None of these are as pretty as that one."

We didn't try on another dress and walked out with the ones we loved.

*   *   *   *

The next week passed, and my dream still hadn't presented itself again. Lucian checked in every day just in case, always hopeful I'd had the chance to try moving in the dream.

My nerves grew more frazzled with each passing day. I worried I'd let him down once I did dream.

Even as Friday evening set in, and Casey came over to hang out, I still couldn't focus on anything else.

"Hey, where are you tonight?" Casey asked.

"What do you mean?"

"You just seem like your mind is somewhere else."

I sighed. "I still haven't dreamed."

"Abby, you really need to let it go. Relax," Casey said.

I held my arms out to my sides, palms up, questioning. "I can't."

He eyed me.

I sighed, placed my hands on either side of my face, and pulled, stretching the skin. "I've never felt more anxious and impatient to have a nightmare in my life, and somehow Lucian expects me to move during it. It just seems impossible."

"I know you can do this." He stood and rubbed my shoulders. "Tell you what. I'll give you a massage before I leave. Then you can fall asleep relaxed." His fingers circled the base of my neck.

"That sounds amazing." I let my head roll back and closed my eyes.

He stopped rubbing. "Good. Then go get ready for bed."

"Do I have to?" I whined.

"Imagine how much better you'll feel in your pajamas."

"You," I said, pointing at him with a lopsided grin. ". . . are very smart."

He smiled. "Go."

I slipped into my PJ's, then let him into my room and flopped down onto my bed face down.

He sat on the edge of my bed as he worked his magic on all the muscles in my back. He took his time on each section, starting with my shoulder blades and working toward my lumbar area. My whole body relaxed into my bed like it was molded to me, and I started to doze.

I don't remember him leaving, but I dreamed that night, vividly. I thrashed awake the next morning, disoriented. It took only a few moments before I realized I hadn't moved. I'd failed.

But as I emerged out of my sleepiness, I remembered what day it was, and my disappointment faded. Dance day!

I hopped out of bed, rushed to pull my dress from the closet, and laid it on the bed.

I couldn't wait to wear it! I only wished Casey would be there to see it.

I bounded down the stars to eat brunch since it was already late in the morning. I'd slept in.

Mom and George were sitting at the breakfast bar, still sipping coffee.

"Morning honey," Mom said.

"Morning." I yawned.

"Pancakes and bacon are waiting for you in the microwave." George set down his mug.

"George made breakfast today," Mom said.

"Wow, getting more culinary by the day!"

My mom and I giggled.

"Oh, sure, tease the guy who made you food." George winked. He shut the newspaper and stood. "I've got to go. Supposed to meet the guys at noon." He kissed my mom on the cheek and left the room.

"Where's he going?" I asked.

"Golfing."

"He plays golf?"

She gave me a strange look. "Yeah, he always has."

How did I not know that? "Oh."

"So, dance tonight, huh?"

"Yep."

"Want me to do your hair? There's a pretty updo I saw in a magazine I've been wanting to try out. It looked easy."

"Yes, please. I've been trying to figure out what to do with it."

"I'll go find the magazine."

She headed upstairs while I finished eating. I glanced at my phone while I ate, wondering what Casey was doing. I typed a quick text to him.

Good morning!

I ran upstairs, tossed my phone on the counter, and hopped in the shower.

After my shower, I spent a good amount of time painting my nails to match my dress.

Mom was ready with a hot curling iron and all the hair things she would need when I finished. I glanced at the picture she had propped against the mirror. All of my hair would be pulled back away from my face, with curls framing my cheeks. More curls would hang down in the back, all complemented by a braid that swooped from the right side to the back.

"Oooh, I really hope this works out. It's so pretty."

"I'll do my best," Mom said.

It fell quiet as Mom started curling. There was something soothing about having someone play with my hair.

"So, Casey's really not coming tonight?" Mom asked.

"Nope."

"How come?"

"The school doesn't let people who aren't students go."

"That's too bad."

"Yeah, it sucks."

In no time, Mom had my wavy hair in much more defined curls, and then she moved to the braid. I watched her work effortlessly as she intertwined my hair. Next came the pins, and she started putting my hair up.

"Close your eyes," she said.

She sprayed my whole head with a thin layer of hair spray before continuing to pin. I stayed quiet, watching her concentrate on styling it just the way she'd planned. After a few more minutes, she stood back and looked at it from different angles.

"I think that's all the pinning. What do you think?" She handed me a mirror to look at the back.

I held it up and looked at both sides of the back of my head.

"It's perfect. You're so good at this."

"Thanks, honey. Now, I think you need just a few finishing touches."

She grabbed a little box and opened it without letting me see what was in it. Then she leaned over my head and pushed a few things into my hair and through the braid.

"There. Now it's perfect."

I picked up the mirror and looked at what she'd done. Several gemstones glistened in my hair.

"Those are so pretty! Where did you get them?"

"Eh, I've had them for a while, saving them for a special occasion."

"Thanks, Mom."

"Oh, psh." She waved me off. "I'll get out of your hair now so you can do your makeup, but I want a picture before you leave!"

She straightened up the counter and turned back to me. Then she smiled and left.

An hour later, I stepped out of my room, ready to go. Mom made sure to get pictures of me on the stairs, the typical before-a-dance photo shoot. And then I headed on my way, by myself.

When I walked into the dance with my hair up and heels on, alone, it made me feel a little silly for even coming. *All dressed up for myself.*

The cafeteria had been decorated so well it was hard to believe it was the same room we ate in every day. Silver fringe curtains hung in all the doorways and in front of some of the windows. White twinkle lights lined all the walls, casting all of the light needed for the whole dance—aside from the disco ball. A single Christmas tree sat on the DJ table, lit up in all white and decked out with only silver decorations.

Then I saw Bailey dancing her heart out, and my doubts faded away. I jumped in next to her, excited for the night to come. She threw her arms around me, and then another set of arms looped around me from behind.

"Ahh! I'm trapped!" I howled.

Alexis swung around to my front, bumping Bailey out of the way without releasing me, and held me at arm's length.

"You look fabulous," she said.

"Thanks!" I said. "Look at you guys. Alexis that color is perfect on you."

"You like?" She twirled around and then bounced away after a guy who held onto her hand.

Bailey danced beside me. I spun around and shook my hips as the beat blasted through the room. My worries drifted away into a bass-filled euphoria. After a few songs, I was winded, and the music changed to a slow song.

The DJ came on the mic. "We're going to slow things down for a bit. Grab your date or maybe that girl you've been eyeing and get out here on the dance floor."

Ryan grabbed Bailey's hand and spun her into him. I stood there as all the couples around me joined up and looped their arms around each other. My eyes fell to the ground. I hoped nobody noticed me as I made my way off the dance floor and to a chair to slouch down and watch.

A boy at the next table smiled at me as I scanned the room.

"Looks like I'm not the only one who came without a date."

I shrugged and faked a chuckle. "Yeah."

He stood and made his way over to me. "Might as well make the best of it." He extended his hand.

I smiled and put my hand in his. We made our way to the edge of the crowd.

"I'm Abby," I said.

"Adam."

It felt strange gripping onto a stranger, even though there was at least six inches between us.

"Are you a sophomore?" I asked.

He shook his head. "Junior."

"Oh, me too. Well, sort of. I'm planning to graduate at the end of the year."

"Wow, that's impressive."

I shrugged. "I'd rather get it all done as soon as I can."

"Wish I could do that," he said.

"Can I cut in?" A familiar voice asked from behind me.

"Casey?" I turned, pulling away from Adam.

"Uh, sure," Adam said. He gave me a nod and let go. I could see he didn't really want to.

Casey's hand slid across my lower back as he came around me. His masculine spice filled my nose.

"What are you doing here?" I asked in shock.

"You didn't think I'd leave you at your dance alone, did you?"

"But you weren't supposed to be able to come. How'd you get in?"

"I have my ways." He winked.

I shook my head.

"So, who was that? Should I be worried?" he asked in a teasing way.

"Adam. Just met him." I glanced over at him, sitting in the place we'd met. Momentarily, I felt bad that he was still alone, but as I cuddled up closer to Casey, I soon forgot.

When the slow songs ended, I spotted Bailey making her way out of the center of the floor.

"Abby! You little sneak! You told me you were coming alone!" she said.

"I thought I was!"

"I need a drink. I'm dying." Bailey fanned her glistening face. She pulled Ryan along behind her. He waved as they passed.

"Someday I want to know how you make stuff like this happen," I said.

"Someday you'll be able to make stuff like this happen for yourself."

In that moment, even with the pumping music and the bodies crowding around us pulsing to the music, I gripped his shirt and pulled him down toward me. Nothing meant more to me than his faith in me. He believed I could do this. It was the first time there wasn't fear in his eyes as he spoke about my future.

I kissed him, melding my body into his, grasping his shirt for stability.

"Ahem. Break it up," A stern voice said.

I pulled back and caught sight of a teacher as she stalked away. With her back turned, I took the opportunity to give Casey another quick peck and let him go.

"I'm thirsty," I said.

"Go sit. I'll get us some waters."

I made my way over to the chair I'd sat in before. I wasn't sitting long when Bailey bounded over to me.

"This is a blast!" she said.

I chuckled. "It's pretty great."

"Why are you sitting here alone? Where's Casey?"

"He's getting us drinks."

"Oh, good. I was worried he left. Come dance when he gets back?"

I nodded, and off she went.

"Was that your boyfriend?" Adam asked.

I turned around. "Whoa, I didn't even see you there."

"That's because I was in stealth mode."

I grinned. "Yeah, he's my boyfriend. I didn't think he could make it."

"You guys look good together."

"Thanks."

When Casey made it back, we downed the water bottles and hit the dance floor again. I had no idea Casey could dance so well. For a brief period, he had the whole floor, with everyone clapping around him. As I watched him, I felt my heart grow. Who knew that this guy would be the one thing I needed. He was the best thing that had ever happened to me.

His eyes found mine, and he made his way back to me. He pulled me in and spun me out so quick I barely had time to respond.

"Having fun?" he whispered in my ear.

"So much."

CHAPTER FOUR

Every step I took echoed around me in the darkness. My heart raced, pumping loudly in my ears. I felt cornered, as if the walls were closing in on me. The ground below me was hard like concrete.

I shook my head, trying to recall what led me here, but everything was fuzzy. This was wrong.

How could I get out? I needed to get out. I shouldn't be here. Then everything started to clear. This was a dream.

I looked at the walls around me, spotting a window, but I felt rooted in place. Move. I urged myself. Nothing happened.

Move.

And then, all at once, my feet went forward, one after the other, until I was standing in front of the window. One of the panes was broken. I kept my hands clear of the break and peered out.

A door opened behind me. Light engulfed the other half of the room. I swung around on my heel to face the light, my back to the window. A figure stood in the doorway, gazing in. I shrank back until my spine slammed against a wall. My back screamed in protest, and a brick dug into my flesh.

I jolted awake. Sweat dripped from my pores. I stood, leaning against the window.

Why am I *standing?*

Never had I woken so startled. I glanced down at my feet. *How did I get here?* Not once had I ever sleepwalked before. *What is happening to me?*

My back ached.

As my heart slowed, I began to think about the dream. *I did it.* I moved in my dream. Then as I looked at where I stood, the reality weighed on me—I walked in the real world too. That couldn't be good. Did I move further than this?

Grabbing a pen and pad, I sat down at my desk. Rubbing my temples, I tried to ease the tension and attempted to remember anything new. I pulled out the first list just in case.

-I moved!
-Window, one pane broken

Then something flashed in my mind. There had been something different. I'd seen a symbol. I doubted I would have even remembered it if I hadn't sat down to write my list. The split-second sight of it flashed in my mind. I couldn't even begin to recreate it, but to me it looked like a snake morphed with a dragon that was twisted up into a 'W.' How could I even begin to describe that to someone without sounding crazy?

-Symbol with golden shimmery eyes in the shape of a 'W'

That wasn't much more than before, but I was hopeful that the symbol would be the saving grace we needed to figure out what this dream meant.

I set the pen down and picked up my phone.

It took two rings for him to answer, then his husky, breathless voice filled my ear.

"Hello," Casey said.

"I did it!" I felt proud as well as anxious.

"Did what?"

"I moved in my dream. I don't know how, but I did it."

He chuckled. "I'm proud of you."

"I would be too, except . . ."

"What?" He sounded worried.

"I woke up standing by my window."

"Really? Like you were sleeping standing up?"

"Yeah."

"Well . . . that doesn't sound too bad." He sounded hopeful.

"No? Well, how did I get there? Did I go anywhere else?"

"Good question."

"I know it's a good question! Casey, I'm freaking out here."

"Relax. I get it. It's a little weird."

"A *little* weird?" I squeaked. My hand still shook as I held the phone. "Why doesn't this bother you at all?"

He sighed. "If everything like this bothered me, it'd be very difficult to be a Protector."

33

I dropped myself into the chair at my desk.

"Every gift presents challenges. We have to master them. It takes time. We all have setbacks. That's all this is," he said.

"So, what am I supposed to do now?"

"I don't know. Maybe Lucian can help."

I groaned. "Okay. I'll talk to you later."

"I love you."

"I love you, too. Bye."

I tossed my phone on the bed and got dressed. Then I picked it up again. I stared at the screen, sighed, and pressed *call*.

"You had the dream," he said after the second ring, completely skipping *'hello'*.

"Yeah," I said.

"How'd it go?"

"Okay, I guess . . . I moved."

"Really?" He sounded excited.

"Yeah, but I moved in person, too."

He was silent a moment. "Interesting."

"Interesting?" I asked.

"Yes. Very."

"Care to elaborate?"

"Can't."

"Why?" I held the phone between my ear and shoulder and crossed my arms. Not that he could see me.

"I have a meeting with Edward right now. I'll catch up with you after school."

"Fine."

It was quiet for longer than I cared for.

"We'll get this figured out. Don't stress about it."

I sighed. "I'll try."

"I'll call you later," he said.

"All right."

He hung up, and I couldn't be sure if he said *goodbye* or not. My mind was elsewhere.

I rested my head in my hands and blew out a breath. This had to get better someday, right?

School would have distract me, at least until Lucian and I could meet later.

First hour went by in the blink of an eye, but by the middle of second hour, my stomach made it's discomfort known. In my haste to leave that morning, I'd forgotten to eat breakfast, and I'd been kicking myself ever since. Focusing on anything but my stomach was next to impossible. By lunchtime, my stomach was rumbling loudly.

After getting my lunch, I found our usual table, which was already full of chatter.

"Abby, you have to come with us tomorrow!" Bailey said as soon as I sat down.

"Where?" I shoved a fry in my mouth.

"We're going to paint pottery," Alexis said.

"Oh yeah? Same place we went?" I asked, turning to Bailey.

"Yep! You'll come, right?"

"Uh, when are you going?" I asked.

"Five?" Bailey asked, looking at each of us.

Everyone nodded in agreement.

"Sure, I'll go," I said.

"It's going to be so much fun!" Bailey squealed.

I sat back in my seat, thinking. At least something good came of today. Plans that didn't involve immortal business. Plans that were *normal.* Just the thought made my stomach flop.

After school, I met Lucian at his house with both lists tucked away in my pocket—a much better place than last time. I handed them to him the moment I walked in the door, and then I breezed past him to the back. It took a few minutes for him to look them over, and I seized the opportunity to shove my feet in the sand. It wasn't sunset yet, but the sun was gradually descending, reflecting orange off the water.

"You saw a specific symbol?" His whole face lit up.

"Yeah."

"Have you ever seen it before?"

"No."

"But you'd recognize it if you saw it again?"

"I'm sure I would."

"Good." He was still staring at the lists as if there was a ton to learn from them.

"I hope you have some good ideas because I don't want to sleepwalk again," I said.

"Well, I do have a plan, if that helps."

"What?"

"Don't try to move again in this dream."

"Why?"

"Well, I think we have enough to go on for now. The symbol will hopefully be all we need."

"Really?"

"You said you'd remember it if you saw it again, right?"

"Yeah."

"Then we just have to find it."

He made it seem so simple, but I doubted it would be. Nothing was simple anymore.

Even little things always ended up complicated. I knew better than to get my hopes up.

He set the notes down and looked at me. "I have something to tell you."

I hated the sound of that. When people said things like that, it usually meant something big, and it usually wasn't good. That was the last thing I needed when I already felt so unnerved.

"I talked to Edward. I know your agreement was that he'd be informed of your progress."

"Yeah . . ."

"I told him you were able to move in your dream after just one try, and he was really impressed."

"Okay . . ." I wasn't sure where this was going because so far this wasn't a surprise.

"He thinks you're ready to move to the next step."

"What do you mean?"

"He wants you to begin training in other areas."

"What kind of training?"

"Martial arts, for one, but a few other things as well. I'm not sure how much Edward wants me to go into it with you before he can talk to you."

This *was* news to me. Not that it wouldn't be useful, I just hadn't expected it.

My eyebrows furrowed. "Why?"

"He didn't say. He just said that he would meet with you to discuss it in detail."

"When?" I asked.

Lucian shrugged. "Just be prepared."

Now that I had begun to get control of my dreams—or so Edward thought—he felt the need to advance my training.

"But it's not like I have anything perfected! I walked in my sleep. That's not exactly something I want to repeat."

"I get that."

"Uh. Whatever," I said, throwing my hands in the air. "It doesn't matter what I think. I'm thrown into this without a choice, and I'm expected to do whatever they want me to just because I can."

"No. You don't *have* to do anything. Edward made it sound like this is what you wanted. Is that not true?" He leaned forward, elbows resting on his knees.

"It is. It was. I don't know anymore. It would be nice to at least have a chance to absorb everything that's going on without adding more. I haven't even figured out the last problem thrown at me. Not to mention, I don't really understand why I need to train for anything. Just because I have a gift doesn't mean I'm one of you. I just wanted to help . . . if I could . . ."

"I can tell Edward you aren't ready," Lucian suggested.

"No, don't do that." The last thing I wanted was for Edward to think I couldn't handle this. What he wanted me to do was important even though I didn't completely understand what it entailed yet.

Ugh!

I pushed my hands into my hair and sighed. "Can I just have a day? One day? Do you have to get back to him right away?"

"Take your time. I can put him off."

I looked Lucian in the eye. I could see he understood.

"Do you ever feel overwhelmed by it all?"

Lucian looked out at the ocean like the answer was written across the waves. I couldn't help but follow his line of sight.

"I used to. It's been a long time since I've felt that way."

"How long did it take you to feel normal again?"

He chuckled. "*Normal?*" He seemed to be thinking about it.

"That long, huh?"

He shrugged. "What is normal? I don't think my life could be considered *normal* by any measurement." He held his arms out. "Just look at where we are."

"Great. So I'm never going to feel normal again."

"That's not what I meant."

I eyed him and crossed my arms.

"What I meant was that normal is relative. My *normal* could be completely different than any other Protector's. It's not like all of us are in line to become an elder. Right?"

"Yeah, I guess so."

"So, normal compared to what you've always been used to? No, you probably won't ever feel that again. Your whole world, your beliefs, they've changed. It'd be crazy to think that things would go back to what they were."

"I guess. I just wish everything didn't have to change."

"Well, everything hasn't changed," he said. "You're still you."

"Someone who resembles me."

He gave me a dirty look.

"Fine. I'm me, but it'd be crazy to think I haven't changed, too, after everything I've been through. Don't you think?"

"Very true. But I'd say that after all you've been through, you're stronger. Am I wrong?"

"No, you're right. I am stronger."

He laughed. "Why do you sound like that's such a horrible thing?"

"It's not the best thing to be excited about."

"You should be proud. Not many could have come out of what you did as well as you did, let alone still be willing to head into a fight that isn't even yours."

I looked up from my lap and watched the waves roll in. I didn't want to continue this conversation. I wasn't even sure I was willing to fight a fight that wasn't mine anymore.

"I just want to take my mind off everything for a while."

"All right. Let's go." He stood up.

"Where are we going?"

"To tour the lighthouse, of course."

My head whipped around to face him where he stood at the edge of the deck.

He bent over, laughing.

My mouth dropped. "That's not funny!" I grabbed one of the throw pillows off the couch and hurled it at him.

"You're too easy," he said, grinning. "But, really, let's go. Is Casey busy?" He walked into the house.

I shook my head. "I don't think so."

"Good."

Lucian grabbed his keys off the counter and held the door to the garage open for me.

We got in his car, and as he drove, I kept expecting him to ask where to go next, but he never did. By the time we pulled into Casey's parking garage, I was really surprised.

"How'd you know where to go?" I asked.

"I'm a Protector. It's our job to know these things." He grinned as he shut off the car.

We walked into the elevator together, and it sent me spiraling into a wave of déjà vu. The last time I rode in this elevator with someone other than Casey . . . that last strange ride had been with Eli. As I thought back to it, I cringed. I could feel the cold elevator wall, the give of the buttons as my back pressed against them. And his lips. His filthy, disgusting, repulsive lips. I stood there, frozen. Unable to pull myself from the memory.

Lucian gripped my arm.

"Abby?" His voice was the loudest I'd ever heard it. But I still couldn't respond. My lips felt cemented shut. My mind locked in the memory.

The elevator doors sprang open. Lucian bent down in front of me.

"Hello!" He waved his hand in front of my face.

A door across the hall opened moments later. Casey's face fell when he saw me—he knew something was wrong—and suddenly it was all too much. I shrank back against the wall and slid to the ground. Everything sounded muffled. I could see feet come toward me, but it was as if they were moving in slow motion. I was swooped up into someone's arms. Casey stood in front of me, which must mean Lucian was carrying me. *How strange.*

Slowly, sound returned. The scrape of the elevator door closing. Lucian's labored breath as he carried me to the door.

"What did you do to her?" Casey asked, his voice accusatory.

I couldn't bring myself to tell him it wasn't Lucian's fault. I couldn't bring myself to do anything. *What is wrong with me?*

"Want to hold the door for me?" Lucian asked.

Casey scrambled to the door and held it open. I bumped about as Lucian made his way into Casey's apartment. He set me on the couch, and Casey dropped down next to me. His hands found mine.

"Abby? What's wrong?" Casey asked. "Talk to me."

His touch. His eyes. I threw my arms around his neck and sobbed. Once the tears started, it was hard to stop them. Minutes passed. Gradually, the emotion began to fade.

I lifted my head, and Lucian stood across the room, looking out the window.

"I'm sorry," I whispered, resting my head on Casey's chest.

"Can I get you something to drink?" Lucian asked.

I'd never seen him so serious. His ever-present grin was gone, and for the first time, I wished it wasn't.

I nodded. "Water?"

Lucian glanced at Casey.

"In the fridge." He nodded toward the kitchen.

Lucian disappeared for a moment before returning with a frosty bottle of water. He sat down in front of me, and Casey sat on the table.

"Care to explain to us what exactly happened back there?" Lucian asked.

I sniffled and stared at the wet spot on Casey's shirt.

"You were fine one minute and then you were gone," Lucian said.

"I'm sorry."

"Don't say you're sorry. There's no reason to be." Casey brushed his hand across the side of my face and lifted my chin.

I sighed. "Remember that time I came here with Eli to help George move?"

Casey's jaw tightened. "You don't have to finish."

Lucian's eyes went to Casey, and his brow furrowed.

I could see he wanted to know. I couldn't blame him. I went completely mental.

"It's fine, Casey."

"No, you don't have to go into this. He's out of your life for good."

I turned to Lucian. "Eli and I came here . . . before everything . . . We were . . . uh . . ."

"Making out," Casey finished for me.

I turned to look at him and wondered if me telling this was bothering him more than me now that I'd regained my sanity. I turned back to Lucian and tried to ignore Casey.

"He had me pressed against the wall. My back pushed buttons, and we ended up landing on Casey's floor . . . mid-heated moment . . . just as he was leaving. It was awkward, and I haven't been in the elevator with anyone except Casey since. It was just too much. It felt like I was back there again. I could feel his hands . . . the buttons . . ." I whispered. "I just couldn't handle the thought of being that way with him . . . after he . . . it just felt too real."

Casey looked away.

"I see," Lucian said, his mouth tight. He stood. "I should go."

Casey squeezed my hand, then released me, and stood. I leaned back against the couch as they left the room together. I could hear them, despite their hushed voices.

"How often does that happen?" Lucian asked. His voice was full of anger.

"Shh . . ." Casey said. "That was the first time. Trust me—I'm as surprised as you."

"She needs time to work through these things."

"I've been trying, but it isn't easy, and Edward isn't all that keen on the idea, either, if you couldn't tell."

"I'll buy her some time with Edward, but you need to help her decompress *now*."

"I know that." I could hear the edge in Casey's voice.

"Good."

The next thing I heard was the chime of the elevator, and the front door closed with a *thud*.

Casey appeared, looking agitated. He stood without saying anything as if he wasn't sure how to proceed.

"I'm fine," I said.

He hesitated, still remaining quiet.

I looked up at him. He looked worried, yet his face held something I'd never seen before. *Uncertainty?*

He sighed, leaned over, and kissed my forehead.

"Are you hungry?" he asked, his face still resting on my head.

I didn't really feel like eating, but my stomach grumbled, so I nodded.

"I'll be right back." He handed me the remote. "Turn on what you want. I should only be a few minutes."

He left the room, but I could hear his voice as it carried from somewhere in the back of the apartment. It sounded like he was on the phone. I sank back into the couch and rested my head back to stare at the ceiling.

I really mucked things up this time. Lucian will probably look at me like I'm fragile from now on. That killed me. I'd been working so hard to be independent and strong. I'd had a fresh start with Lucian, and now that had been ruined all because of a stupid elevator.

And Casey? The fact that Eli still affected me so much was hard for us both, but to hear details he probably never wanted to know about what went on in the elevator before the doors slid open?

I hated that either of them saw me that way, like an invalid.

When Casey stepped back into the room, he'd changed into sweat pants and a ribbed tank top. His muscles bulged as he made his way over to me.

"I don't know what came over me."

"Stress. You've been through a lot, and you haven't taken enough time for yourself. To heal."

"Well, that hasn't really been an option."

He cocked his head.

"What would I have been able to pull back on?" I asked, challenging him.

"You didn't have to go back to work so soon."

"It would have raised too many questions if I didn't."

"Who cares?"

"My parents!" I shouted. I shrank back into the couch, feeling terrible. I'd never yelled at him like that before. I couldn't say I'd ever yelled at anyone like that before.

What is wrong with me?

I bit my lip. "I'm sorry," I whispered. I looked down at my hands. *I'm messing everything up.* "I should go." I stood.

Shoot! I don't have my car.

Casey put his hands on my shoulders. "Stop."

I looked up at him. A single tear slid down my face.

"What's wrong with me?"

"Nothing. Nothing is wrong with you. Sit down."

I sat and brought my knees up to my chest. How could an elevator cause so many problems?

One stupid elevator.

Casey walked around the couch and pulled me back against it. He rubbed my shoulders. At first, it didn't do much, but soon my muscles began to loosen, and the tension start to ebb away. My whole body relaxed.

There was a knock at the door. Casey kissed the side of my head. "Be right back."

A few minutes later, he returned with bags of food and plates. The smell emanated in, and my mouth watered.

Casey handed me a plate and laid out all the food in front of us. Fried chicken, mashed potatoes and gravy, macaroni and cheese, and biscuits. Comfort food.

"I'm going with Bailey and the others to a pottery place tomorrow," I said.

"Oh yeah? That'll be nice to get out with them. You haven't done much with Bailey lately."

"Nope, we've been too busy."

Or maybe that was just me.

CHAPTER FIVE

The next day after work, I went home and showered to get the smell of stale coffee out of my hair. Bailey and the others would meet me at the pottery place at five o'clock. I was sure this would be just what I needed to get out of my funk.

When I walked in, the smell of paint assaulted me at the door. I saw my friends crowded around a large table near the back. Alexis already held a ceramic piece in front of her, while the other two talked and pointed to the wall, no doubt still trying to decide what to paint.

"Hey, guys."

"Oh, good! You're here." Bailey grabbed me by the elbow and pulled me to the pottery wall. "I can't decide. You *have* to help me."

She held up a ballerina bank and a coffee mug. I stared at the two pieces.

"If it were me, I'd choose the mug. You'll use it more."

She eyed the pieces. "You're so right!" She set the ballerina down and skipped back to the table with the mug clutched in her hands.

Breanne sidled up beside me. "Glad I'm not the only who hasn't decided what to paint yet."

I smiled but didn't tell her that I'd picked out my piece before I even came. "What are you trying to decide between?" I asked.

She looked at me sheepishly. "There's nothing that's caught my eye yet."

I quickly found the same box Bailey and I had painted last time. "How about this? Me and Bailey have made these before. They turned out really pretty."

She nodded with a smile. "I like it."

I went over and grabbed a platter. This would be my mom's Christmas present. I smiled, thinking about the things she might use it for. It had been a long time since I'd made her a gift.

Bailey eyed the platter when I got back to the table. "That's a big piece to paint," she said.

"Yeah, it's for my mom for Christmas. I already got her something, but . . ." I shrugged. "She'll get two gifts."

"That's a good idea! Why didn't I think of that? This mug just turned into my dad's Christmas present!" Bailey said, sounding thrilled with the idea.

Soon, teal paint was spread over my entire platter. Then I decided that I'd do a diamond border on the lip in brown. Before I was even halfway done, Bailey, Alexis, and Breanne had finished theirs, paid, returned to the table, and sat down with their purses in their laps.

"You guys don't have to wait for me. I'll probably be a while."

"Are you sure?" Alexis asked, looking uncertain.

"Of course."

"Breanne and I were going to see a movie. Bailey do you want to come? Starts in twenty minutes next door."

"Uh . . ." Bailey hesitated, looking from me to Alexis.

"Go, Bailey. I'm fine. Really."

"I should stay."

"No, you should go to the movie. Don't feel like you have to sit here with me," I said.

She looked at me as if she were still debating. I nodded, smiling.

"All right," she said. "See you Monday?"

"Yep."

She gave my shoulders a quick squeeze, and the three of them bounded out.

The noises around me faded into a low murmur of white noise as I continued painting. I relished the time. When I'd finished every detail, I felt completely relaxed. Not once did I think about Edward or my nightmares. I thought only of my brush strokes. It was the best time I'd had all week.

When I walked out, I decided to catch a movie by myself, for the first time *ever*, but when I rounded the corner, I came face-to-face with Edward.

I groaned. *So much for relaxation.*

"Hello, Abby," he said.

"What are you doing here?" I crossed my arms.

"We need to talk."

Edward clasped his hands in front of himself. When I didn't answer, he continued, "Obviously, I can't force you to talk to me. But I do wish you would, if not now, soon."

I stood my ground, staring at him, debating if I should stay or bolt. It was tempting to just brush him off and go to the movies.

Edward never faltered.

I sighed and crossed my arms. "Fine. Where?"

Edward put his hand out, gesturing me to turn around, and we started walking to the parking lot.

Of course, somewhere private.

He stopped and opened the door for me. I turned to look at him again.

"It won't be long. I promise," he said.

I sank into the seat of his pristine car and was hit with the smell of rich leather. I didn't feel like I should touch anything, it was so clean. Edward slipped into the driver's seat, and we headed out of the lot.

We were silent for a couple miles before I couldn't take it any longer.

"What is it you wanted to talk to me about?" I asked.

"Lucian is unwilling to talk about you. To be honest, it's coming out of left field, so to speak. He's usually very direct and doesn't often change his mind. But now, he says he was wrong, that you haven't advanced like he'd thought. I would like to know from *you* how you're feeling."

"I'm fine. I wish everyone would stop worrying about me."

"Are their concerns valid?"

I remained quiet for a moment and stared out the window, trying to think of what to say. I had always been compelled to tell Edward the truth. That hadn't changed. "Maybe after yesterday."

"What happened yesterday?"

"Uh . . . I guess you could say I had a little meltdown. It wasn't a big deal, though."

"What do you mean by *meltdown*?" His calm voice remained even and mellow, much more than I felt on the inside.

"It was just stress. I felt like I was in an elevator with Eli. A flashback that felt a little too real. No big deal."

"Sounds like post-traumatic stress."

"No. Absolutely not. I'm fine."

Edward eyed me. "I hope you're being honest with me because I'm about to ask a lot of you."

"It was a moment of weakness, nothing more."

"You're sure?"

"I'm fine."

"Good. Lucian told me that he explained some of what I want to move forward with, at your wish, that is."

"He didn't say much."

"I want you to work for me."

I hesitated. "What does that mean?"

"For a long time, there have been good and bad Protectors. I've been trying to find the best way to determine if Protectors are still following our guidelines or if they have their own agenda. It can be incredibly tempting to do what you want when you are a gifted immortal. And it can sometimes be difficult to prove. That's where you come in. I've never met anyone gifted, yet unlike us. I want to put you in the field to find Protectors who have turned their backs on our values."

"But how would I be able to do anything?"

"I'm still working on those details. Eventually, after you've graduated, I would like to assign a suspect Protector to you. That would give you the up-close-and-personal connection you need without throwing up any red flags."

"How am I any different than anyone else?" I asked.

"You are mortal. Bad Protectors won't know that you know anything about them. Then there's your gift. It gives you an upper hand. I have an inkling that your dreams will help show you the bad in each case before anything happens, and that is how I hope to catch them."

"I see." I looked out the window and tried to hide my surprise. *Work for Edward?* "That is a lot."

"I'll give you some time to think about it." He pulled the car into a parking space. I glanced over, and we were parked right next to my car. *How did I miss the drive back?*

"Okay."

"Don't be a stranger. If you have questions, don't be afraid to ask."

I nodded, slipped out of his car, and climbed into mine. I sat for a few minutes, letting it all sink in. *Work for Edward?*

I knew he wanted my help, but somehow I'd only expected him to want to know what happened in my dreams.

I grabbed my phone.

"Hey," Casey's soothing voice answered my call. "How was painting?"

"It was really good . . . until Edward showed up."

$*$ $*$ $*$ $*$

Casey pulled into the space next to mine, and I got out to meet him. "I'm so glad you're here," I said.

He walked over and put his arm around me as he gave me a quick peck on the cheek. I held him longer than normal, soaking in all the comfort his arms gave me.

"I missed you today." I snuggled into his chest as we walked.

"I missed you too. What happened? You've got me on pins and needles."

"Edward wants me to work for him," I said.

"Work for him? Doing what?" The perplexed look on his face reflected my own feelings.

"Finding out if Protectors are still protecting, or if they've gone off on their own, discarding the Protector's standards, I guess."

"What?"

"He wants me to go in as if I have no idea about this world. I guess you could say I'd be a spy."

"Abby, you can't. Please tell me you aren't even considering it." Casey stopped walking and turned to face me.

"I'd be lying."

"Talk to the team. Please. They won't want you to do it either. This isn't the right thing for you."

"Why?"

"Do you know how dangerous problem Protectors can be?"

I glared at him. If anyone knew how dangerous a twisted immortal could be, it was me. "Umm . . . I think I have an idea."

He sighed, rubbing his brow. "Of course you do. I'm sorry. I just can't sit back and watch you walk into more of the problems that you've been trying so hard to escape."

"I get that, but if not me, who? Edward thinks my gift will be a big help, and it's not like there are a ton of gifted mortals walking around. Maybe if I do this, I can help someone like me. Maybe I can stop them from going through what I went through."

"But, Abby, that's not something that happens a lot. It's rare for a Protector to go bad. Really rare. You are certainly a magnet for them, though."

"Exactly."

"Promise me you won't agree right away. At least give yourself time to think about it."

I nodded. "I promise."

We decided to see a movie together since we were already there. Casey bought the tickets, and we walked into the theater hand-in-hand. At first, it was hard to focus on the movie, but as I cuddled up to him, I began to relax.

On the way back to my house, Casey picked up food. When I pulled into the driveway after beating him back, I sat there, watching the top of my convertible slide away and the night surround me. Only minutes passed before Casey pulled in and handed me the food. He threw his leg over the door and pushed himself up and over into the passenger seat. We ate in my car in my driveway. It was our own, quicker version of a picnic, and of course, with the top down, it felt romantic. The stars sparkled above us in the clear sky all while the heated seats kept us warm.

"This is good," I said.

"Mmm-hmm," Casey mumbled.

It was quiet for a while as we both digested the crazy evening that had unfolded around us.

"Thanks for coming tonight. I'm not sure what I'd do without you," I said.

"There's nowhere I'd rather be."

When we finished, Casey grabbed all the garbage and tossed it in the big bin by the garage. He walked me to my doorstep and kissed me goodbye. As he walked away, I sensed he was hesitant to leave, but then, like nothing, he continued on.

I wondered if he'd wanted to say something but changed his mind. Maybe he wanted to say more about Edward's plan.

I thought about his suggestion of talking to the team before I decided. I couldn't deny that it was a good idea, and I had every intention of doing so. I knew they were a bit more neutral toward Edward than Casey was, and that made them the perfect people to ask.

The next day, after work, I came home, made some mac and cheese, and ate in the dining room with a book in my hand.   I must have been so into it that I didn't even hear the doorbell. Casey peeked his head into the room.

"Hey," he said.

He had an ear-to-ear grin on his face.

"Hey . . . what's with that face?" I closed my book and looked him over.

Ferdinand and Luke jumped out from behind him.

"Surprise!" Luke shouted.

"Get some shoes on, and let's go," Casey said, almost giddy.

"I'm in sweatpants."

"That's perfect," Luke said.

I popped my hip and put my hand on it as I left the room. "What do you guys have up your sleeves?"

Casey reached out, grabbing my shoulders, and spun me around. "Shoes."

I glanced over my shoulder at the three guys standing behind me, all with goofy grins on their faces.

"Go!" they all said in unison.

"Okay, okay! I'm going."

I jogged upstairs, found the first pair of flip flops I could, and threw them on, despite the fact that it was winter.

When I got back downstairs, I popped my head into the living room. Mom and George were curled up watching a movie in their PJ's.

"I'm going out with the guys, okay?"

"Okay, honey. Be home by curfew," she called.

The guys stood in the doorway. Casey and Luke threw an arm around me and pulled me to the car. Ferdinand hopped in the driver's seat.

I laced my fingers into Casey's, sat back, and let them surprise me with whatever they'd planned. As he drove, it became clear he was headed toward Casey's apartment. Except Ferdinand didn't turn into the parking garage but, instead, passed it. He drove further down along the lake that sat at the base of the apartment building. I often looked down at the water from Casey's window, and I'd never seen so many people gathering at the water's edge. The crowd seemed to be growing by the minute.

"What is this?" I asked as he turned into a parking lot that seemed almost full.

The guys ignored me as they grabbed a box, cooler, and blankets from the trunk.

"Come on—we have to hurry."

They jogged across the field to a dock. A few boats were waiting, tied to it.

Luke jumped onto the closest one to us.

"We're here," he announced.

Casey helped me step aboard. My mind still spun. *What are we doing?*

Brad called out, "Ready? 3, 2 . . .1!"

The entire boat lit up. Christmas lights were strung across the boat, lining the walls in thin rows. On the bow, a blow-up snowman came to life and lifted from the floor.

"Wow, this is amazing. What is all this for?"

"A boat light parade," Brad said.

"That's a thing?" I asked.

"Oh, yeah it is. We've won two years in a row." Brad pumped his fist.

"We would have won last year, too, if it weren't for the dead battery . . ."

"Let it go, Luke," Brad said.

"Fine. We're going to win this year. That's all that matters."

Ferdinand shook his head. "And how do you know that?" He crossed his arms.

"Because I've got a plan." Luke's smirk was contagious.

I shivered against the cold breeze that swept over the boat. Casey grabbed one of the blankets and put it around my shoulders.

"Right . . ." Ferdinand lifted the cooler into the boat.

Luke leaned over. "Don't listen to him. Wanna help me?"

"Sure," I said. "With what?"

He turned me toward the back of the boat and pushed me up the stairs to the upper deck of the huge boat. He grabbed a box before following me up.

Inside the box was some wire, a few strings of lights, and two costumes. Santa Claus and a present.

What did I sign up for?

"Hand me those wires," Luke said.

One by one, I handed Luke each wire. Slowly, a Christmas tree shape emerged.

"You can sit," Luke said as he worked, fitting and bending the pieces together.

"I'm all right."

He moved forward and pulled the box off the seat closest to him. "Sit. Relax." He stopped, waiting for me to sit.

I gave him a weird look and sat. He went back to work.

What is his deal?

Then it hit me. He knew.

"Casey told you about my . . . reaction. In the elevator."

"We don't keep those kinds of secrets from each other, but don't worry—it doesn't leave us four," he said it casually, yet it felt so revealing.

I looked at my hands. It was bad enough Casey and Lucian saw it firsthand, but now they all knew.

"Edward wants me to work for him."

Luke went rigid and stood up. "What?" His open mouth and furrowed brows told me that maybe I'd been wrong to think they'd have a different opinion than Casey.

"Yeah. That's how I felt at first."

"What does he want you to do?"

"He wants me to find the bad Protectors. Be a spy of sorts, I guess." I braced for his reaction, but, at most, his face twisted. I didn't know what that meant. I waited for him to speak. For once, he didn't jump in to talk right away. "Say something."

"I don't know what to say."

I glanced over the rail, watching Ferdinand goofing around at the front of the boat.

"I'm the king of the world," he yelled.

I giggled at him.

Luke looked over at me. "What does Casey think?"

I turned my attention back to him, my lips tight, but didn't say anything.

"That's what I thought."

"But I want to know what *you* think about it," I said.

He rubbed his forehead. "I don't know. I'm not sure what Edward has in mind, but it sounds dangerous, and being that you don't have immortality . . . I don't think it's a good idea to put you in the field with people who are trained to do a lot of damage."

"So, you don't think I should?"

He looked at me as if I were asking him how I looked and he didn't want to say the wrong thing.

"I just wonder how he can promise you safety. I mean, he's putting you in the field, right? Or am I wrong?"

"No," I grumbled.

"What were you hoping I'd say?"

"I don't know. It always seemed like Casey had something against Edward, so I thought he was being biased."

He chuckled. "Oh, he has something against Edward all right, but when it comes to this, he's right. I wouldn't want to see anything happen to you. You've already been through too much."

"I know."

"We can't make the choice for you. Only you can do that. We're hardwired to protect, so seeing danger and not trying to stop it would go against our instincts."

"Yeah . . ." I hesitated. "Can you keep this between us? At least for now? I'll tell them . . . after I decide what to do."

"Sure. It's between us, for now. I really hope you think hard before you decide."

"I will."

He turned back to the tree he was constructing, and it was quiet until he placed the last piece in place—the star.

"Hand me a string of lights?"

I pulled the whole bundle of lights from the box and worked to untangle it. When the first strand was freed, I handed it to him. As I worked, I found one strand that was all yellow—for the star, I assumed.

"Want to wrap some of them?" he asked without looking up.

I stepped over, watching him and the way he worked them around the wire. Then I copied what he was doing. In the time it took me to do one, he finished three, and it was done except for the star he was working on.

He stepped back and looked it over.

"Ready?"

I nodded, and my fingertips brushed my lips.

He grabbed the plug, and a sly grin spread across his face.

A hand found my lower back.

"You're just in time," Luke said.

He pushed the plug into the extension cord, and the tree lit up so brightly I had to shield my eyes.

"Wow, dude. That's a lot of lights."

"Yep. We're going to win." He couldn't have looked prouder.

Luke turned back to the box as the rest of the guys came to see his creation.

"Now for the finishing touches." He held up the two costumes I'd seen earlier. "You in, Abby?"

"Me?"

All the guys looked at me, huge smiles on their faces.

Luke nodded.

I stared at the costumes in his hands.

"Oh, all right. I'll do it."

"Yes! See, we're *so* gonna win!"

He tossed me the present costume. I turned to the rest of the guys to ask where to change. All of them were holding back sniggers. Casey looked down, one hand covering his mouth, the other pointing toward a door to the left of us.

I slipped inside and tried to ignore the laughter that erupted once it closed.

I glanced around the room. There was a bed, two nightstands, a dresser, and a full-length mirror. It was a gorgeous room. The all-white bedding looked really inviting in the chilly night.

I lifted my shirt over my head and slipped into the costume. It was then that I noticed the battery pack tucked into the pocket.

Oh man.

I closed my eyes. Then flipped the switch. I paused, bracing myself for what I would see, and looked in the mirror. Lights twinkled all over the costume, making me stand out just as much as the Christmas tree. I would never live this down.

I knew they would all be waiting as soon as the door opened. I closed my eyes, took a deep breath, and stepped out. I waited, but when I heard nothing, I opened one eye. All the guys turned around. Each immediately excused themselves in fits of laughter, claiming they had things to get ready.

Except Luke, who was just slipping into the bright red Santa coat, completing his costume.

"Are you ready?" he asked with a twinkle in his eye.

I nodded, and with that, all of the white fur that lined his costume lit up. Flashing bright white lights twinkled in time with the Christmas tree. Luke made one quick adjustment on my battery pack, and mine flashed along with his too. We were sure to stand out.

I heard the guys below, moving about and calling to each other. Then, with a small lurch, we started moving. I grabbed the railing as I stumbled.

Boats lined up ahead and behind us in a neat row, despite the wake bumping them about.

In the distance, I could see a huge crowd that lined the edges of the water and went back as far as I could see.

The floodlights around the crowd suddenly went out, and a cheer went up.

There were so many really well-lit boats. The competition must be pretty steep. I hoped, for Luke's sake, we won.

One by one, each boat moved forward for all to see. Soon, we were next, waiting just enough time to allow sufficient space.

Luke pulled me to the front deck. "Make sure you wave a lot." He adjusted the positioning of my lights until they were just the way he wanted them and stood back. He gave a quick nod and turned to the crowd.

I bit my lip. *At least nobody out there knows me.*

The boat chugged forward.

As we drew closer to the crowds, the cheering grew louder. I smiled at them and waved.

Luke danced around next to me, jumping and shaking his tushie. I giggled at him. Then I threw out my fear, took his cue, and joined in alongside him. I bounced around in a circle, shaking my whole body and waving like a giant goof.

It seemed like such a short time, and it was over. I panted and gripped my cramping side.

"Oh my gosh, that was so much fun!"

"You were amazing!" He high-fived me.

Once the parade ended, all the boats returned to the dock for the awarding of the winner. As our boat coasted across the water, I ducked into the room and slipped out of the costume. I felt a lot better in my own clothes.

We pulled into our slip, where the judges were waiting with a first-place plaque.

"Congratulations! Santa and the present were the best part of the parade," one of them said before they walked away.

"Heck yeah they were!" Luke fist pumped and danced around the boat, pointing to each of the guys. "Told ya! Told ya!"

They let him have his fun and set to work cleaning up the boat and preparing to disembark. I pitched in where I could, but mostly I just got in the way. Eventually, I gave up and stepped onto the dock to wait.

"Hey, you guys want to come back to my place and order pizza to celebrate?" Casey asked.

His question was met with a round of yesses.

"You too?" he asked me as he stepped onto the dock.

"Sure."

*　　　*　　　*　　　*

We filed into Casey's apartment and shed our layers of jackets and hats at the door. The warmth of his apartment settled into my bones. My stomach groaned.

Casey pulled out menus, and the hungry guys dominated ordering, so I sat back and waited in the living room. They would order enough for me.

As each sat down around the table with me, it remained quiet. Exhaustion and hunger seemed to be hitting us all.

"Should we play cards or something?" I asked.

Before anyone could answer, Casey jumped in. "Did Abby tell any of you the news?" "News?" Brad asked.

News? What news?

Casey didn't give me a choice to say anything before he blurted it out. "Edward wants her to work for him."

My jaw dropped, but I was quick to clamp it shut. Luke looked at me and then at Casey.

What is Casey doing?

That was my news. Or it should have been. I squirmed my seat, unsure if I should speak or leave.

"What!" Ferdinand said. It wasn't a question.

"What does he want her to do?" Brad asked.

"He wants her to fish out the bad Protectors," Luke said. "And I'm not sure she wanted all of us to know about it until she'd made up her mind." He was looking directly at Casey. Angry.

"She's part of this team. It's important that everyone knows what's going on."

"It's okay." I glanced down at my hands.

"Why does he want Abby? Shouldn't it be a Protector's job?"

"Because of her gift," Luke said.

"And since I'm not a Protector, they'll be more likely to trust me," I finished for him.

Brad shook his head and blew out a breath. "I don't like it."

"See," Casey said.

"What are you doing, Casey? Are you hoping that we're all going to side with you and push her into what you want? It's her choice!" Luke said, raising his voice.

"So, you think she should do it?" Casey asked.

"I didn't say that. But getting the team to side with you isn't going to stop her if she decides to do it."

"I know that. She's free to make her own choices. I just wanted her to know what everyone else thinks before she decides."

"And what does everyone think?" I asked.

All eyes were on me. I knew they might be afraid to say how they felt, so I eyed each of them and waited for someone to speak up.

There was a knock at the door, and Luke went to get the food and was back a second later.

"Like I said before, I don't like it. It's very dangerous dealing with people like that," Brad said.

"I agree, but again, I'm with you either way." Luke reached over and squeezed my hand.

"I don't want you to. You've already faced so much. It's finally over. It's time for you to move on. Time for you to be happy," Ferdinand said.

Casey looked thrilled that everyone agreed with him. Though their opinions did nothing to change my mind. It almost irritated me to hear them. I pointedly looked each of them in the eye.

If Casey thought for one second he could pressure me into saying *no*, he had another thing coming.

"And what if I've already made up my mind?" I asked. "I've decided to go ahead with it."

All of them stopped and stared at me. Casey's look of anguish made me sick to my stomach. I knew it wasn't the answer he wanted or expected, especially after everyone had just sided with him.

"I'll be with you every step of the way." Luke broke the silence. His eyes never left me.

"Thanks," I said.

He nodded and went back to eating.

The rest of the guys ate, too, but they didn't say anything else about it. Eventually, Ferdinand brought up football, and the chatter began again.

Casey didn't talk to me the rest of the night. In a way, I didn't blame him. I understood where he was coming from. He didn't want me hurt. But it was my choice, and he needed to accept that.

It was Brad who hopped out of the driver's seat and walked me to my door that night after dinner. And I felt a twinge of guilt.

"Just give him some time," Brad said. "He'll come around. He's just in shock and worried."

I nodded.

He gave me a quick hug and was gone.

CHAPTER SIX

I hoped that after Casey took time to sleep on it, the shock would wear off. But the next day, when I hadn't heard from him by dinner, I concluded that he still couldn't handle it. I threw myself into bed and fought the frustration. *I didn't do anything wrong.*

I grabbed my phone and called my dad. It rang twice before he picked up.

"Hey Dad."

"Oh, honey, it's good to hear from you."

"Christmas is next week! Is everything coming together for you to come?" I asked.

"Of course. Nothing could keep me away."

"Good." I smiled to myself.

"Have you finished shopping?" he asked.

"Yeah, in November."

"Just like your mother, always so prepared," he said in adoration.

"Yep!"

"I bet they're already wrapped and under the tree."

I giggled. "A Christmas tree wouldn't be a Christmas tree without presents underneath."

"It sure wouldn't."

The line fell quiet. "Are you busy?" I asked.

"Oh, I'm just looking at the ordering sheets. I should probably let you go so I can get this done, but I'm so glad you called. I needed that."

"All right, Dad. I love you."

"I love you too, honey."

"Bye."

I felt so much better after talking to Dad. He always seemed to put me in a good mood.

*   *   *   *

The next evening I sat, waiting, in front of Lucian's house just as he'd asked me to. Casey still hadn't called, and I was grateful for the distraction. Lucian seemed excited for whatever he'd planned. When he'd said to dress in black running clothes, I knew it was sure to be an interesting night.

He swung his car into the garage ten minutes late.

"You know, when you tell someone to meet you, usually you're there when they arrive."

"Yeah, yeah. My meeting ran late. Come on, I have to change real quick."

"Make me wait even longer . . ." I sighed.

He stopped at the door, not allowing me to enter. "Did I just hear you joke twice in a row?"

I stuck my tongue out at him. "Just hurry up, would you?"

Even though he was making me wait, I couldn't help but take advantage of his glorious backyard. The sunset left a dull glow in the sky, with just enough light to illumine a few waves coming in.

Lucian emerged from the back of the house. I looked him over. He was dressed in black jogging clothes to match mine. Headphones dangled from his phone.

"So, what is it you have planned for me?" I asked.

"A little run. Sound too strenuous?"

"How little?"

A wicked grin settled on his face.

"I figured we'd start out with a jog around the neighborhood, and then we could wander the warehouses."

"Is that allowed?" I asked, remembering the fences that surrounded them. The last thing I wanted was to get caught doing something we weren't supposed to be doing.

He shrugged and tapped his headphones. "We'll play dumb."

That thought gave me nerves I couldn't shake.

He tossed me a pair of headphones. "Just plug them in. Don't turn on the music."

He took off out the door, leaving me in the dust. I picked up the pace and caught up to him in no time, but it took its toll. I was already panting.

It was harder to *keep* pace, and I fell behind. Lucian slowed down to stay with me, and I took advantage of it by slowing even more.

"What? Is running not your thing?" He hardly sounded winded.

"What . . . gave you . . . that idea?" I said through breaths, sarcasm trailing from each word.

He shook his head.

Our circle through the neighborhood was bringing us closer to the warehouses. My nerves escalated, making me nauseated.

"Are you sure about this?" I asked.

"What's the worst that can happen?"

The gate surrounding the complex of warehouses was just ahead of us. There wasn't an opening, and I wondered if he expected me to climb it. *That wouldn't end well.* Then I spotted a place where the fence had been cut. It wasn't noticeable from afar, and I couldn't be sure, but I suspected that Lucian had come ahead of time to take care of that.

He slipped through first and held it open for me to squeeze through. I caught myself on a sharp wire, and a pool of blood rolled down my arm. I bit my lip and pressed the bottom of my shirt against it to stop it from dripping. The blood kept coming, I rolled up my sleeve, hoping the pressure would make it stop, or at least keep it from dripping everywhere.

"You okay?" Lucian asked.

"I'm fine. Just a scratch," I lied through the pain.

For once, someone listened to what I said. He dodged in front of me and continued forward, picking up the pace to a notch faster than a walk. I propelled myself forward, trotting along next to him.

I doubted anyone would believe I was a jogger. I was panting— even with the slow gait I maintained. I tried to calm my breathing to no avail.

Lucian grabbed my arm and pulled me forward, shoving me against the building with his body. His chest heaved with each breath. He peeked around the corner from where we'd come.

"Go," he whispered, pointing in the opposite direction. "Stay against the wall."

A beam of light bounced around as the holder drew closer. Anxiety swept through me. *If they catch us, what will they do?*

I took one step, but my feet froze to the ground. Lucian ran right into me. He grunted, pushing me forward, kicking me into gear. I rushed around the next corner, glancing around. Nothing looked familiar so far, and the symbol I was looking for had yet to present itself.

Using the cover of the building, Lucian took the opportunity to sidestep around me to get ahead. He grabbed my hand, pulling me along with him, running until we were two buildings over.

I doubled over, clutching my side. "The next time you suggest a covert op in which jogging is our cover, I won't participate!" I wheezed.

"Oh, come on. You'll be fine. Now, keep your eyes open," he hissed.

He was all business and, for a moment, I missed his wisecracking. Just for a moment before I came to my senses, whimpered, and kept moving.

The warehouse yard was far larger than I'd realized. After weaving between a few more buildings, we came to another fence—the end of the road.

"You didn't see anything familiar?" he asked, easing to a stop.

I shook my head.

He grimaced. "All right. Let's go back the opposite way. Maybe we'll see something we missed from the other side."

I nodded, ready to follow. He turned like he was going to take off, but then whirled back around. I almost ran into him.

"We have a higher chance of running into the guard this way. Be ready to duck and cover."

I sighed.

My eyes darted about, watching for any shred of light. We rounded the first building, and I held my breath until I knew the coast was clear. We were so close to getting out, and I had a sneaking suspicion that our luck was running out.

I stepped up the pace and sped past Lucian, hoping that the faster we ran, the sooner we could get this over with. Lucian followed suit at first, but as we neared the third building, he tried to slow me down. I pressed on.

As I jogged around the next corner, Lucian grabbed me from behind, covering my mouth with his hand. My back slammed against his chest, knocking the wind from my lungs. Lucian's grip tightened as he pulled me back around the corner. My heart pounded. My cut screamed in protest as his arm pressed against it. I bit my tongue to stop myself from crying out.

"He turned his flashlight off," Lucian whispered in my ear. He leaned around me, trying to gain a better view. A moment passed before he stepped out. "Slower this time, okay?"

He wasn't happy with me. *Good job, Abby.*

I kept close to him. *Two more.* He jogged along until a shout sounded behind us. I whipped around to see a guard running toward us, his flashlight shining. Lucian didn't hesitate.

"Run!"

Lunging after him, I stumbled but remained on my feet if only by miracle. He beat me to the gate and held it open for me. I squeezed through as fast as I could, and Lucian pushed me forward as he threw himself through the opening.

"Go! Go!"

We sprinted until we were two streets over, near Lucian's house, and I could run no more. I slowed down, letting him pass me. He held the door wide open when I got there, and I jogged through it before collapsing on his floor, panting.

"What were you thinking, running ahead? You're lucky we didn't get caught."

I shrugged.

"You're going to get me in trouble with stunts like that." He shook his head. I could see his mischievous grin returning. He wasn't really mad.

"I can't believe we got away," I said, still feeling my heart racing.

He put his back to the wall and slid to the floor across from me, his breathing still erratic.

"So, you didn't see anything?"

I shook my head. "Nope."

He brought his knees up and rested his arms on them. "I really hoped that was the place. It made sense—you'll be by it a lot more."

I could tell he was deep in thought. Finally, he stood and reached down to help me up. As I reached for his hand, the red smear across my arm caught his eye.

"That doesn't look so good," he said.

"Oh. I forgot all about it."

"Come on."

I followed him into the kitchen, and he handed me Band-Aids and ointment. Once I cleaned the cut, I realized it was worse than I'd thought. The edges pulled open with each movement of my arm.

Lucian looked at it and whistled through his teeth. "You got yourself good. I think you'd be best off to use a butterfly on that one. Need any help?"

I shook my head. He wasn't treating me like glass, and I didn't want him to start, but I figured out soon enough that putting a butterfly on one-handed wasn't exactly a piece of cake.

I tried to flatten it on my arm for the third time with one hand, my fingers stretching before I gave up.

"Actually, can you help me with this?" I asked.

He held out his hand, and I dropped the bandage in it. "Hold still." He pinched the cut together, his rough fingertips scratching the already-irritated skin.

I winced.

"Done."

I inspected his handiwork. "Thanks."

He nodded. "Hungry?"

"Starving. Someone made me run." I cocked my head to the side and pursed my lips.

He stopped and turned to look at me. "Man, listen to that sarcasm. You're beginning to sound like me! I'll go order food. Why don't you invite Casey over?" He left the room.

I hadn't told Lucian about meeting with Edward, nor had I told him Casey and I had been giving each other the silent treatment for two days because of it.

At first, I was upset with Casey, and I still wasn't pleased with how he'd handled the situation, but I was ready to put it behind us if he could. Maybe tonight would be a good icebreaker. I slipped into my sweater, pulled my phone from my pants pocket, and pressed Casey's speed dial. I felt butterflies in my stomach, wondering if he'd even answer. On the third ring, his voice came on the line.

"Hello."

"Hey!"

"What are you doing?" He was distracted, his voice monotone and unfocused.

"I'm at Lucian's. Are you hungry?"

"Ah . . ." He paused. I could hear voices in the background. Some didn't sound happy.

"Casey?"

"Oh. Umm . . . yeah, I could eat. What's up?"

"We're ordering food, and we thought you might want to join us."

"Ah . . ." He paused again.

I couldn't help but wonder what was holding his attention. "Casey?"

"Yeah. I'll be there in, say, thirty minutes? Text me the address."

"Is everything okay?"

"What? Oh . . . yeah, of course. See you in a bit."

He was acting strangely, but it didn't seem to be directed at me. I shrugged it off and texted him the address before returning to the living room where Lucian was finishing up on the phone.

I stood by the back door, gazing out at the beach. The darkness swallowed most of it in shadows, letting only bits of it be seen in the moonlight.

"Forty-five minutes," Lucian said, breaking me from my thoughts of Casey's weirdness and worry that tonight would be awkward.

"Huh?"

"The food? It'll be here in forty-five minutes."

"Oh. Good. Casey will be here in thirty."

"Hope you don't mind—I invited my girlfriend to join us. You like playing cards or board games?"

"Love board games. I haven't played one in a long time."

We picked through all of Lucian's games, leaving just three out when the doorbell rang and the front door opened.

"Hello?" a woman's voice called.

She stepped into the room. Her long blonde hair hung straight all the way to her hips, and her blue eyes looked like crystals, sparkling when the light hit them just right.

"Hey." Lucian stepped forward and kissed her cheek. He settled his arm around her waist. "Abby, this is my girlfriend, Willow. Willow, this is Abby."

"It's so good to meet you, Abby." Willow's voice was unique, brisk and scratchy, but I thought it sounded pretty. She stood taller than me, but still Lucian was taller.

I stood there, awestruck, when I realized I should have said something. "Uh . . . you too." I smiled extra wide, hoping to compensate for my momentary lapse. Knocking echoed in the entry.

"I'll get it," I said.

When I pulled the door open, Casey stood there. He looked nervous with his hands shoved in his pockets.

"Hey," I said.

I stepped back and let him walk in. Lucian and Willow still stood where I'd left them.

"Hi," Casey said. He turned to me, expectant.

"Oh! This is Casey. Casey this is Willow. And you've already met Lucin." My cheeks heated. *Oops.*

"Good to see you again," Lucian said, holding out a hand.

Casey took it. "You too."

Lucian eyed me. "You okay?"

I nodded quickly.

Willow and Lucian were amazing together—it wasn't hard to see from the moment she arrived. Her eyes often fell on him as she spoke, and a grin always found its way to her lips when his eyes met hers. Lucian's hand never left her back.

She was witty and poised, the perfect match to his snarky self. I liked her a lot.

"Before I forget, thanks for working with Abby. I was surprised when Abby told me who Edward assigned to help her."

"It's what I'm here for."

"Not really." Casey laughed.

"No, not usually," Lucian said, grinning. "To be honest, Edward didn't want just anyone working with her. He thinks she's got a lot of potential. And after what I've seen so far, I can't argue."

I blushed. The three of them were staring at me, and I felt like I was under a spotlight.

"She's talented for sure." A grin lit up Casey's face.

"Are you the one who taught her those mad martial arts skills?" Lucian asked.

I blew out the drink in my mouth all over the floor. My head shot up, my eyes as big as hockey pucks. "I'm so sorry!"

I jumped up and ran to the kitchen, feeling even more embarrassed. After grabbing cleaning supplies, I rushed back into the living room to clean up the mess I'd made.

Lucian and Casey had already dabbed up most of the mess with napkins when I returned.

"What do you mean?" Casey asked, giving me a strange look before turning his attention back to Lucian.

"Dude, she is fierce. She laid me out!"

"What?" Casey asked. Confusion deepened the lines on his face.

"I'm surprised she didn't tell you!"

"It' wasn't a big deal," I muttered, trying my best to downplay it.

"What happened?" Willow asked.

"I made the mistake of grabbing her arm. I underestimated her. She executed those maneuvers perfectly. Couldn't have taught her better myself."

"Go Abby!" Willow cheered and high-fived me.

"I was going to say good job on the training . . . I assumed it was you," Lucian said.

"Ah . . . yep, that was me." Casey looked like he didn't know whether he should be proud or worried.

"Should we play a game?" I asked, hoping to take the attention off of me.

After I lost the first two games, Willow grabbed my arm.

"Let the boys chat for a while. Come outside and talk. I'd like to get to know the infamous Abby a little better."

"I don't know about infamous," I said, following her outside to the porch. I slipped my shoes off and let the sand-dusted wood tickle my feet.

"Well, I've sure heard a lot about you. And not all has been from Lucian. That makes you famous in my book." She winked. "I always wondered what you looked like."

I looked down at myself.

"Like me, I guess."

As much as I liked Willow, I hated that everyone seemed to know all about the girl named Abby, yet I knew nothing about them. It seemed unfair. My cheeks warmed as I stared out at the water. I could almost make out the foam that tipped the waves as they crashed on the beach.

"So, are the rumors true?" she asked.

"What rumors?" Anxiety rose up inside me. The last thing I wanted to do was talk about Eli. It brought out so many emotions that were hard to mask.

"You know, the thing with Eli and the train?" Her inquisitive stare was so innocent, yet penetrating. She had no idea how painful it was to think about.

I sighed. "Yeah. They're true."

"Wow."

"I know, but can we not go into detail? It's not exactly a pleasant memory."

"Of course. Sorry to be nosy."

"It's fine. I understand the curiosity." I didn't really understand, but I wanted to be friends, so I put my feelings aside and made myself move on.

"How long have you and Lucian been together?" I asked.

"Forever. Sometimes it's hard to remember what my life was like before him."

She peered out at the water. Quiet fell between us. I didn't hear him approach, but when Casey slipped his arms around my waist, I felt at home. It felt so good after the silence the last few days.

"Mind if I borrow Abby?" he asked Willow, resting his chin on my shoulder.

She winked. "Not at all."

I watched her as she walked back inside. Lucian moved around the living room, straightening up the table and putting away the board games.

Casey turned me toward the steps. "Let's go for a walk."

"Lead the way."

My bare feet sank into the cool sand. He took me down to the water, and we let the cold waves wash over our feet.

"What do you think?" I asked gesturing around us. "It's pretty amazing, isn't it?"

"I'm surprised you haven't moved in," he teased.

We walked a bit more before he spoke again. "I'm glad you invited me. I wasn't sure if you were going to talk to me again after the way I acted. I feel bad about how the parade evening ended. I know it was all my fault." He paused. "I've been fighting with the team all day about it."

"Wait, what? Why?"

"I don't want to go into it all, but they're mad about how I treated you. And they're right. No matter how I feel. I shouldn't have acted that way."

I remained quiet, my lips tight. I hated the idea that they were fighting, but it made me feel good that the team was standing up for me. *Why does this have to be so confusing?*

He leaned over to look at me before he stopped me altogether. "Abby?"

"You know, the last time we were on the beach together wasn't exactly a good memory."

Once, he'd followed me to the beach and waited for Eli to leave before he made an appearance. I'd felt someone watching me for a while. Felt goosebumps rise on my arms.

Then, when I first saw him, I was so excited that I ran straight over to him. He told me then that Eli wasn't who I thought he was, that it was all an act. I'd been so mad at him. But it turned out that everything he said was true. He was protecting me.

The moonlight lit his half grin before he looked at the ground, embarrassed.

"Another one of my not-so-fine moments."

"I don't know," I said, thinking. "Now that I know what you were trying to do, I think it's kind of sweet."

His head lifted, and his dimples appeared.

"Really?"

I nodded. "Now, what do you say we make a new memory on the beach?"

I stood on tip toe, wrapped my arms around his neck, and kissed him. He responded, tilting his head down to meet mine. He squeezed me closer. Slowly, I pulled back, feeling breathless, and nestled my head into his neck, breathing in his spiced masculine scent. The cold water splashed around our ankles. Goosebumps rose on my whole body.

"Ah!" I jumped out of his arms, hopping from foot to foot until I was out of the crisp water's reach. Casey followed, chuckling.

We walked a bit farther until I could see the distant gleam of the lighthouse and looked on in awe of its beauty. "We should get back. It's getting late."

He spun me like we were dancing until I faced Lucian's, and we began our trek back.

When we came back inside, Willow and Lucian were snuggled up on the couch.

"Man. You're going to have to help me get my hands on a place like this!" Casey said.

Lucian laughed. "I don't know. These are quite hard to come by. Took a lot of pulled strings to get this place."

"I bet."

"You guys go see the lighthouse?" Lucian asked.

My face tinted. His mischievous smirk grew.

I ignored Lucian, hoping Casey would too. "We should go, Casey, I'm tired."

Casey's eyes narrowed. "Lighthouse?"

I squirmed. Grabbing Casey's arm, I tried to pull him from the room.

"Yeah, the lighthouse down the beach . . . ooh she made you turn around before you got to it, didn't she?" Lucian howled.

My stomach dropped.

"We really should go. I'm exhausted. Someone made me go running." I shot daggers with my eyes in Lucian's direction.

"Hey, it's good for you," Lucian said.

"Yeah, yeah." Grabbing my bag, I pushed a very confused Casey toward the door. "Thanks for tonight."

"Sorry we didn't find the warehouse," Lucian said.

Casey shot me another strange look.

"Don't worry about it. I'm just glad we didn't get caught. It was nice meeting you, Willow!"

Lucian chuckled. "Yeah, me too. Make sure you keep your arm clean. It's a pretty gnarly cut."

I cringed, imagining Casey's reaction. "I will."

I stepped out and waved as I walked to my car. Casey trailed behind. I held my breath, awaiting his onslaught of questions.

"What was that all about? A lighthouse? What did you almost get caught doing? What's wrong with your arm?" Casey hissed beside my car.

I gave one last wave to Lucian before he shut the door. Then I turned back to Casey to explain.

"I'm afraid of going inside lighthouses, okay? It's not a big deal."

"Why?"

I sighed and looked off in the distance.

"Tell me," he said. He wrapped his hand around mine.

"Because they're haunted," I whispered.

Casey started to laugh but caught himself

"See? That's why I don't tell people! They think I'm crazy."

"I'm sorry. It's not funny," he said, despite the grin on his face. "It's cute."

"It's not cute!"

His grin grew. "So, how did he know about it?"

"Did you see the lighthouse in the distance when we were walking on the beach?

He shook his head.

"Lucian and I went for a walk once, and I saw it in the distance. I mentioned how I thought it was pretty, so he said we should go check it out."

"And you wouldn't."

I shook my head. "It's so embarrassing."

"Nah, it's no big deal, just like you said. What about your arm? And getting caught? What was that about?"

I slid my sweater off my shoulder, exposing the Band-Aid. "We tried to find the warehouse from my dream."

"Oh my gosh, Abby!" Casey gasped. He reached out and gingerly touched the edges.

"It's not that bad."

"How did you try to find the warehouse? I don't understand."

"We went for a run." I shrugged. "Hence the black running clothes."

"Okay?" He waited for me to continue.

I gestured to the gated warehouses. "I think Lucian cut a hole in the gate a few blocks down. That's how I cut my arm. There was a sharp piece sticking out I didn't see. Typically clumsiness." I took a deep breath. "Anyway, we slipped in without being seen. On our way back, the guard chased us, but we were able to get away."

"What?" His smile was gone, and he sounded mad.

"It wasn't a big deal."

He ran his hands through his hair. "Abby, you're going to give me a heart attack one of these days."

He reached out and pulled me close.

"Oh, please. I was with Lucian. Besides, I'm a fast runner." I winked.

"Can you just not do this kind of thing anymore?"

With what I was signing up for with Edward, I knew I couldn't keep any kind of promises, but I wasn't going to drudge that up again.

"No promises."

"I can't even leave you for two days without you getting yourself into trouble." He backed away, shaking his head. "Get home before you get yourself in more trouble."

"Yes, sir," I said, giggling.

CHAPTER SEVEN

Mom, George, and I were finishing up my favorite Christmas movie when I saw Dad pull up in front of the house.

I bolted out the front door. "Dad!"

"Hey, Abbs!" He rounded the car and opened the trunk.

"Need any help carrying things in? Maybe some with pretty paper on them?"

He grinned. "Always the snoop. I've got it all, I think."

Unfortunately, this visit would be short, and it was booked solid with all of my favorite Christmas activities. With Mom and George joining us, there was bound to be lots of awkward moments.

Here's to our first combined Christmas!

I took a deep breath and threw the door open, "Dad's here!"

George came over first and shook Dad's hand. "Good to see you again. Need any help?"

Dad shook his head. "I've got it. Thanks." He hoisted the bag higher on his shoulder and headed toward the stairs. "The guest room still in the same place?"

"Yeah." Mom cleared her throat. "Make yourself comfortable."

I could see this was weird for her, but she was trying.

"We're going to see Christmas lights as soon as you're ready, Dad. I'm getting the hot chocolate ready right now."

Dad chuckled as I left the room, and I heard his footsteps on the stairs. All was right in my world.

We drove neighborhood after neighborhood with George at the wheel, Dad sitting right next to me. It was cozy in a weird sort of way.

I stuck my head out the window to get a closer look at some of the houses I liked the most.

"Oooh, Mom! Look! They have a whole cookie family!"

"How cute is that!" she said. "We need to step up our decorations next year."

Other than a handful of remarks from Mom and Dad, I did all of the talking. I tried not to let their silence make things feel strained.

After an hour, our hot chocolates were gone, and George drove us all back home.

I sighed as the silence stretched on inside the house. Eventually, George and Mom excused themselves to go to bed.

Dad waited until they'd gone before he spoke. "Well, that was a bit awkward, wasn't it?"

I raised my eyebrows and looked at him.

"Yeah . . . " He blew out a breath.

"It's okay," I said.

He smiled down at me, dropped his arm around my shoulders, and leaned over. "So, how do you like him?"

I thought of George. Thought of all the times he played stepdad, and not well. Thought of the time he came to me in the middle of the night after my nightmare. Of our middle-of-the-night chats. And then all the times he made my mom smile.

"I think he's a good one," I said.

He rubbed my arm absently. "Good. And you're okay with it all?"

"Yeah. I am."

He nodded. "I'm glad. I think . . . it's good that she's happy."

"Me too."

The next day—Christmas Eve—we built gingerbread houses. Casey even joined us. Of all of them, Mom's was my favorite. She always had a knack for decorating.

Casey and Dad cleaned up the mess on the dining room table while Mom, George, and I finished cooking our huge Christmas dinner. It felt great, all of us working together, just like Christmas always did growing up. Except that we'd added two new people to the mix.

Once the table had been loaded with all the food and set for the five of us, I looked in awe around the table. It was a moment I wanted to remember for a long time. I grabbed my phone.

"Everyone look over here and smile." I held up the phone and snapped a picture. Then I turned to Casey. Before I could say anything, he stood and held out his hand to take my phone. I made my way over to my dad and stood behind him.

"Say cheese," Casey said.

"Cheese!"

"Okay, silly face," Casey said.

I stuck my tongue out and crossed my eyes and waited for the flash.

We were all still giggling when we dug into the food.

"So, Casey what are your plans for Christmas?" Dad asked.

"Uh . . ." He looked caught off guard. "Well, my family doesn't live in town, but I have some close friends that I get together with every year."

"That sounds nice," Mom said.

Casey nodded.

The room fell quiet, aside from forks clinking on plates.

"Okay, favorite Christmas memory, and *go*!" George pointed at me.

"Ooh, that's a hard one. Let me think . . . ah . . . okay, so one year when I was about eight, I got a bike for Christmas. After we had a big Christmas lunch, Mom, Dad, and I took a bike ride. A really long one. Man, we had to have been gone for hours. We ended up at the beach, and we watched the sunset before we biked home, looking at Christmas lights on the way."

"Oh, I remember that," Mom said. "That was so relaxing."

"Yeah, I seem to remember the reason we stayed at the beach for so long was because your mom was too tired to continue riding." Dad laughed.

"Oh yeah!" I covered my mouth as laughter took over mid-bite. "Her legs were sore for like a week!"

"Hey! Let's not pick on Mom!" Mom said, even though she was trying to hide her giggles.

George turned to Mom. "What about you?"

"Oh, I've got one!" A mischievous look gleamed in her eyes. "When Abby was about four, all she wanted for Christmas was a dollhouse bigger than her. Christmas morning, she came rushing downstairs, spotted that dollhouse next to the tree, and she was so excited with her jumping up and down, she peed her pants right there in front of the tree."

My mouth dropped. "*Mom*!"

Everyone started laughing.

"I think that one takes the cake." Casey gave me a sideways look.

I smacked his shoulder. "Rude!" I couldn't help but simper—it was a *little* funny.

When everyone was done, Mom and George volunteered to do the dishes. Dad jumped up to start clearing the table.

"I should go," Casey whispered.

I stood up and walked with him to the door. "Thanks for coming for dinner. It was so nice having you here."

He leaned down and kissed me. Pulling me further into the entry toward the door, he deepened his kiss, pinning me against the wall. I squeezed his shirt in my hands, bringing him closer. And then he pulled away far too fast for my liking. I gripped his shirt tighter, not letting him get too far away. His lips rose at the corners.

"I should go," he said.

I puckered my lips and closed my eyes. I felt a rumble in his chest. He gave me a quick last peck. I let go, and he was gone.

*   *   *   *

Christmas morning, we tore into brightly wrapped packages until the living room was littered with a rainbow of paper. My favorite gift by far was a gorgeous silver necklace with a single silver dollar charm on it from Dad. It was perfect.

The part that came next I'd dreaded since before the weekend even began. Dad had to leave. He loaded the gifts I gave him into his bag, kissed my forehead one last time, and walked to his car.

"Bye, Abbs."

I watched his car drive away and felt his absence deeply. Then I grabbed my keys and headed for Casey's. The last thing I planned to do was sit at home thinking about Dad not being there.

Hours later, Casey and I were curled up on his couch, vegging out for the first time in months, when my phone rang.

"Hey Mom," I said.

"Where are you?" she asked. Her voice scared me.

I sat straight up. "Casey's. What's wrong?"

"Your dad was in an accident."

I jumped up. "What? Is he okay?"

Casey was on alert, mouthing, *'What's wrong?'* I ignored him.

"I'm not really sure." She paused. "They said he was stable and headed to the hospital."

My heart dropped. "He didn't call you himself?"

She hesitated, confirming my fear before she even responded. "No."

"I have to go. What hospital?"

Casey was already up with keys in his hand.

I hung up the instant she told me where he was. My mind reeled. I was hours away while my dad was hurting.

"What happened?" Casey asked, holding the door for me.

Casey

"My dad was in a car accident. I have to go to California." Abby brushed past me to the elevator.

"I'll drive you."

She pressed the elevator button over and over in what I could only view as desperation.

Nothing could happen to her father. She already dealt with so much.

Not this.

Not now.

"No. You don't have to go." Her hands shook, though she tried to hide it.

"You're in no shape to drive. Let me drive you."

When we reached the first floor, she rushed forward, almost crashing into one of the elevator doors. At the doors to the garages, I reached to grab the door for her, but before I could, both opened on their own.

Did I do that?

I turned back to the doors that were now closing. What just happened?

I must be losing my mind.

"Abby, wait up."

She was a car length away from me now, practically jogging.

Running ahead, I stopped in front of her, gripping her shoulders. A tear rolled down her face.

"Hey, he'll be alright."

"I just have to get to him."

"We will."

Abby

I leaned into Casey's arms for just a moment, letting my tears dry. I sniffed.

Casey opened the door for me and walked to his side of the car. It didn't even register that he was inside until we were backing out of the parking space. I put my seatbelt on and leaned back into the headrest. I breathed in and out deeply, trying to calm myself.

Casey drove faster than I would have dared, for which I couldn't have been more grateful. But still, the drive seemed to take forever. Six hours was a long time, especially when all you wanted was to be there already. Minutes seemed to pass like hours.

I watched out the window as we left the city behind. Desert stretched before us and beside us as far as the eye could see.

With all that space outside, it suddenly felt stuffy in the car, restricting almost. I laid my head back against the seat and closed my eyes, trying to make it go away.

Wind rushed into the car, blowing my hair around my face.

"Thanks, it was getting really stuffy in here."

"Huh?" Casey asked.

"For rolling the window down."

"Ah . . . I didn't roll anything down," Casey said.

I sat up and looked at him. His confused face stared back at me.

"That's weird."

I pressed the buttons, making the window go up and down. It worked just fine—no glitches. I shrugged.

"You should try to sleep," Casey said. "It will make the time seem like it's going faster"

I nodded, closing my eyes.

<u>Casey</u>

Abby stilled as she laid back against her seat. The wind tousled her hair around her face.

What in the world was going on? The door and now the window? Both opened without a single person touching them. My head spun through scenario after scenario.

Minutes turned to an hour, and I still couldn't get it out of my head.

I checked on her out of the corner of my eye, and the rise and fall of her chest told me she was sound asleep.

This was no coincidence. She brushed it off so easily. Too easily. Stress and worry must be clouding her judgment. If she were in her right mind, I doubted she would have brushed it off at all. This type of thing might be normal in my world, but not in hers.

One possibility kept pushing its way to the forefront of my mind. It was the most likely cause, and once she found out, I couldn't be sure how she would react.

I kept my mouth shut. She didn't need anything else right now.

First, she needed to know her dad was okay. For now, that's all that mattered.

Abby

Six and a half hours later, Casey nudged me awake as he pulled up in front of the hospital. I jumped out before I was fully awake, not even waiting for the car to stop rolling. The sun had begun to sink behind buildings.

I hit the ground running, only barely hearing Casey call out behind me. "I'll park and meet you inside."

Inside the hospital, with its white walls and sterile smell, I came to a dark-haired secretary sitting behind a desk in the emergency department. She looked up at me from behind her glasses.

"I'm looking for my dad. He was in an accident."

"Last name?"

"Martin."

After running a search on her computer, she led me to a room down the hallway and to the right.

Dad sat upright in the emergency room bed. His leg was in a temporary cast, his arm rested in a sling, and his forehead was blue and purple with a gash butterflied together at the center.

"Dad?" I whimpered.

"Abbs? What are you doing here?"

"Someone called Mom. They said you'd been in an accident. I had to make sure you were okay."

"I'm fine, honey. You could have called, silly."

"I didn't know how bad you were. I thought since someone called for you . . ."

He lifted his good arm, motioning for me to sit with him. "I'm fine. Broken leg, broken wrist, and a bump on the noggin. It's going to take a lot more than this to get rid of me, kiddo."

He wrapped his arm around me and kissed the top of my head.

"What happened?" I asked.

"Oh, somebody cut in front of me. I guess they misjudged the distance and clipped my bumper. Spun me around and off the road into the ditch. I'm lucky I didn't roll, or at least that's what the officer on scene said."

"I'm so glad you're okay."

"Did you come all this way by yourself?"

"No," Casey said from the doorway. "I drove. She was too worried . . . I didn't want her driving."

"I appreciate that. Your mom does know you're here, right?" He cocked his head to the side and raised his eyebrows.

I pressed my finger to my lip. "Uh, I think so?"

Dad shot me a sideways look.

"I guess . . . I demanded to know where you were and hung up . . . so maybe not? But I did say I needed to make sure you were okay."

"Oh, Abby," Dad said. "You better go call her."

"All right."

It took only a few minutes to call my mom and let her know. At first, she wasn't pleased, but she calmed down when I told her Casey came with me.

"Mom said to get better quickly, and if you need anything to let her know."

Dad nodded. He stretched in the bed. "If I didn't know any better, I'd think I'd been here days instead of hours, this bed is so uncomfortable!"

"Oh, I remember that," I said thinking of my stay in a hospital bed. I shuddered at the thought.

"I bet you do," Dad said, his face taking on a grim hue.

"When do you get out?" Casey asked.

"Ah, the nurse said I could leave as soon as she brought me my discharge papers"—he checked his watch—"a half hour ago. Actually, since you guys are here, would you mind driving me home? My car didn't fare well in the wreck, and I don't think I'm going to be driving anytime soon with this leg. I was going to call a friend . . . "

"Of course we can," Casey said right away.

"On second thought, it's getting kind of late. Maybe you guys should just stay the night."

I turned to Casey. He nodded.

I squealed and clapped my hands. "I'll text Mom and let her know."

"Why don't you let me call her instead?"

"Okay."

This was shaping up to be a great impromptu trip. Dad was okay and I got to stay another night with him in my old house, all the while Casey was here. Complete bliss.

We got Dad home and inside. I stopped in the entry and breathed in the familiar scent. Nothing had changed. Not a single thing had been moved since I was last here.

Using a crutch was difficult for Dad with his broken wrist, but he seemed to be getting it down. Still, I followed him up the stairs just in case.

"I hope you don't mind, but I'm going to go to bed. I'm exhausted, and . . . all of this"—Dad said, motioning to his whole body—"hurts."

"Are you hungry?" I asked. "It's dinnertime. Well, past dinnertime."

"They fed me at the hospital. Couldn't take pain medicine without food."

"Okay." I gave him a gentle hug, and he hobbled off to bed.

After he left, I turned to Casey and slid my arms around him, nestling my head against his chest. "Thank you."

He kissed the top of my head, and I could feel him inhale deeply. "I'm just glad your dad is okay."

"Me too."

"I'm starving," he said.

"Go out?"

"Lead the way."

As we headed out of the neighborhood, I thought of Kelly and how we used to ride our bikes this way to go to the beach. I wished there was time to meet up with her, but I hadn't spoken to her in months. As much as I hated to admit it, I had no idea how she was even doing or even if she'd want to see me. I couldn't help but feel that she was better off without me, anyway. All the problems that inevitably followed me around would just put her in harm's way, just like Bailey.

Of course, it would be worse now. I'd signed up for this. It was all-encompassing. My whole life.

After we grabbed some burgers, we sat outside at a table to eat. Casey was unusually quiet.

"Is everything okay?" I asked.

He hesitated, searching my face. His stare was intense. What was he looking for?

"Casey? What's going on?"

I stopped eating. I couldn't stomach food when he was acting so strangely.

He wiped his hand on his napkin and set it down. "I think you might have another gift."

"What are you talking about?"

"Earlier, I went to open the door for you to go out to the parking garage. Both doors opened without me touching them. At first I wondered if I initiated my gift without realizing. And let me tell you, that's a stretch—that hasn't happened in years, not since I've gained control. Then, in the car, the window. Nobody touched it."

"Those are just coincidences. Maybe the wind pushed open the door, and the window . . . maybe a wire got crossed." I grasped at any idea that popped into my head to explain why it would have happened. Anything, of course, except what he was suggesting.

"No, Abby, that doesn't happen."

I picked at my food. Casey would never bring something like this to me, not unless he was sure. Tears welled in my eyes. I turned away, trying to hide them.

"I think because you were so emotional and stressed today, it brought forth your gift. Your mind was in turmoil. You did things without even realizing. A lot of times that's how it happens."

I shook my head and stared at the ceiling. I couldn't look him in the eye.

"Abby, say something."

"What am I supposed to say?" I turned to face him. A single tear streaked down my face.

Why did it have to be me? Somehow it felt like this life was meant for someone else. I couldn't possibly have the ability to master another gift. It was one more thing that set me apart from everyone else, and I just couldn't be comfortable with that.

He moved to my side, encasing me in his arms. "This isn't a bad thing. If anything, this will give you even more protection."

"It *is a* bad thing. It's one more thing to try to figure out. It's one more thing that makes me not normal, yet not a Protector, either. What am I? I have no place. I don't fit in with anyone."

"Your place is with me. Always."

I rolled my eyes. "You know what I mean."

"Hey, most people would be ecstatic that they could make things happen with their mind."

I sighed and dropped my head into my hands. "Is that what I did? I don't even know."

"I think so. You were thinking about it being stuffy in the car, right? So, you wanted the window down, and down it went."

"Yeah, but I don't remember even thinking about the door."

"You probably did, you just didn't realize. You were upset."

I shoved a french fry in my mouth. "Can we talk about this later?"

He nodded and changed the subject.

He took me to the beach that night after dinner, not for long. Just long enough to help me clear my head. There was something about breathing the salt air that eased my nerves.

"I wish I could make this easier for you." Casey held me around the shoulders, resting his chin on my head.

"I know."

"You know I'm here for you, though. Every step of the way. I'll do whatever I can to help you."

"I think I need to figure this one out on my own."

Casey pulled away and looked down at me. "Are you sure?"

I nodded, biting my lip. I needed to do this for me, my own way, for once.

"Okay, but if you change your mind . . ." He trailed off, his voice getting lost in the wind.

"I know." I looked up into the sky. "Oh, and Casey? Can we keep this between us for now?"

*   *   *   *

We hit the road back home the next morning after I made sure Dad ate breakfast. I kissed him on the cheek and told him to find someone to help him out until he got back on his feet, but I doubted he would.

Throughout the drive, I found myself unable to think of anything but this new gift. For a while now, Edward had told me that new gifts might reveal themselves. I always doubted him. In hindsight, that had been silly. He was an immortal Protector. He would know a bit more about gifts than I would But of course, we were both in uncharted territory, so neither of us really had a clue.

I glanced at the window, thinking of yesterday, then turned back to Casey. He was focused on the road. I leaned back against my seat, just as I had the day before, and closed my eyes. In my head, I willed the window down. I waited a few moments and opened one eye. Nothing happened.

I sighed.

Some gift.

CHAPTER EIGHT

Clutching my phone, I paced the room. I'd already made up my mind. Why was this so hard? My jittery hands clenched and unclenched.

If my parents knew what I've planned, I'd never be allowed to leave the house again. Ever.

I sighed, pressed Edward's number, and held my breath.

This was it.

"Hello." His smooth voice came through the phone.

"Hi, Edward. It's Abby."

"How are you?"

"I'm good."

"What do I owe the pleasure of this call?"

"Well . . ." I paused.

He waited, patient as always, for me to continue.

"I've decided to help you with your . . . umm . . . problem."

He didn't respond right away, and I grew worried he no longer needed me.

"That is, unless things have changed . . ." I said, leaving it hanging, giving him the opportunity to back out.

"Oh, no, no, no. Please excuse my silence. I simply needed to consider how to proceed. When can you meet?"

"After school? I have to work, but I have about an hour and a half in between."

"Meet me in front of your work as soon as you can get there. I'll be waiting."

"Okay."

"I look forward to it." The phone clicked, ending our call.

There. I did it. No turning back now.

As the day rolled on, I felt more at ease. This had to be the right choice if destiny had brought it to me. It must be. Things like this didn't happen by chance. It must be fate.

The day passed in a whirlwind of schoolwork and boring lectures. I daydreamed about what my life would be like in a year. After graduation, I'd be working with Edward if all went as planned.

To avoid a fight, I didn't tell Casey I was meeting with Edward before work, and as I headed to the meeting, I began to stress that that had been short-sighted.

I saw Edward's car the moment I pulled into the lot. He stepped out and held the passenger door open before I even got out of my car.

"Somewhere private?" I asked as I slid into his car, even though I already knew the answer. Everything, it seemed, with the Protectors needed to be done in private. It was important to keep their identity hidden.

He nodded.

Of course.

Silence filled the car until the engine roared to life. He waited until he swung the car out of the lot.

"I have to admit, I was surprised by your answer," he said.

"Why?"

"I expected a bit more resistance. You don't usually agree to things so easily."

I immediately felt defensive. "That's not true. I just don't like to do things when people try to force me."

"Noted."

He was silent again as he changed lanes and turned. I recognized where he was going right away, but I said nothing. Instead, I fiddled with my hands, anxiously waiting for him to get to the point.

"While I was surprised, I can't say that I'm disappointed. Quite the opposite, in fact. But I suppose you aren't here to discuss my feelings."

I smiled, trying to be polite.

The car rolled to a stop in front of Lucian's house.

"Why Lucian's?" I asked.

"We do need him for your training."

"Oh."

Lucian was waiting at the front door with a warm smile unlike his normal sarcastic grin.

"Edward." He nodded. "Hey, Abby."

Edward breezed right past him like he owned the place, while I hesitated, waiting for Lucian. He motioned me forward, ahead of him. I rolled my eyes, and he chuckled.

We sat down on the deck—my favorite place. Sitting between them made me feel so inferior. Power radiated from them, despite the normalcy they appeared to exude.

"I gave Lucian the plan for your training already, and he's agreed to work with you for an extended amount of time."

Lucian nodded, grinning. He looked all too pleased with this. That could only mean one thing—he would be making me work. Hard.

"I wanted to go over some of it with you so you could ask questions," Edward said.

I nodded, urging him to continue.

"First of all, I want you to begin working out. Running, lifting weights, the whole deal."

I groaned.

"What? You thought it was going to be easy?" Lucian grinned.

"As part of that workout regimine, we will implement kickboxing and self-defense. Again, Lucian has all the details. In addition to physical training, we will train you to think like us by introducing various scenarios both real and constructed. There will be tests of that knowledge, so always be prepared. Never let your guard down."

"I never do," I said.

Edward raised his eyebrows. "You sound sure of this."

I crossed my arms and nodded.

"I do hope that's true." He glanced back down at the papers in his hands.

I didn't like the sound of that.

"Now, about your job." He looked back at me, unsure. "I'll allow you to keep it for now, but know that eventually it will be too much to do both."

I have to quit my job?

"Oh . . ." I felt dejected at the idea of having to give up something I enjoyed.

I don't know why I didn't think of this before. It made sense. Having time for both plus school didn't really seem possible. But what was I supposed to tell my mom?

He set the papers aside. "You'll be paid for your time, of course."

"I'm not worried about that."

His brow creased, but then he shook it off again.

He turned to Lucian. "I trust you'll explain everything in detail as it becomes relevant."

Lucian nodded without hesitation.

It was interesting to see him around Edward. His whole presence was altered. Serious and focused. Such a change from his usual smiley, playful self. I grinned. It amused me seeing him that way.

Edward handed me a calendar. "Now, until we phase out the coffee house, you'll need to commit to at least three days a week of training after school."

Three days. I would have zero free time to spend with Casey. One more reason he was going to hate this.

I sighed. "Okay."

"Please let Lucian know which days. I'll leave that for you two to decide." Edward stood. "One last thing. Your dreams. You'll still work with Lucian on them as well. Please let me know when a dream presents itself. Have there been any new ones?"

I shook my head. "No, only the same one, in the warehouse."

"Help her summon the dreams." Edward turned to Lucian. His head shifted back to me. "Do you have any questions?"

"Uh . . ." I shook my head.

"Please let me know if you think of any. I have to go. Lucian will bring you back to work. I do hope that's okay."

I nodded when I couldn't find words fast enough, but he didn't see. He left without another glance.

I turned back to Lucian when I heard the door shut. "You are going to enjoy this far too much."

He smirked. "You bet I am."

I rolled my eyes. "Get me back to work now, would ya?"

*　　*　　*　　*

All I could think about the rest of the day was Edward's training plan. One sentence scared me the most: *'Help her summon the dreams.'*

Willing myself to dream had been so fruitless before that I felt like it would make my dreams nonexistent.

I worried I'd be a huge disappointment. How could I ever live up to his expectations? Edward was surrounded by greatness every day. I could never measure up.

After work, I went to Casey's without calling. I needed to talk to him about the meeting with Edward, but when he didn't answer the door, I sat down on his welcome mat and called him.

There was an answer on the fourth ring, but the voice on the line made me hang up right away. I checked the screen and felt my heart drop into my stomach. *Why was a girl answering Casey's phone?*

A knot formed in my chest. Everything in me tensed. I had to get out of there. I jumped up and pressed the *down* button over and over, urging it to arrive faster. The second the doors opened, I darted inside, willing it to move swiftly.

Not again.

I couldn't feel this again.

Eli had lied to me. Had Casey? Is that what this was?

When the doors opened at the bottom, I took off running and collided with Casey. He stood in front of the doors waiting, alone.

"Abby." He stumbled backward. "I didn't know you were coming over."

I couldn't speak. I froze, rigid in his arms. He stepped forward into the elevator, bringing me with him, and up we went. I scooted to his side. He gave me a one-sided hug and then looked at me strangely when I didn't hug back.

"What's wrong?" he asked.

"I . . . tried to call you."

"Oh yeah? I guess I didn't hear it." He fumbled through his pockets in search of his phone, then stopped. "It's not here."

"A girl answered." I searched his eyes. I needed to find something—anything—that showed me that he was who I thought he was.

"Oh, you didn't think . . ." He paused. "Abby, I was at Brad's. My phone must have fallen out into his couch or something. Wouldn't be the first time."

"Who answered, then?"

"Probably Jessica, Brad's girlfriend."

"Oh." My cheeks heated. I felt so stupid for even letting my mind go there.

Why did I immediately assume something so dark? People lost their phones all the time.

Eli. That's why. I groaned.

"Abby, I'd never cheat on you, if that's what you thought."

I didn't respond. He reached for me.

I threw my arms around his neck. "I'm sorry. I've just been lied to . . . I don't know why I assumed that. You've never done anything . . . to make me think anything like that."

He paused, pulling me in. "I get it. People haven't exactly been honest with you, and you've been through a betrayal only you can understand. But those people aren't me. I'm not Eli." He stepped back and held out his hand. "Let me see your phone."

He called his phone with mine. It didn't seem to have rung long before he spoke. "Hey Jess, can I talk to Brad? It's Casey." He paused. "Hey, I left my phone there. I'll just swing by in the morning to get it. If anything comes up, let Edward know I don't have it. Yeah . . . thanks."

I breathed deep and felt the muscles in my shoulders loosen.

"There. I'll have it back tomorrow morning," he said.

He let us into the apartment. I followed behind him, still feeling shaken. I went to the fridge and grabbed a water, guzzling half of it without taking a breath.

"How was your day?" he asked.

And then, like a ton of bricks on my shoulders, everything came back to me.

"Oh, it was good. That's actually why I came over."

"Yeah?"

"Yeah. Um . . . can we sit on the couch?" I pointed toward the living room.

He gave me a weird look but headed to the couch without saying a word.

"I had a meeting with Edward today. I gave him my answer this morning."

He sighed and rubbed his forehead. "I really wish you wouldn't do this."

"I know. But I have to."

"You don't."

"I do. I wish I could explain it. I feel pulled to help. I mean, I've been given these gifts. What else am I going to do with them?"

He shrugged.

"Exactly. I have to at least see what this path holds for me."

When I didn't respond, he relented. "How did the meeting go?"

"Good, I think. Lucian will be training me."

"Well, at least I know you're learning from one of the best."

"I have to train with him three times a week. It's going to be a lot."

"I knew it would be. It always is. Are you really sure this is what you want?"

I nodded.

"Okay."

That night as I crawled into bed, I couldn't help but think that our conversation went better than I'd expected. Casey seemed to accept it. I knew he wasn't happy about it, but he was trying, and that's all that mattered.

I picked up a tennis ball from under my bed and chucked it at the wall. It rebounded back into my hand. I continued tossing it, letting it be a constant rhythm in the background of my thoughts.

Now, if I could just master my new gift, that would be super helpful.

I tossed the tennis ball again and back it came, right into my hand. I looked at the yellow-green ball. Rolling it around, I watched the way it moved. I imagined it lifting into the air. I thought hard, hoping, just maybe, it would lift, but nothing happened. I sighed and threw it again.

This time, I rolled over and let it fall to the floor.

CHAPTER NINE

Lucian's thick arm gripped me around the waist just before my back slammed to the ground. I gasped for air and choked on it when it surged into my lungs.

Lucian looked back at me with smug eyes.

"I thought you said you were ready for anything?" he asked as though he were innocent.

My eyes watered.

"How am I supposed to be ready for something you haven't shown me?" I grumbled through gritted teeth. My anger bubbled to the surface.

This was our very first training session, and he didn't hold back. Not one bit.

He pulled me to my feet.

"Oh? Your enemies have a habit of explaining their next move beforehand?" He stood there with his hands on his hips. Sweat rolled down his temples.

I rolled my eyes. "Point taken."

I flounced onto the desk and sat down on the couch, holding my ribs.

"Wait a minute, what are you doing?"

"Taking a break! What does it look like?"

"There are no breaks."

"You just laid me out and knocked every bit of air out of me! I'm taking a break!"

Lucian shook his head. "Edward's not going to like it when I tell him you don't follow commands well."

I smirked. "Edward already knows that."

Leaning back, I put my head in my hands and watched him squirm. I took a few cleansing breaths, waiting for the pain to subside, and then stood.

"There. I took my break, and now I'm up. Happy?" I brushed past him to the beach.

He advanced on me. This time, I was ready. I bent my knees, bracing for the impact. As he came closer, I bent forward, grabbed hold of his hips, and thrust up with all my might. His legs went up, and then, all at once, he came down on top of me. We crumpled in a heap in the sand.

"Ow." I whimpered when he rolled off of me.

"I think you had the right idea on that one. Your execution just needs a little work."

He stood, brushing off the sand like it didn't even hurt. Of course, he'd landed on me—it probably didn't hurt that bad.

Four more times I hit the sand—and three of those times, sand launched into my mouth. I'd had enough. From the ground, I kicked Lucian in the back of his knees. He fell as his legs gave out beneath him.

"There. I took you down. We can call it a day."

He didn't want me to see it, but he was amused.

"Have you learned anything about the different ways that someone could get the jump on you?"

"Yes."

"Good. Now that you've realized you *aren't* always ready, I can teach you how to get yourself out of a situation where you've been taken off guard."

I sighed.

We weren't done.

Casey

Pace. That's all I could do. The knot in my stomach refused to unclench. It twisted my gut, filling my throat with bile.

It was only first day of training, and I couldn't keep my cool. This wasn't even what I most feared, and this was my reaction?

Lucian was well-prepared to train her—that much comforted me—but soon, sooner than I cared for, Edward planned to throw her into something dangerous. Something I worried would be too much for her to handle. Something in which I couldn't help her.

I fought with myself daily not to open my mouth, each time wondering if maybe *this* would be the time I could somehow convince her to back out. But I stopped myself. All it would do was lead us into yet another fight.

I had only one other choice. It was the only way I could be sure that she would be as safe as possible. And I didn't like it.

Not a single bit.

Abby

The next day, I hopped out of bed faster than I should have. My muscles screamed in protest. My knees buckled under the pressure, and I fell back onto my springy mattress.

I winced as my fingertips pressed into my ribcage. Dark bruises stood out on my pale flesh. Blow after blow had taken its toll on my small body.

Saturday. That used to mean time to relax, but now it meant work, followed by training, and then maybe, if I was lucky, time to spend with Casey if I wasn't too tired.

Good thing I work with coffee.

On my way out the door, I stopped in the kitchen to grab breakfast. Mom was washing dishes when I strode in.

"Good morning, honey."

"Morning."

"There's some bacon in the microwave."

I grabbed the last of it and chugged a glass of orange juice.

"Gotta go," I said.

"You have to work?" she asked.

"Yep."

"Okay, I'll see you later."

My shift went slowly, as if time were at an almost standstill. Something about Saturday's made time pass just a bit slower.

After my shift, I headed to the park where Lucian had told me to meet him. I was relieved when I saw the mound of tacos piled in the center of the table. My stomach grumbled as I remembered the deliciousness that waited inside the wrappers.

"Oh my gosh, Lucian, you are my favorite person right now. Those smell . . . so good."

I dropped my bag and slumped onto the bench, snatching the closest taco. Ready to devour it, I leaned over to take a bite, when a hand landed on my shoulder. I jumped, almost dropping the taco, and spun around.

Casey smiled back at me.

"Oh my gosh. What are you doing here?"

He sat down next to me.

"I'm sorry I've given you so much trouble about your decision to join forces with Edward. I should have supported you. I won't stand in your way again," Casey said.

"Okay . . ."

"I'll be helping with your training from now on."

"Really? Does Edward know?"

He smiled. "Of course."

I threw my arms around him, squeezing.

"Wow. And you knew?" I asked Lucian.

He nodded but continued eating without reaction.

This was the best news I'd heard all week.

Lucian gave me a half hour to eat and let my food settle before our run. I stopped after two tacos. I knew a full stomach and running wouldn't mix. It felt like no time had passed when Lucian stood up.

"Let's go."

I groaned.

He lifted his arms above his head, stretching to each side. He brought each leg up behind him, then jogged in place a couple times. I mirrored him. Then he took off.

I shot Casey a help-me look and hightailed it after him.

Eight laps around the park later, I was panting.

"That's it for today, right?" I gasped between breaths when I caught up to Lucian at the Ramada.

Lucian laughed out loud.

I rolled my eyes.

"Does she roll her eyes this much at you?" Lucian asked Casey.

He chuckled and shook his head. "She saves those just for you, man."

Lucian pulled out a pair of boxing gloves and a couple pads that looked like they slipped on someone's hands. He handed those to Casey and helped me slip my hands into the gloves.

"Today, you get to beat up your boyfriend."

"I think I'm going to like today." I shot Casey a mischievous grin.

Lucian showed me the proper way to stand and throw a couple punches at Casey's padded hands. I watched the way the pads flexed around his fist. My eyebrows raised. I doubted my strength could even come close.

I stepped in front of Casey, ready. I took a deep breath and started nailing him with an assortment of punches, high and low. He blocked every one with the pads. Lucian stopped me a few times to correct my foot placement and the way I swung.

Casey accepted the barrage of punches when a little girl walked up to us.

"What are you doing?" she asked, her pigtails bobbing side to side.

"Uh . . ." I froze. I couldn't figure out what to tell her. *Practicing to protect myself against immortals gone bad* just didn't work.

Lucian stepped forward, bumping me to the side. "She's training to be a policewoman someday. What do you want to be when you grow up?"

While she explained that she wanted to be a unicorn with sparkly rainbow hair, I zoned in on Casey as he slid out of the mitts and gestured for me to do the same. He looked worried. My heart rate picked up. He nodded toward the parking lot.

It was time to go.

I waved at the little girl as Casey ushered me to the car and Lucian followed behind. Casey took my keys, and Lucian gestured for me to get into his car.

By the time I was buckled in and the car was pulling out of the parking lot, my hands shook. An adrenaline response to an unknown danger was probably the most useless reaction my body ever had.

"What was that about?" I asked.

"That was my bad. We shouldn't have been training there. I got comfortable. If a Protector sees other Protectors training a mortal, what's that going to look like?"

I hadn't thought of that.

"Was she a Protector?" I asked.

He shook his head. "But that doesn't mean that she doesn't have Protector's around her. Chances are she doesn't. It's not like we're everywhere. But the minute we let our guard down is the minute your cover is blown." He blew out a breath. "I never even saw her coming. Sneaky little thing."

"Me neither."

I stared out the window. I'd never realized how easily my cover could be blown. Never even realized how many factors went into my training. Maybe Edward was right. Maybe my guard was down sometimes.

*   *   *   *

The next day, my phone rang just as I was leaving school.
"Hello?"
"Abby, I think I found it." Lucian sounded excited.
"Found what?" I asked.
"The warehouse. Can you meet me?"
"I have to work."
Lucian grumbled. "When do you get off?"
"Eight."
"I'll pick you up."
Then I heard a click and knew he was gone. *Guess I don't have a choice.*

Hours later, I was scrubbing syrup off the clear window barrier when Lucian and Casey walked into the coffee house. I smiled. Nothing made me happier than to know Casey would be helping along the way. My time wouldn't have to be as divided trying to fit him into my hectic schedule. Or wasted trying to catch him up.

"I'll be off in five," I said.

They nodded and sat down.

I watched them huddle together, talking in hushed voices. No doubt my name was being thrown around. I wished I knew what they were saying.

I threw together drinks for all of us to surprise them and clocked out.

"Thanks," they said at the same time when I handed them their drinks. We walked out the door.

"What were you guys talking about?" I asked.

"Just about where this place is," Lucian said.

"Where is it?"

"You'll see."

It took ten minutes to get there, but when we pulled in, I recognized where we were. These buildings were where the elders had met with me the very first time I met Edward. Lucian kept driving past the familiar building. I watched it as we passed. It looked deserted.

We pulled into a parking lot a small distance from it. After we passed two more buildings, it came into view. The very last building. The dragon emblem stared me in the face. I gasped. Even in the dark, it shimmered.

"Oh my god."

"That's it, isn't it?" Lucian asked.

He stopped the car. Headlights shone on the building in two white orbs.

"Yeah. I can't believe you found it."

"There's only one building that you can see that emblem from. That one," he said, pointing.

My stomach flopped.

"Let's get out of here," Casey said. "I don't want to chance anyone seeing us here. We still have no idea what this dream means."

"Agreed," I said

I leaned back against the seat. We'd found it. Now the pressure to figure it all out weighed heavy on me.

Why was I there? What was I hiding from? Who was in the doorway? What did it all mean?

*   *   *   *

As I let myself into my house that night, my phone rang. I fumbled with my purse and keys trying to answer it.

"Hello?" I said, my voice winded as I juggled everything.

"Hey, Abbs. Did I get you at a bad time?" Dad said.

"No, I'm just getting home. Got my hands full. What's up?"

"I've got some great news."

"What?" I shut the door behind me and paused in the entryway.

"I'm coming for a visit next weekend."

"Really?" I squealed. "Wait, what about your leg?"

"Doctor cleared me to fly—he just doesn't want me driving that far yet. I'm using a cane now."

"That's great. How long do I get you?"

"Not long," he said, his voice changing. "I fly in Saturday morning and leave Sunday morning."

"Boo."

"I know, I wish it was longer, but I figured short was better than nothing. The truth is that spring's right around the corner, I'm not sure when I'll be able to get away again. Heck, it'll probably be for your graduation."

"It'll be good to see you, though. Should I get any big plans together?" I asked

"Uh . . . I'm not sure how much I'll be up to with my leg. How about low-key—lunch, maybe a movie? That kind of thing."

"You've got it."

"Great. I miss you so much."

"I miss you too."

"I should go. I need to make dinner. It's getting late."

"It is late! Go eat! I love you."

"I love you too, Abbs. Bye."

I hung up the phone and called to Mom in celebration. "Dad's coming for a visit next weekend!"

CHAPTER TEN

It was a slow afternoon in the café, which meant lots of deep cleaning. A bucket of piping hot water never left my side as I tore apart half of the espresso machine to give it a thorough scrubbing.

The door chimed, and George walked in. My surprise wasn't well concealed.

"Hey," I said. It sounded like more of a question than a greeting.

"Hey."

"Did you want a drink?" I asked.

He shook his head.

"Then . . . did you need something?" I asked in full barista mode.

"I thought we could go for a drive when you got off work."

"Umm . . . all right. Twenty minutes."

"I'll wait." He went over to a table by the window and sat down.

This was so out of the ordinary. I couldn't grasp why he'd want to take me for a drive.

Then a thought struck me. Did he want to marry my mom? My heart beat faster. They had been together for a while now, and they were living together. It was the only thing that he could want to talk to me about, *right?* I wasn't sure I was ready for *that* permanent with George. What would I say?

Walking out with him to his car, nerves really hit me. It wasn't often that I was alone with George, and sometimes that still made me uncomfortable, despite that he lived with us. I wondered sometimes if it would ever be completely comfortable between us.

He entered the freeway a short while later, and I felt surprised that we'd be traveling somewhere far enough to require the freeway.

I bit my lip.

"Where are we going?" I asked. "I didn't realize it'd be so far."

"Oh, just for a drive. I don't really have a place in mind."

I held my hands together and remained quiet, waiting for him to get to the point.

After ten more miles, I grew frustrated.

"What is it that you wanted to talk to me about?" I asked, failing to hide my aggravation.

"Tsk, tsk. Impatience." He paused to steal a glance. "I'm joking."

I halfheartedly chuckled and wrapped my arms around myself.

George exited the freeway and pulled into a deserted dirt parking lot that led to a trailhead. After he stopped the car, he turned to me.

"Let's go," he said.

"Go? It's almost dark."

"So?"

He paused for a second as he unbuckled his seatbelt, then stepped out of the car and shut the door. My heart pounded as he walked to my side of the car. It took me all of a split second to decide something felt off. I hit the *lock* button and jumped into the driver's seat.

Lucky for me, the keys still hung in the ignition. The car roared to life with the twist of my wrist.

I cracked the passenger window, just enough for him to hear me, as he began to pound on it.

"Give me one good reason why I shouldn't drive away right now," I demanded through clenched teeth.

"Whoa. Abby, what's the matter?"

"You took me for a drive. Now we're looking up at a trailhead, and I don't know why. Heck, I don't even really know where we are."

George's fingertips protruded into the car as he gripped the glass. He leaned down to look in the window, gazing directly into my eyes. He remained quiet as if he was thinking. Or maybe he was waiting for something. Waiting for me to second-guess myself.

"Not once have you asked me to do anything with you. Ever. Why now?"

He shook his head. "I just wanted to get to know you."

"Bull! I'm not buying that!" I threw the car into reverse.

He looked down at the ground as a grin spread across his face, and he began shaking his head.

"What? Why is this funny?" Anger boiled within me. My arms shook as I clutched the steering wheel.

"I told Edward that there was no way I'd get you to come."

I froze. *Edward?* "What did you say?"

He looked up at me.

I relented and unlocked the doors. He sighed as he sat down beside me.

"I'm listening." My eyes searched his face. Had I really heard that right? Did he really say *Edward?*

"Test."

I gasped. "What?"

He turned to look at me, his face sincere. "This was a test."

I let out a loud, rumbling sigh and banged my hands against the steering wheel.

"You did good."

"I did good?" I whipped my head toward him.

"Yeah."

"Are you kidding me? Who are you to even judge—how do you even know Edward? You took me to a trailhead like this as a *test?* Seriously? Do you know how twisted that is?"

"I know, I know. That's precisely why I didn't want to do this!" I could hear an edge of frustration in his tone.

I stared at him.

"Abby, I'm a Protector. I mean, I was. I'm sorry I didn't tell you this sooner, but I figured that, like most people, you had no idea who we were. And then I met Eli and Casey. From then on, I wondered how much you knew. To have one Protector as a friend could be chance, but two?" He shook his head. "I should have said something."

"So you've known about Eli and Casey all this time?"

He nodded.

"I'm retired, but I can still sense fellow Protectors."

"They never mentioned anything about you . . ."

"Ah, yeah. They wouldn't." He glanced at me, pausing. "They don't know. See, I asked for that part of me to be obscured to other Protectors, as well as any other immortal. They see nothing more than plain old me. Nothing special, if you get my drift."

I shook my head. It hurt. How many more surprises were in store for me?

"I wanted to settle down. Live a normal life. You know? I wanted exactly what I've found with your mom. And you."

"But when you realized who Eli and Casey were, why didn't you say something?"

"I didn't know how much you knew. It wasn't until your "accident," "—he held up his fingers in air quotes—"that I realized how deep you really were." He glanced out the window. "I ran into Edward at the hospital . . . he explained everything. Your situation was so abnormal; I wasn't sure what to do."

"So you left."

He nodded, looking ashamed. "I did go back to work, but I could have stayed. It just caught me off guard. I'm sorry. I tried so hard to get away from that life, to really settle down and move on. I wasn't ready to face it again. I didn't know how. Not like this. Anyway, Edward thought it would be better if you didn't know—you know, like an extra Protector watching out for you, one you had no idea was even there."

"So Edward convinced you not to tell me?"

"He made it seem like a good idea, and at first, I thought he was right. As months passed, I regretted it, but how could I tell you then? After I'd hidden it for so long."

Steam may as well have been coming out of my ears. "I'm so tired of people keeping things from me!"

I threw open the door, feeling the need to get away from him, as if distance would solve this.

George got out of the car. I could feel him standing behind me. Goosebumps prickled on my skin even though I wasn't cold.

"At the time, I thought he was right. That having an extra person watching out for you wouldn't be a bad thing. With you in the hospital, I wanted to protect you. I'm sorry."

"And you couldn't do that with me knowing?"

His head drooped. "It wasn't well-thought out. I was wrong."

After everything I'd just learned, I wasn't sure who I was most mad at—Edward for keeping me in the dark *again* or George for not telling me who he was and testing me like this.

"Can you just take me back to my car?" I asked, barely above a whisper.

The ride was silent. I stared out the window, trying to keep myself from looking in George's direction until we pulled up to the elevator at Casey's apartment.

"Why are we here? I have to get my car."

"You're in no shape to drive. You can get it later. I'll drive you if you need me to."

"Fine." I got out and shut the door.

There was something about the stillness of the elevator. As soon as the doors shut and I began to rise, tears rushed down my face. I leaned against the wall, putting hands up to cover my vulnerability. When the doors opened, I hurried forward, grabbing Casey's doorknob without thinking and bolting inside.

It dawned on me the instant the door shut behind me that Casey wasn't expecting me, and I shrank against the door, embarrassed. Music filled the apartment. I felt so stupid. I rubbed the tears from my blurry eyes and peeked around the corner. Casey stood at the sink doing dishes in nothing but his boxers. His hips swayed back and forth to the beat. I covered my mouth, stifling a giggle.

I stood there watching him as I wiped the tears from my eyes. Then he shut off the water and turned around. The second he saw me, he jumped back into the counter.

"Abby! What the heck?" Then as if a switch flipped, his whole expression changed. "What's wrong?"

He lunged forward. His wet hands found my hips as he searched my eyes.

"People won't stop keeping things from me. I'm just so over it."

He sighed and pulled me over to the couch. "What do you mean? Who's keeping things from you?"

"George and Edward." I sniffed.

"What?" He looked at me with a confused expression, and I knew exactly how he felt.

"George is a retired Protector," I said, rolling my eyes.

"What?"

I just stared at him. "Yep, that about sums up my reaction." I blew my nose into a tissue.

"How? He has no . . . remnants of it."

"I guess he wanted to be 'normal.' Can't say I blame him, but it'd have been nice to know a long time ago."

"Whoa. I didn't know that was even possible." He sank back into the couch, deep in thought.

"He said it was some kind of favor from the elders."

"How did you find out?"

"A test. Edward decided that my first test should come from George since it's the least expected. Stupidest idea ever."

"Jerk." He spat.

I laughed. "Tell me about it."

"What was the test?"

"George came to my work and asked me to go for a drive. It seemed weird, but it's George, you know? So I went. Everything was fine until he stopped at a trailhead and suggested we take a hike. I mean, come on, it's dusk. Nothing about that seemed right. I mean, he's never asked me to do anything *ever*, and the first time he does, it's a nighttime hike? No. The second he got out, I jumped in the driver's seat, locked him out, and demanded he tell me what was going on or I'd leave him there."

Casey snorted. "I'd have loved to have seen that," he said through fits of laughter.

His laughter made my lips curl.

"But wait, if he wanted to be normal, how did he even get into this with Edward in the first place?"

"I guess Edward and George ran into each other at the hospital after my 'accident.' That's when George found out how much I knew about Protectors. That's what he'd been waiting to find out before he said anything about his past."

"So, why didn't he tell you then?"

"Edward."

Casey shook his head. "Of course. Always the root of everything. You know, it's not too late to back out."

"I'm not backing out. Maybe Edward will start taking me seriously now."

"Maybe." But I could tell he didn't mean it.

I glanced down, all at once fully aware that I was sitting half in his lap and he was only wearing boxers. "I'm sorry I just barged in . . ."

His gaze followed mine down his body. My cheeks tinted. He slid my legs off his lap. "I'll go put some clothes on." He started to leave the room but turned around. "And you are welcome to barge in here anytime." He took another step, then stopped again. "I should probably give you a key."

He seemed to consider this thoroughly as he left the room.

He trusted me enough to give me a key? That was huge.

Moments later, he returned wearing sweatpants. He was still sliding a t-shirt over his head.

"You didn't have to put a shirt on," I said under my breath.

Casey tried to hide the blush on his face by turning his back, but he wasn't fooling me.

I shook my head, smiling.

*   *   *   *

Four days later, Casey stood at ready. I took a deep breath, preparing myself for yet another blow. This was the second day in a row that we were going head to head, and the two days before I'd spent weight training to prepare myself for it. Casey was going easy on me—I'd taken a beating the day before.

My muscles ached.

"Okay," I said, breathing heavy.

Casey lunged, grabbing me around the shoulders. Before I could slip out of his grip, he threw his foot out, hitting me in the back of the knees and knocking me flat on my butt. He landed on top of me in one swift move, pinning me to the ground.

In the sand, my fall was cushioned, but every move ground sand into my sore skin. I didn't give him another chance to get a grip on me.

Using my feet, I propelled myself downward through his legs and swung myself up. Thrusting myself forward, I grabbed hold of his neck, putting him in a chokehold. I threw myself backward to make it that much harder for him to escape. I landed hard on my butt again, and Casey landed on top of me, the headlock still in place. I sucked in a breath through my teeth as pain rippled down my spine.

"Good," Lucian said. "However, I'd like to see you gain control much quicker than that."

I lay there, letting the pain subside. They gave me a few minutes between each maneuver. Just enough to regain my breath and strength.

I reached into the sand under me and rubbed my lower back, hoping to alleviate a bit of the radiating pain there. "I'm not sure I can once he comes at me."

"Don't wait for him to make a move. If you're always waiting for someone else to make the first move, you'll always be playing catch-up."

"Let's go again," I said.

Casey stood, brushing himself off. He was still bent over when I came at him. I laid him out on his back and fought to flip him to his stomach. I needed to get his arms behind his back in order to gain control. I struggled as the sand shifted beneath us. All at once, my feet slipped out from under me as Casey overtook me. He flipped me onto my back, knocking the air from my lungs, and pinned me at the neck under one arm. I felt my airway begin to close and tapped his arm three times, and he let up.

I sat up, coughing.

Lucian shook his head. "She doesn't have enough strength."

Casey shook his head. "I think working on this more today is going to just wind up causing her more bruises."

"I agree. Let's call it a day." Lucian folded his arms.

Casey pulled me to my feet.

"You okay?" he asked when I bent over, holding my knees.

I huffed, feeling the pressure in my chest. "I'm fine."

He put his hand on the small of my back. I held my side and stood up.

"I need a hot tub." I groaned.

He chuckled. "Come on."

"Carry me . . . " I said just to whine. But when he scooped me up in his arms, I realized, of course he would carry me if I asked. "I was only kidding."

"I know," he said, a hint of amusement in his tone.

Casey walked into Lucian's house and then made his way straight to the front door.

"Bye Lucian." He called.

"Bye!" I yelled.

I heard Lucian's muffled reply just as the door swung shut behind us.

"Where are we going?" I asked.

"You'll see."

After he pulled into the parking garage of his apartment building, I turned to him. "Your apartment?"

Casey stayed quiet, but his grin widened.

He squeezed my side, causing me to squeal and then immediately wince.

"Sorry."

Inside, Casey took a right turn instead of getting on the elevator. He looped his fingers in mine. At the end of the hallway, he backed into a door, pushing it open enough for me to walk in next to him. The humid smell of chlorine hit my nostrils. *His apartment has a pool and hot tub! How did I not know that?* I wanted to just throw myself in, but I hesitated, frowning.

"I don't have a swimsuit."

"You're wearing a sports bra under your shirt, right?"

I nodded.

"Shorts," he said, pointing at my elastic shorts. "And your sports bra. Instant swimsuit."

"I knew I kept you around for a reason." I stood on tiptoe to kiss his cheek.

"Go ahead, get in. I'll go change and be right back. Need anything?"

"Water?"

"You got it." He disappeared as I pulled off my shirt.

I glanced at my reflection in the mirror. Bruises in different shades spotted my abdomen and ribs. A few on my arms and legs stared back at me as well, but they weren't as bad or as painful. I debated whether I should just leave my shirt on. Nobody would understand the marks on my body if they saw them. But since I was alone, I decided to just leave it off and hope nobody else decided to take a swim.

Easing myself into the hot tub, goosebumps rose on my arms as the heat penetrated my muscles. I slid all the way in, leaned back against the wall, and closed my eyes. It was hard to believe anything was better than this.

The door opened and shut.

"That was quick," I said.

Feet shuffled behind me. I opened my eyes, ready to greet Casey when someone grabbed me from behind by the shoulders and head. The pressure of their body weighed down on me, pressing me forward and under the water. My arms and legs flailed violently.

I couldn't breathe. I needed to get it together. I brought my knees up and pushed off the step, throwing the assailant off balance. They stumbled backward and slammed into the wall. They grunted. *Him.* I felt him fall onto the step, losing the one advantage he had. I spun and dropped my feet from beneath me, yanking myself free from his grasp.

In the split second it took to come up for air, he stood, towering above me. His brown hair stuck to his forehead. I could hear Lucian in my head, directing me. *'Make the first move.'* Without thinking, I threw a low punch, connecting where it counted. He doubled over, holding his groin.

Jumping up on the seat, I positioned myself behind him. I leaped on his back and jerked him off balance. I wrapped my arms around his neck in an attempt to put him in a chokehold. He stumbled forward but caught himself before he went under. My knees slammed into the step.

"Oww!" I cried out.

My grip loosened. I was losing my leverage. Seizing my only opportunity, I grabbed his head and slammed it into the pool deck. I braced to do it again when he yelled out.

"Test!"

I froze but didn't let go.

"What did you just say?"

"Test."

My world spun. I let go and backed away until my back hit the wall of the hot tub. Nausea filled me, and I choked back bile that rose in my throat. He turned around, and his green eyes locked on me. Somehow those eyes felt familiar—too familiar. Blood dripped from his forehead.

The door opened, and Casey stepped in. His smiled faded the minute he saw me pressed against the side of the hot tub, chest heaving. His eyes flew to the guy who stood in front of me.

"What the . . ."

The guy put his hands up. "I'm only following orders." He hopped up on the step and got out dripping wet. He squared himself in front of Casey. "Don't be mad, Case.'"

Casey dropped everything he was carrying and landed a right hook on the guy's face. He stumbled. Casey gave him a good shove, knocking him on his butt. Then Casey threw himself into the hot tub. He grabbed my shoulders, looking me over.

"Are you okay?"

"F-fine. Do you guys know each other?" I asked.

He grimaced. "That's my brother."

Brother?

The lengths at which Edward was willing to go was shocking. Using the people we cared about most to test my abilities irked me.

I turned to his brother. He sat where he'd landed, watching us.

"I'm sorry," he said.

I shook my head. Turning to get out, I grabbing the railing and stepped up, but a strangled cry escaped my lips. Casey didn't try to boost me out but instead came around in front of me and held out his hand. He lifted me out of the water and handed me a towel.

His brother looked me over. "I didn't know." His eyes roamed over all the bruising.

"Of course you didn't! That's why you don't just jump in without assessing!" Casey barked.

"I didn't have a choice. I had orders!."

"Casey! It's fine," I said.

"No it's not!"

"This is what I signed up for!" I said.

"No. You signed up to go undercover. Not to get beat up when you have your guard down in a place like *my* apartment."

"Trust me, I don't like this any more than you do, but I understand why he's testing me like this! Would you rather I get into a situation where I'm in over my head and it be too late?"

"She's right, and you know it, Casey. This is the only way to know if she's ready."

Casey pushed his hand into his hair and pointed a finger at his brother. "You don't get a say in this."

"You may be mad that I did this, but would you have wanted it to be anyone else? You know I wouldn't have really hurt her."

Casey looked him in the eyes. He looked reluctant to agree. But eventually, he turned to me. "Abby, this is my brother Cade. Cade, this is Abby."

"I've been looking forward to meeting you, Abby, though I didn't dream it would be right after I attacked you. I'm sorry again. Looks like it was bad timing—you seem to have already taken quite the beating." He pointed to my bruises.

Casey's jaw tensed. "Those are from training."

I slipped my shirt on, feeling self-conscious.

Cade's eyebrows rose. "Geez, I guess that's a difference from having immortal healing."

I sat down and inspected my knees. Scrapes, more bruises, and a little blood—nothing terrible.

"Casey, can I go upstairs and lie down?" I asked.

Casey stood and gathered everything up, and the three of us went upstairs.

After changing into a pair of Casey's sweats—something that was becoming a regular thing—I climbed into his bed and snuggled into the very center. I breathed in his scent that lingered on the sheets. It made me feel at home like I did in his arms.

I could hear Casey and Cade's deep voices echoing through the vents in the apartment, yet I couldn't understand what they were saying. I hoped Casey wouldn't hold this against Cade. Granted, it wasn't the way I would have liked to meet him. But I didn't blame him. Not like I did George. He hadn't been living a lie in my house.

My eyelids began to droop listening to the steady rumble of their voices. Eventually, I couldn't fight the exhaustion anymore.

The *click* of a door closing lifted the heavy veil of sleep that encompassed me. I rolled over, trying to find the light without success. As I opened my eyes, I found the sun no longer streamed through the window.

"Are you awake?" Casey whispered.

"Yeah," I said, my voice husky.

"I made dinner. You hungry?"

"Mmhmm . . ."

"You have to get up then," he said.

I grabbed hold of his waist, pulling him into the bed next to me.

"First I need a hug."

He sank down, allowing me to scoot closer to him and snuggle into his chest. I started to drift back to sleep. He didn't give me long before he nudged me again.

"Cade's still here."

I sat upright in a flash, then winced. "Why didn't you say that sooner? How long was I out?"

"An hour."

"You should have woken me up earlier," I said.

"Relax. Cade made you something."

He eased out of the room, leaving me to pry myself out of his very soft bed.

"Good morning sleepyhead," Cade said as I entered the kitchen. "How are you feeling?"

"Sore," I said, stretching my arms in front of my body.

"Maybe this will help." He handed me a round white plastic jar. I twisted off the cap and peeked inside. The smell was pungent.

"Eww. What is it?" I asked.

"A special remedy," he said with a smirk.

Casey raised his eyebrows at Cade and shook his head.

"Just rub it on your bruises. It will help."

"Ah. Thanks."

Throughout dinner, I couldn't help but notice the similarities between Casey and Cade. Their mannerisms in the way they ate and spoke mirrored each other. I loved seeing Casey with his brother. There was a happiness about him. Any hint of anger was long gone.

"How long has it been since you've seen each other?" I asked.

"What's it been, Case? Three years?"

"Yeah. Three."

"Wow, that's such a long time."

"It's not so bad. Time goes fast," Cade said.

"So, have you been on assignment for the last three years?" I asked.

"About. The last three or four months now I've been on a break."

"But you guys talk on the phone still, right?" I asked.

"Oh yeah. We talk on the phone a lot." He paused, grinning at Casey. "Ever more so since he met you, Abby."

"What?" My eyes shot to Casey.

He blushed. "Not that much more."

"You are quite the challenge," Cade said.

My mouth dropped, but I quickly shut it. "What?"

"He's exaggerating," Casey said.

But when his cheeks tinted, I couldn't stop myself from wondering what they said about me—what he said about me.

"Well, I hope I'm not that bad."

"You're worth every struggle," Casey said.

I blushed and dropped my gaze to my plate.

"I've never heard Casey so happy. I'm really glad he has you."

The room silenced. Casey stood.

"Okay, enough mushy-gushy stuff. Who wants ice cream?"

I sighed, grateful for Casey's diversion. I hated being the center of attention.

"Me!" Cade and I said at the same time.

"So, where have you been living?" I asked.

"My last assignment was in Texas, but since then I've been traveling. For now, I don't have a home base."

"That sounds like a lot of fun."

"Gotta do it while you've got the time. Right, Case'?"

"Someday," he said as he set three bowls on the table.

A silent look passed between them, and then it was gone. My brow furrowed. *What was that?*

I shoveled another bite of ice cream in my mouth, and a brain freeze struck. I couldn't hear a word they said anymore until it finally passed.

"Where are you staying?" Casey asked.

"A hotel—one of the best, of course."

"You know you could stay here." Casey gestured toward the couch.

"Nah, you don't have an on-staff masseuse." He grinned.

Cade's spoon clinked in the bottom of the bowl. He glanced at his watch and slid out of his chair. "Actually, I should go."

I stood out of habit. He leaned down and gave me a small, soft hug. "It was good to meet you."

"Yeah. It was nice to meet you. Next time, let's try not to let it end in blood being spilled." I glanced up at the butterfly bandage on his eyebrow.

"It's a plan."

He gave Casey a big bear hug with a slap on the back, and then he was gone.

*   *   *   *

At home, my body ached just to move. Climbing the stairs to my room caused tears to fill my eyes.

I stripped down and showered, then I spread Cade's cream everywhere that hurt—which didn't leave much *uncovered*. I crossed my fingers, hoping the cream would do something. Anything.

Exhaustion pulled me to sleep as I lay in bed. I willed my bedroom light off so I didn't have to move.

Off it went. I jerked my head in the direction of the light switch. *I did it!*

I thought hard and tried to repeat it. *Turn on.*
Nothing happened.
"Urgh."
I rolled over, facing away from the switch, crossed my arms, and fell asleep.
In the morning, I dressed and jogged down the stairs before realizing nothing hurt. Not. One. Thing. How was that even possible? I lifted my shirt. Not a single bruise remained.
I typed a text to Casey.
Cade is a genius!
His cream not only took away the pain, but it healed all of the bruises. I may as well have been immortal—my body healed overnight. I could never go without this cream again. Ever.

CHAPTER ELEVEN

A single set footsteps echoed on the concrete floor—mine. My back pressed into the wall, and my chest heaved. The walls seemed to close in on me. I was cornered with no escape. Inching my way further into the dark room, I hid. I wanted nobody to find me. Why was I here?

I shook my head, trying to recall what brought me here. My mind was a blur. This was wrong. I needed to get out. I shouldn't be here. All at once, everything started to clear. This was a dream.

I looked at the walls around me, spotting a window. I urged myself forward. One of the panes was broken. I kept my hands clear of the break and looked out.

A door creaked behind me. Light flooded half of the empty room. I spun around to face the light, my back pressed to the window. A figure lingered in the doorway.

My heart hammered against my chest. I needed to get away. I needed out. I shouldn't be here.

Without warning, I couldn't breathe. I couldn't move. I struggled . . .

Gasping for air, I sat up, pushing the weight off my face. My pillow fell to the floor. Why was my pillow over my face?

Darkness amplified the clock on my nightstand. Three in the morning. I groaned.

No way would I be able to sleep after that. I rolled out of bed and padded downstairs. At the foot of the stairs, I froze. The TV was off, but the sound of someone in the kitchen had me second-guessing going in there. I clutched the railing until my knuckles hurt. I debated running back upstairs.

What was I doing? This was the kind of thing I'd been training for.

I took a deep breath and tiptoed forward. Then, I thought better and grabbed an umbrella from the hook next to the stairs, just in case. I clung to the umbrella like a bat. The noises grew louder as I approached the doorway. At the last second, I jumped out, ready to swing.

George dropped a loaf of bread on the floor and threw his arms in the air. "Whoa, whoa, Abby. It's me."

I dropped the umbrella. "Dang it, George! You scared the crap out of me!"

"I'm sorry. I was just making a snack."

"Geez! Normally you have the TV on. I thought you went to bed."

"I was going up after this." He pointed to his snack.

"Why are you always up in the middle of the night, anyway?" I realized how annoyed I sounded, but that's exactly how I felt. Why did he have to be up right now? I needed a few minutes to myself, not another scare. My chest ached as the adrenaline wore off for the second time.

"I don't sleep well at night," he said. But I sensed there was more to it. I left it alone. "What are you doing up? Another nightmare?"

I considered ignoring his question. He wasn't exactly my favorite person at the moment. I threw open the freezer and grabbed the orange sherbet, stalling.

"Yes . . . " I swooped up the bread and set it on the counter next to him.

"Want to talk about it?"

I eyed him. He worked with Edward. He kept things from me. How could I trust him with anything?

"I haven't been very honest with you. I'm sorry for that. I am on your side though. It may not look that way right now. I get it if you don't want to talk to me, though."

It took only a few minutes to throw together a bowl of ice cream. I sat down at the bar across from him.

"Did Edward tell you anything about my dreams?"

The puzzled expression on his face told me all I needed to know.

I sighed. *Might as well tell him everything. If he's really going to be on my side, he needs to know.*

"My nightmares aren't just normal nightmares. Edward says I'm gifted."

"How can that be?" He set his snack down and turned toward me.

I shrugged. "Your guess is as good as mine."

"What gift do you have?"

"My nightmares show me things that will happen at some point. All of them so far have been of a moment where I was fighting for my life."

"All of them?"

"Yep."

"And you've just had another?"

"To be fair, I've been having it for a while. This time . . ." I paused. "I couldn't breathe. When I woke up, my pillow somehow covered my face."

"Are you okay?"

"Fine. I just couldn't sleep after that."

"I don't blame you. So, this is why you've been so surrounded by Protectors?"

"I'm surprised Edward didn't go into all of this with you."

"I'm not. Edward only gives need-to-know information, and all I needed to know was that you were helping out and needed training."

I shook my head. "Sounds like Edward."

"Would it be asking too much to know what you're training for? I've been wondering. I've never heard of any non-Protector helping out before."

"That's because it doesn't happen. I'm going undercover to figure out who's using their gifts for things on their own agenda."

"The rogue Protectors . . ." He let out a whistle. "That's like sticking your hand in a beehive."

"So I've been told."

"I don't like it."

I rolled my eyes. "Well, you aren't the first."

"I'm sure I'm not. There's no way I could talk you out of it?"

I shook my head. "If anyone could, it would have been Casey. And he tried."

George nodded. "You'll let me know if you need help?"

"I'll be fine."

I set my bowl in the sink.

"Thanks for telling me."

"I should go upstairs. Maybe sleep . . . if I can. My dad will be here in the morning."

He nodded, and I went upstairs hoping I wouldn't regret telling him everything.

I couldn't wait for my dad to get here. He planned to be here by late morning, and I got the weekend off from all training. *Thank you, Dad!*

*   *   *   *

Dad arrived at the house just before lunchtime in his rental car. I opened the door before he could even knock.

"Hey Abbs!" he said in the doorway, his bag in one hand and his cane in the other.

"Dad!" I threw my arms around his neck. "I've missed you so much!"

"I've missed you too, sweetie." His stubble scratched my cheek as he hugged me back. Then his gaze shifted, and he pulled away. "Hello."

George stood back, just in view. I let go. George stepped forward with his hand outstretched. Dad accepted it without hesitation.

"Good to see you again," Dad said.

"You too," George said. "How was the flight?"

"Uneventful, not too much turbulence."

"That's good."

The room fell silent. I looked from George to my dad and back again.

"Well . . . should we get to lunch?"

"Sure. I'm starved." Dad turned back to George. "I'll see ya."

George waved and went back to the kitchen.

I sighed. *Awkward.*

Dad threw his arm around me, and we walked to the car. He seemed to be getting around really well—he hardly used the cane.

After lunch, we went to a movie and then for the only adventure his short trip and injured leg would allow—Tempe Town Lake. We sat lakeside as the reflection of the sun disappeared from the water.

"Casey lives right over there," I said pointing at his building.

"It's nice."

"Very. You should see the view." I thought for a second. Then I grabbed his arm and pulled him up. "Come on!"

We rode the elevator to Casey's floor in silence. My lips pressed tightly together as I held my breath. I hated this elevator. It took too much energy to suppress the terrible memories it invoked. One day, I hoped, none of this would remain, and stepping inside would be no different than going anywhere else.

I shook off the bad vibes as I walked out of the elevator on Casey's floor. I knocked on his door, hoping he was home, and Brad opened it.

"Hey."

"Hey, is Casey here?"

Brad pushed the door open. All the guys were crowded around a table playing cards.

"Sorry to interrupt . . ." I said.

Casey jumped up and rushed over.

"Hey guys," Casey said. He gave me a tight squeeze and whispered in my ear, "I didn't know you were coming by."

"Me neither. We were walking by the lake, and I told my dad about the amazing view from up here and thought I'd come see if I could show him."

"Of course. Come on."

Casey pulled me inside and to the living room, Dad following along behind us.

"You don't play poker, do you?" Casey asked my dad.

"I do enjoy a good game of poker every now and then."

"Would you care to join us?" Casey asked.

I loved that he was including my dad. I stood back, watching them chat, the glorious view behind them, and just felt so at home.

"Uh . . ." He blew out a breath, glancing at his watch. "One game. I've got to hit the road in an hour or so."

*　　　*　　　*　　　*

I hated waking up the next morning knowing that Dad was waking up in California. Life had to go on, and unfortunately his life was in California and mine was here.

Downstairs, Mom sat at the counter eating breakfast. George was nowhere in sight.

"Good morning, honey."

"Morning," I said.

"Ready for school?"

"Yep." I grabbed a banana and my keys and headed for the door. "I'll see you later!"

Daydreams occupied my mind for much of the school day. At one point during math, my last class of the day, I stared at the whiteboard markers and wondered if my gift would work. Up until now, practice had been hit or miss.

I concentrated that entire hour on the markers, only moving them twice the whole time while the class was focused on the teacher. I felt like I might be on the brink of getting it down when the final bell rang. I jumped in my seat.

Progress. I breathed a sigh of relief as I exited the school. Maybe I could get this down. Tonight, when I had more time alone, I had a good feeling I'd get it.

I rushed home and sneaked a quick snack before I left for Lucian's.

I knocked on his door when I arrived, and he pulled it open moments later. "You know you don't have to knock. I know it's you."

"Yeah, well that seems weird."

He shook his head. "Whatever. Let's get to it." He placed his earbuds into his ears as he strode out to the beach.

This was easier now that we had a routine. I knew what to expect. All workouts started with a run. As much as I hated running, I didn't feel like I'd die after the first five minutes anymore, and each day got easier. Still, I couldn't keep up with Lucian. His physique was fantastic—only immortals could match.

Twenty minutes later, he turned back and headed in a different direction. He was so far ahead, I couldn't ask him where he was going. I followed behind him and pushed myself to catch up, but eventually he eased to a stop in a deserted parking lot—deserted, that is, except for the giant inflatable obstacle course set up in the field next to it. As we got closer, I could see Casey sitting on it with his legs pulled up in front of him. He stood up as we approached. A stopwatch hung at his neck.

"What in the world? I didn't know you were coming today."

Casey nodded and laughed as I came closer. Lucian climbed right up onto it, got into a starting position, and turned back to me.

"Climb up. We decided to take it easy today since *someone* had the weekend off."

I ignored his comment and focused on the obstacle course in front of me. I hadn't been on one of these in years. *This might actually be fun.*

I wasn't sure how this trained me, but I rolled myself onto the blow-up landing pad and found myself stuck, unable to get to my feet. I felt like a huge roly-poly. Deep belly laughs overcame my whole body.

"Ahh . . . I can't get up!" The laughter almost engulfed my words.

Lucian shook his head. "You're helpless."

Lucian lifted me up while Casey pushed up on my back, making me feel even more like a beached whale. My laughter didn't help one bit. After a good struggle, the three of us were able to right me on my feet.

Lucian looked at Casey with a smirk. "Maybe she can't do this after all."

Casey shrugged, amused.

"Oh, hush! I can do it."

"Prove it."

I crouched down and readied myself.

"Go!" Casey called.

I took off through the first tunnel and fell flat on my face as I came out on the other side. *Well, that was graceful.*

Lucian glanced back, a sly smile on his face as he hoisted himself up the obstacle wall. I scrambled to my feet and hurried after him. He beat me by twenty-five seconds.

"Well, you did it. I'll give you that," Lucian said as I climbed off.

"Let's go again."

"This time try not to fall on your face."

"Ha. Very funny."

Casey stood back, laughing. I glared at him.

"You two enjoy this way too much."

We got back into position, and when Casey said, "Go," I raced forward, clearing the first tunnel without falling. Then, on the second hill, I slipped and tumbled backward from the top. Lucian beat me again.

Casey didn't even say by how much, which told me it was a lot.

On the next go, Lucian remained one step ahead of me, beating me by ten seconds.

"Dang it!" I grunted.

Their faces turned red, but they restrained their laughter.

"'Good thing I didn't take you to the real obstacle course," Lucian said. "This would have been really bloody by now."

"Again!" I said.

Lucian followed me to the start. His silence as he climbed up was enough to let me know how smug he was, but what he didn't know was that I had no intention of losing again—even if that meant playing a little dirty.

We braced ourselves to go again. I sprang into action the second I heard Casey's voice. I couldn't even be certain he'd actually said *go*. I lunged at Lucian, grabbed his waist, and flung him backward. I used the momentum to throw myself forward. Halfway up the first wall, Lucian grabbed my foot and yanked me down. I landed on my shoulder with a bounce. Scrambling to my feet, I jumped up the wall, but before I could grab Lucian, he was over the top. I flipped myself over, and as I landed, I caught Lucian by the ankle just enough to trip him. On my hands and knees, I crawled past him weaving between the barriers. In a flash, Lucian came down in front of me.

"Did you just jump over me?" I yelled.

He turned back just for a split second and winked. I smacked the bounce house and jumped out the side. I got to the finish line just as Lucian did.

"Aw, what? You gave up?"

"I can't even beat you when I cheat. What's the point?"

"The point is to get faster every time. Endurance. Believe it or not, this is very good cardio, and that's good because you need a break from the harder things. Now, get back to the beginning. You're going against Casey."

It was more fun racing Casey, though I wasn't all that sure if he was going easy on me. Even still, he beat me more times than not, while I came in inches behind him.

I felt like every time I was a disappointment. Each time it seemed like I would never get better. But then, out of nowhere, I started coming in at the same time as Casey, and our times got faster.

At the end of the day, the three of us went to Casey's apartment and ordered pizza. We took it down to the hot tub and spent the evening unwinding, but I knew the next day wouldn't be easy—my muscles already protested. Who would have thought I would be so sore . . . everywhere.

After easing my muscles in the hot tub, I couldn't wait to get home to use the cream Cade had made me. In my eyes, it was the best thing ever created.

CHAPTER TWELVE

Weeks passed in the blink of an eye. Eat. Sleep. School. Work. Train. And then it started all over again. Sometimes in a different order. Often in the few minutes before I fell asleep, I would call my dad to check on him. He was doing so much better now and walking without the cane.

"Don't you worry about me—you just worry about having fun with your friends," he always said.

Have a social life? Ha. What was that? Bailey rarely called anymore, though I couldn't say if it was because I'd turned her down too many times or if she herself was too busy. As for Casey, if he hadn't changed his mind about this whole thing and started helping with my training, I don't know when I would have gotten to see him. I couldn't remember the last date we went on. The Christmas dance, maybe?

I walked into school that morning feeling good and ready to start the day. Boredom struck as I sat listening to the third teacher of the day drone on and on. We already had this down—well, most of us anyway. The one who didn't were forcing the rest to review.

My head lolled into my hand as I tried to keep myself awake. Glancing over at the large desk in the corner of the room, I noticed a stack of books and papers teetering on the edge. My head straightened as I looked more closely at the mess waiting to happen.

A solution to my boredom?

My eyes flicked here and there around the room. Satisfied nobody was watching me, I concentrated on the stack. With a loud *thud* and a flurry of papers, everything crashed to the floor.

Yes! I did it!

I smirked as the entire class jumped. Our teacher scrambled to try to clean up the mess with the help of a few students, but the bell rang before it was done.

I breathed a sigh of relief. Why hadn't I thought to do that sooner?

"That was crazy," Bailey said.

"Sure was."

"What's with that grin?" she asked.

"Oh, nothing."

She rolled her eyes.

"What? Can't I just be happy we got out of there and got to miss the last few minutes of review?"

"Sure," Bailey said. But I could tell she wasn't sure she believed me.

Throughout the rest of the day, I searched for opportunities to practice again, but I didn't find one until the last class of the day. I dropped my pen on the floor, and it rolled under the desk next to me.

I groaned. The teacher stood at the front of the room talking. I laid my head on my desk—
the only way I could see my pen—and concentrated hard just like before. At first the pen just twitched, but then it rolled my way, just within reach. I plucked it off the floor, feeling accomplished.

The bell rang, and I grabbed my bag as I walked out the door.

I thought of Casey asking every so often about my new gift, and about Lucian, who didn't know. I couldn't wait to surprise both of them when the moment was right. I'd mastered it all by myself.

But for now, I had to meet with Edward. It was just him and me this time, which had me more curious than ever. Usually Lucian joined us, and often Casey, too, but not today.

I couldn't stop fidgeting, while I waited for Edward to tell me why he'd wanted to meet. The serious yet happy stare he wore gave little away, as usual.

Edward handed me an I.D.

"Ashley Brooks? What's this for?" I asked.

"Your first mission."

"Already?"

"I think you've proved yourself by passing the tests. Especially with George. If you were able to detect something off with him, you have the instinct that, I'll be honest, I was concerned you didn't possess. Cade also spoke highly of your ability to protect yourself, especially in surroundings where you felt secure. I've discussed it with Lucian. He feels your training has gone well, which leads me to believe you are ready. Am I mistaken?"

I shook my head. Looking over the I.D., I noticed the picture was me, but everything else wasn't. It even said the wrong eye color.

"This says I'm twenty-three."

"Indeed it does."

He reached over and handed me a cell phone. "You'll need this as well."

Butterflies fluttered in my stomach.

"What am I doing?" I asked.

"You're going to a nightclub. I received a tip that there may be illegal things happening at a club run by castoffs. You're going to find out if it's true."

"What do I have to do?"

"Ask around. Find out who's behind it. That's it. We need proof."

"What am I asking for?"

Edward hesitated. "Just ask around. Find out *what* you can get your hands on—drugs or whatever else they may offer—and from who."

I balked. "Oh, is that all? Like it's so easy for me to talk to people and ask for drugs."

"More than likely this person will present himself to you. I know you can do this. Consider it acting. I think you've played your role well when the time called for it in the past."

He seemed so sure, however, I remained uncertain. How did one even start to ask about drugs?

Edward handed me a wad of cash.

"For a new outfit and anything you need at the club."

I sighed.

Hours later with my hair done, I stood in front of the bright lights of a gray building wearing one of the skimpiest outfits I'd donned in my life. The ground pulsed from the music within. I flounced right up to the door the way Edward had instructed me to. The bouncer took one look at me and waved me through so I bypassed the line that sprawled to the end of the building. The other clubbers grumbled as I walked in before them.

I couldn't deny that it felt good.

The music and strobe lights hit me like a wall, making me falter in my heels. Taking a deep breath, I readjusted my black skirt and crop top and flipped my hair. *It's just acting. I can do this.*

A wave of nausea washed over me as I walked to the bar. I pushed my shoulders back and held my chin high. I felt eyes on me from all over. It was the last push I needed to let myself go. I grinned and allowed an extra spring in my step.

Leaning over the bar, I batted my eyes at the bartender. He came right over, dimples showing.

"What can I get ya?" he asked.

"Something fruity, perhaps," a gentleman said, cutting in next to me. He flashed a smile. "On me." He was dressed in black slacks, a maroon dress shirt, and black tie. He had short black hair and light brown eyes that popped against the maroon. For a moment, I lost myself in his eyes.

"Hi," he said.

I clamped my mouth shut, suddenly back where I should be. I felt flustered already, and I hadn't even spoken to him. With a deep breath, I leaned into the bar and turned back to the bartender, taking a moment to compose myself. "A soda would be great. Cola, please."

When I turned back to Mr. Dreamy, his gaze hadn't strayed from me.

"Thanks," I said.

"Don't mention it. I'm Drake."

"Ab-Ashley," I said.

"I've never seen you in here before."

"First time."

"What do you think?"

I glanced around. "It's nice."

The bartender returned with my cola fitted with a cute umbrella with two cherries stuck to it, and slid it across the bar.

"Care to join me?" he asked, holding out his hand.

My throat went dry. *'More than likely this person in question will present himself to you'* Edward's words rang in my head. I grabbed my drink and gulped down two big swallows.

With the drink clutched in one hand, I placed the other in his. "Lead the way."

After dancing two songs, I pointed to a table on this side of the dance floor.

He shook his head. "I have a better idea."

He placed his hand on the small of my back. All I could think of was Casey and how it should be his hand there. I didn't know how long I could keep this up for. It felt so wrong on so many levels. I pushed Casey from my mind. *It's just a job.*

Instead of leading me to a table, the man brought me to a darkened staircase. He stepped in front of me and began to climb. I hesitated. Something about going upstairs made me uneasy.

"Where are you taking me?" I asked. I pushed a playful grin to my lips, trying to not cause a stir.

"Upstairs, there's tables. It's quieter. We don't have to go up if you'd rather—"

"No, it's fine," I said, cutting him off.

Glancing back at the pulsing crowd, I sighed. My training better be enough. It might just come to that once I went up these stairs.

The higher I climbed, the quieter the music became, until it faded to a distant rumble.

At the top, there were private areas throughout a large room. Some even had curtains that could be closed.

He stopped at the furthest one and closed the curtain behind us, jolting my nerves. My skirt, once again, felt too short, and my heels felt too tall. I fidgeted with my clothes, trying to cover myself some before I gave up and sat down.

"Tell me about yourself." He leaned back into the cushions, at ease. I envied people for whom charisma came easy. I could only hope my fake confidence would get me through the night.

"What do you want to know?" I purred in a way I didn't know possible.

"What should I know?" He grinned.

"You should know that you look amazing in that color."

His smile broadened. "Playing coy, I see."

"Never." I held my straw to my lips long after taking a drink.

"Do you live in the area?" he asked.

I nodded. "Not far. You?"

"I feel like I live here sometimes."

I grinned and fidgeted with the umbrella. Then I took a deep breath. "So . . . what kind of fun does this club offer?"

His grin faded, and his eyes flashed. *Was that annoyance?* He slid his empty glass away after he downed the last of the amber liquid.

"What have you heard?" he asked. He was no longer flirting. He wasn't happy.

I sat up straighter, feeling the hair on the back of my neck rise.

"Nothing," I said. "I just thought there might be a little extra fun behind the scenes, if you know what I mean."

"We don't do that here," he thundered.

"O-o-okay," I stuttered. "I didn't mean anything." I set my glass on the table and stood.

He eyed me as if he were weighing what to do, and then his face softened.

"I'm sorry. I guess I'm a little defensive."

"Why?" I asked without thinking. "I mean, if that's not too personal."

"Well, there were some people here that were offering some things . . . illegal things, but I removed them. This isn't that kind of place. That's the last thing I want in my club. I don't want people to get the wrong idea."

"I get that." I looked down at my hands.

"I didn't mean to get angry. I have a lot on the line. I hate that my name's been dragged through the mud."

"I shouldn't have asked. I'm sorry. I should go." I stood.

"No, please don't. Forgive me. Let's go downstairs. I'll buy you another drink." He held the curtain to the side.

I hesitated. My eyes locked on his. The sincerity they held struck me. He was no criminal.

"Another one of these," I said, raising my empty glass.

He grinned as the tension melted away from his face. "You've got it."

"So, you're the owner?" I asked as we walked.

"Ah, yeah."

"This place is pretty cool. Lots of space."

"Thanks." He looked around. "I took an empty warehouse and turned it into my vision. It's a labor of love really."

"I hope I find something I'm so passionate about."

He gave me a strange look. My forehead began to sweat. *What am I doing?*

"I just mean"—I stumbled to try to fix what I'd said—"what I'm doing now isn't what I want to do forever."

He nodded. "What do you do now?"

"I work at a coffee house."

After we got our drinks, we found a table by the dance floor, and some of his employees joined us. He seemed to be really good friends with all of them. Eventually, after listening to them talk for a while about all kinds of things, from the charity work they did as a group to last night's basketball game, I felt certain the rumors Edward heard were no longer true.

It was time for me to get out here.

When Drake was engrossed in conversation, I tried to slip away, but he grabbed my arm when I'd taken only a few steps.

"You aren't taking off, are you?" he asked.

I shook my head, unable to find the words. "Uh . . . bathroom?"

"Great." He pointed to the side of the bar, showing me where it was.

I waited until his attention was back with his friends, and then I moved toward the bathroom. At the very last second, I slipped into the crowd and out the front door.

Edward's beautiful car pulled up to the curb right away. I dropped into the seat and slammed the door. He pulled away before I could even buckle in.

"What did you learn?" he asked without wasting a moment.

I rolled my eyes but kept most of my annoyance to myself.

"This place is clean," I said.

"I know."

"It sounds like there was a problem, but the owner found out and put a stop to it. Wait . . . what?"

Edward nodded. "Good. You did good."

"I did *good*? What do you mean *'you know'*?"

"We investigated this place a few months ago. Drake approached me and explained he had a problem, wanted us to help him figure it out. We did. The problem was handled."

"What the hell was this, then?"

"A trial run."

"Are you kidding me?"

"I had to be sure you could pull something like this off. This mission was zero-risk, and I know how Drake runs his business. He introduces himself to all the new faces."

"You tricked me."

"No, Abby. I tested you."

I crossed my arms and shook my head. "Are we about done with these tests? I've had enough."

"Yes, we're done now. You did very well."

I couldn't wait to get out of this car and away from Edward. Thankfully, he took me to Casey's. There was no way I could go home looking like this. I'd be grounded for life. It was probably for the better, anyway—my whole body still shook with anger.

Casey waited by the elevator. I wondered how long he'd been waiting there. I grabbed my bag out of the back and grunted a goodbye to Edward. But he didn't even lift his eyes from the road ahead of him.

Before I made it to the elevator, Casey enveloped me in a huge hug. I didn't have hands to hug him back, so they were smashed in between us with my bag and purse, making for the most awkward hug ever.

"You're trembling. Are you okay?"

"I can't help it," I said through my teeth.

"Why? What happened?"

"It was another stupid test!" I shouted louder than I meant to.

Casey looked around, checking if anyone was watching before turning back to me. "What do you mean? How could it have been a test? That doesn't make sense."

"The owner of the club I went to asked Edward to investigate it for him a few months ago. They caught the person and stopped the problem. He just used the scenario to send me in to see how I would do working undercover."

"What?" He shook his head. "I'm sorry."

I stabbed the elevator with my finger. "I just want to get out of these clothes so I can be done with it."

He wrapped his arm around me, then looked me over and shook his head. "Agreed. These clothes aren't you."

"Tell me about it."

*　　　*　　　*　　　*

The next day, Casey picked me up to go to Lucian's to train.

I wasn't in a great mood. I felt restless. Call it pent-up frustration from the day before or maybe just the pressure to be what I needed to be all the time. It almost felt like I couldn't breathe. My nerves swirled in my stomach, churning with ferocity.

On the drive over, I didn't talk much except to reply to Casey's questions.

"Are you okay?" he asked when he shut off the car in front of Lucian's.

I nodded. "I'm just anxious or something today."

"Does this have anything to do with last night?" He paused. "Or your gift?"

"Maybe . . ."

I turned toward the door, and it unlocked. I reached for the handle and froze. Casey hadn't moved. Slowly, I turned around. Casey was watching me.

"I did that, didn't I?"

He nodded. "You're getting it down more, aren't you?"

I ignored him and got out. *That wasn't control.*

What I needed most right now was to hit something. That would really make me feel better.

I threw open the door and stormed in.

"Ready Lucian?" I called into the house. I paused only a second, but when he didn't immediately show himself, I continued on. "I'm getting started."

I walked straight through the house and out the back door. I took off without waiting. I knew the drill: run, then train. Might as well get it out of the way.

I took our usual path and turned back at the lighthouse. Lucian never joined me, but after a good run in the salty air, I felt a bit readier to face this—as ready as I'd ever be, anyway.

I jogged up the steps and went inside. Lucian and Casey were huddled together in the living room and stopped talking the moment I stepped inside.

I put my hand on my hip. "I assume he told you?" I asked, panting.

"He did," Lucian said, his grin gone.

"Did you already know my mission was fake?" I asked.

Lucian shook his head. "No. I understand why you're angry. I would be too." He paused. "But in a way, I think Edward did you a favor."

"What?"

"The first mission is always scary, and then the second one isn't as bad, until one day the nerves are gone altogether."

"You think I needed a trial run?"

"No. I didn't say that. But what's done is done. We can sulk about it, or we can learn from it. Although Edward's tactics are a bit unethical at times, he does know what he's doing."

I groaned.

"Shall we get started on your training for today?" Lucian asked.

"Yes, please. Do I get to hit things?"

CHAPTER THIRTEEN

After a week of getting my butt kicked in training and answering a zillion what-if questions about how I would handle myself in any situation, including some of the most outrageous, unbelievable scenarios, I was looking forward to spending some alone time with Casey. He promised me a date at his place.

As I drove, I debated going home to change but decided against it. Casey would understand. Workout clothes were all I wore lately.

My body ached. My head throbbed.

When I pulled into the garage, I saw Casey waiting for me next to the elevator.

"Hey," I said.

He strolled over and wrapped his arms around me.

"Hi," he said.

He lifted me up and kissed me one sweet time, then reconsidered and kissed me again, longer this time.

Slowly, he lowered me back to the ground.

"Come on."

He took me by my hand and led me to his apartment. At his front door, he stopped and turned around.

"Close your eyes."

"What? Why?" I asked, giving him a skeptical look.

He shook his head. "Just do it."

I smiled and obliged, shutting my eyes tight. I could hear the keys in the lock and then the door handle. Casey held my hand and pulled me inside. The door closed behind us.

"Can I open them now?" I asked.

"Wait . . ." There were footsteps. "Okay . . . now."

The room was dark except for candles lit in all directions. His dining room table was set for two with silver covers over the plates. Two tall white candles burned on either side of a small vase of red roses.

"Casey . . . " I breathed.

"Sit." He pulled out my chair.

Instead of sitting, I reached around his neck and kissed him. "Thank you. This is beautiful."

The shyness he rarely let me see came out as he glanced down and blushed. He lifted the cover from my plate, revealing a small pizza.

"Oh my gosh." I giggled, taking my seat.

He grinned and sat across from me. "Your favorite."

"Now I feel bad I didn't go home and change."

"You look beautiful."

I turned away, unable to maintain eye contact when he complimented me.

"So, what's the special occasion?" I asked, changing the subject.

"Do I need one to do something special for you?"

My cheeks flushed.

He reached across the table and brushed the top of my hand. "You mean everything to me, Abby. I never knew true happiness until I met you. I don't spend enough time showing you."

"Kicking my butt on the beach doesn't count?" I smirked.

He pursed his lips.

"I'm kidding."

"Dance with me?"

He grabbed a remote, and soft, slow music began to play. He stood and held out his hand. With a smile, he led me over to the floor-length windows and locked one hand in mine while the other found my waist.

The world seemed to drift away when I was in his arms. The music carried me, and I let myself get lost in this moment. This was all that mattered right now. No matter what the future held, we always had each other. I rested my head on his shoulder.

I lifted myself on my toes and kissed him. Holding the back of his neck, I pulled him closer.

He boosted me up, and my feet left the ground and wrapped around him. He held me there, kissing me with so much intensity. Slowly, he stepped toward the couch without breaking the kiss.

He sat down with me straddling his lap. Our kiss deepened. Heat spread through my body. Casey's hands pressed against my lower back, pulling me closer. He gripped my loose-fitting tank top. I reached down, tugging at his shirt.

Sitting back, our eyes met, and the passion in his matched mine. I lifted his shirt over his head and gazed down at him. His chiseled chest rose and fell with his quick breaths. I ran my hand down from his chest to his abs.

Casey reached up, cupping my chin in his hands, and pulled me down to meet his kiss. This time it was rushed and needy.

His hands slid down my back, gripping at my shirt in his hands. It tightened against my skin, and then, just like that, he released it and flattened his hands against my back. His kiss turned tender and soft. He was pulling away, leaving me breathless. I leaned against his chest, letting my breathing settle before sliding off his lap and laying my head on his stomach. My finger traced the contours in his abs.

"There's chocolate cake," Casey said after our breathing returned to normal.

"What? And you didn't start the night with that? You're holding out on me!"

He shrugged, smiling, and leaned over to grab his shirt. I eyed him as he straightened it out, getting ready to pull it over his head. Focusing on the shirt, I shot it out of his hand. It landed across the room.

Casey froze.

"You perfected it?" His shocked expression made me smile.

I nodded. He jumped up, pulling me along with him. He squeezed me and swung me around. "Does Lucian know?"

"No, I wanted to show you first."

His face lit up. "This is the best news I've heard all week!"

He kissed me on the cheek and headed to the kitchen. When he returned, he had two plates with huge pieces of chocolate cake. He forked off the first bite and held it up.

"To the amazing girl who never stops surprising me."

I savored every bite of my cake, and when it was gone, we settled back into the couch together. Casey trailed his fingers up and down my back, relaxing me.

My phone rang, startling me from my zen in the crook of Casey's arm. I held the phone to reveal the screen: *unavailable*. Only Protectors called me from unavailable numbers. Casey's fingers stopped.

I groaned. "Hello."

Casey sat still. I could tell he was trying to hear the other side of the call.

"Abby, excuse my interruption," Edward said, "but I have a mission for you. Unfortunately it's time-sensitive. Where are you?"

I sat up straight. "Uh, I'm at Casey's."

Casey leaned forward, planting his elbows on his knees. He was already on alert and worried.

"I'll be there in ten minutes." There was a *click* on the line.

"So much for a relaxing night," I muttered.

Just as he said, Edward arrived ten minutes later. "Thank you for meeting with me."

Did we have a choice?

"What can we do for you?" Casey asked.

"A man's gone missing," Edward said. "A mortal. I assigned a Protector to this person a week ago. Now I can't even contact the Protector."

"Well, how am I supposed to help?" I asked.

"With the help of another Protector, you're going to go into the absent Protector's main hangout. The Protector going in with you will know who you are, and she will know the Protector we're looking for."

"Why do you need me? I mean, if this Protector knows who you're looking for and where he hangs out?"

Edward's lips pulled tight. "She's going to pretend she's trying to dispose of her . . . assignment."

"I'm playing hostage?"

"More or less."

Casey sat back, shaking his head, but he didn't speak.

"Why?" I asked.

"We're hoping that he'll take you to his hiding place. We think that's where he may be keeping the missing man."

"Who will I be with?" I asked.

"You can come in now," Edward called toward the front door.

I could hear the door open and the click of heels on the tile.

"What's up, cupcake?" Willow strutted into the room.

"Willow?"

"At your service. Well, for pretend, anyway." She winked. She leaned her tush against the edge of the couch. "You ready to kick some butt with me?"

"I think so."

"When do they start?" Casey asked, his mouth set in a thin line.

"Tonight. Now."

"There's a sleazy bar downtown that they all hang out in. That's where we're going."

"We hope this will be a quick, easy mission," Edward said.

"You ready?" Willow asked.

I glanced down at my sweats. "Ah . . ."

"Your clothes are fine." Willow said.

"Okay, then."

I gave Casey a quick kiss. He gripped my arm, and his green eyes bore into mine. I felt his worry deep in my core.

"I'll be alright," I whispered.

He released my arm and gazed at the floor. I grabbed my phone off the table.

"Text my mom and clear it with her to stay here for the night? A movie marathon with a bunch of friends, maybe?"

I pressed it into his hand and stood.

I nodded to Edward and followed Willow out of the apartment. I glanced back at Casey and Edward sitting quietly across from each other. Then I pushed myself out the door.

Once we arrived at Willow's car, she opened the trunk and pulled out rope, handcuffs, and a small pocketknife.

"Uh . . . what's all that?" I asked.

"Gotta make it believable." She shrugged. "Climb in."

I groaned but obliged.

"Okay, put up your feet."

I propped them on the tail light and imagined what someone might think if they saw this. How would it look that I willingly climbed into a trunk and let someone tie me up?

Willow pushed my feet down. They landed with a *thud*, and I couldn't move them apart. Rope dug into my ankles when I tried.

"Before I forget." She handed me the knife. "Hide this anywhere they won't look."

My mouth dropped.

"Yes, I mean your bra."

She turned around as if something was really interesting across the parking garage. Before she turned back, I reached up my shirt and settled the pocketknife against the side of my underwire where my arm would conceal it.

I held out my hands, and when she turned back toward me, she smiled. She clamped the handcuffs down on my wrists.

"Now for the trick. These are play cuffs." She pointed to the release. "Press this, and off they come. There's one on each side."

"Okay." I waited for her to go on.

"You good?"

"Uh . . ." I nodded.

Then she shut the trunk, and I was trapped in darkness. Complete darkness. The car pulled away, and I tried to look around. A sliver of light shone through from the backseat with each passing street.

My stomach tingled. They were putting me right in the fire.

Maybe it *had* been a good idea to start with a trial run.

I rolled my body toward the back seat, welcoming the small draft that whispered my way through the crack. Even at night, it was hot in here. Sweat ran down my forehead.

The car swung right and then a quick left before the engine cut off. I heard a door slam as the car shook. Willow slapped the trunk.

My heart raced harder with each passing minute as I awaited her return. What was happening in there? Would she come back alone or with our target? Selfishly, I hoped alone, though I knew that would only extend the time it took us to solve this mystery.

More time passed. A few car doors opened and closed, and gravel crunched beneath someone's feet.

Then voices. They came closer and closer, getting louder with each breath.

"I just don't know what to do with her. I can't take one more minute of her constant babble."

There was deep chuckle. "How'd you know to come to me?"

"A friend."

Keys clicked into the trunk, and it popped open, just a little at first. Light blinded me.

"Close it. Let's go."

The trunk slammed shut once again, followed by the sound of two doors. Willow's car vibrated to life.

Though his voice was muffled, I could hear him directing her where to go, but other than that, they remained quiet.

"Right there. The dirt road."

"You're sure this is it?" Willow asked. I could hear the skepticism in her voice.

"Of course. It's not like this is the first time."

His words sent shivers down my spine. How many times *had* he needed this place?

The road got bumpier, jolting me. The car slowed.

"What are you doing?" the man's voice came again. He sounded annoyed.

"Slowing down. It's really bumpy."

"No, keep up the speed. I don't have time to go slow."

Willow pressed the car faster. The washboard road vibrated the car, giving me an instant headache.

The car swerved around a bend in the road, and I slid to one side of the trunk. My head whacked against the metal side.

"Stop there."

The car shuddered to a stop. My bound hands pressed against the back seat. The seat came loose, slightly moving forward.

I bit my lip.

The trunk sprang open, but the darkness still surrounded me. I closed my eyes and pretended to be unconscious.

Willow reached in to find my hands. I stirred. Just as her hand gripped mine, it was yanked away again. The guy pushed her to the side.

"Let me."

His fingernails dug into my sides as he lifted me from the trunk and flung me over his shoulder, leaving my arms dangling near his behind. I wanted to yell out, but I clamped my mouth shut and let my body go limp. I refused to make this easy on him.

He trekked into the forest. It grew darker, if that was even possible, the deeper into the trees we went. The smell of pine tickled my nose.

He began to breathe uneven as he maneuvered around large rocks and downed logs. Then, just like that, he stopped.

Before I knew what he was doing, he bent over and dropped me on the ground. For the split second of free fall, a knot formed in my throat. His eyes twinkled with delight at my fear, like he enjoyed watching.

Without my hands free, my tailbone broke my fall. My spine slammed down, jarring every vertebrae. My only saving grace was a large heap of pine needles—that is, except for the rock underneath them that dug deep in my leg. I yelled out, unable to bite back the pain.

"Ah, she's awake now. Just in time."

He slid his feet back and forth on the ground until he revealed a flat board. He bent and lifted it away, tossing it to the side.

"Get in." He growled.

I shook my head.

Willow sidestepped and stared at me, open-mouthed.

Oops.

He snarled at me. "All of them. So ungrateful."

He grabbed my hair.

"Wait, wait!" I yelled. "I'll go!"

He let go.

"Go then."

Scooting my butt along the ground like an inchworm, I moved toward the hole in the ground. Just as I slipped my legs into the hole, a groan from within startled me. In the dark, I couldn't see the bottom.

I whipped around to look at Willow, who grinned. She'd heard. She put her finger to her lips.

I nodded.

She lunged forward, then right before my eyes, she disappeared. My eyes darted back and forth, unsure what I'd just witnessed.

Where did she go?

Seconds later, she appeared behind him, a huge stick in her hand.

He was oblivious, his eyes trained on me.

"Go!" he yelled at me. His loud voice startled me.

At that, Willow hit him on the side of his head with a branch. A dumbfounded look overtook his face. He swung around.

"You stupid broad." He spat.

She ducked out of the way of a blow headed straight for her face. She landed a kick to his stomach, and he stumbled backward. This only seemed to irritate him further. He stood up, shook his shoulders, and advanced again.

She held the stick like a bat.

"Come on—batter needs a target." Willow taunted him.

She swung as hard as she could as he came at her. My heart raced, worried that she might miss.

At the last minute, he bent, and the stick flew from her hand as he collided with her stomach. They landed in a heap on the ground, Willow at the bottom. The stick skittered just a few feet from me.

Willow struggled underneath him as he aimed blow after blow at her.

She needed me.

Slipping out of the handcuffs and wiggling my feet free of the ropes, I grabbed the stick, shifting its weight in my hand.

Then, I ran forward, giving him no chance to catch me. I swung hard. The stick hit him square in the temple, and he went slack as he tumbled to the ground in a heap.

Willow shoved him off.

"Ugh. Could he have been any more arrogant? Thanks for that."

I nodded.

"Give me those?" Willow asked, pointing to the discarded cuffs.

I tossed them to her, and she fastened them to his wrists.

"Just in case," she said.

"Hello?" I called down into the hole.

Another groan came from inside.

"Do you have a flashlight?" I asked.

She tossed me her phone. I shined the flashlight down into the hole. A man lay bound with rope, mouth gagged.

I handed off the rope to Willow.

"Pull us up?" I asked.

She nodded.

I took a deep breath and jumped.

The pain in my shins burned, blinding me momentarily. I double forward, trying to balance, grabbing my knees.

The man who lay before me looked old enough to be my dad. It seemed a bit odd that it was me coming to his rescue.

I bent, the knife in my hand.

"Hi. I'm Abby. I'm going to cut these. Okay?"

I waited for him to acknowledge me.

He nodded.

Once his hands were free, he pulled the gag from his mouth.

"I never thought . . . anyone . . . would find me," he said in a raspy voice.

I called up to Willow. "Are you ready?"

"Yep."

I knotted the bottom of the rope and held it steady.

"Step on." I told him.

"You first," he said.

"No, go."

"It'll be a lot easier for her to pull me up with your help."

I stared at him. He grabbed hold of the rope. His kind eyes urged me on.

Inch by inch, Willow lifted me from the hole. Within minutes, we'd pulled him up and out and were headed back to the car with the rogue Protector dragging behind us.

I realized I'd never asked what his name was, but at this point, I didn't care.

"Who are you guys? How did you know where to find me?" the man asked.

"Let's just say a little birdie told us," Willow said.

"Well, shouldn't we be calling the police?"

Willow and I glanced at each other.

"Nope," we said in unison.

It was dawn when we pulled up at the elders' headquarters to drop off the rogue Protector and his victim.

Edward was waiting outside with a few other people I'd never seen before. He was beaming. He went straight to helping the hostage out.

"Bruce, it's good to see you."

So, that's his name.

"Do I know you?" he asked.

"Oh, no. I'm just here to look out for people like you. Let's get you inside so Miranda can make sure you're okay. Then we'll get you back home in no time."

"Uh, okay." Bruce stared at all of us. He looked unsure as he walked away.

Miranda led him inside, and Edward turned back to us. "Good work, ladies." His smile was the biggest I'd ever seen it.

Someone else made his way around the car and pulled the bad Protector out.

"Go home. Get some sleep," Edward said.

Willow drove away from the elders' building. Above us, the night sky was beginning to lighten, and the stars faded with each passing minute.

"How are you feeling?" Willow asked.

"Exhausted."

She chuckled. "Yeah. Me too, but I meant about everything. How are you feeling about what we had to do tonight?"

I thought about her question.

"It wasn't what I expected—you know, being the bait and all—but I'm feeling good. No regrets."

She nodded.

She pulled into the parking garage at Casey's and stopped next to the elevator.

I waved as I shut the door behind me.

"Abby," Willow called out the open window. "You did really good tonight."

"Thanks. You too."

Her lips curled. "I hope so."

I hadn't realized how silly it sounded for me to compliment her on her job until it was already out of my mouth.

I rushed to the elevator to escape the awkwardness. Once I was inside, I slipped the key to Casey's apartment from my pocket. I didn't want to wake him. I couldn't wait until I could claim his couch and sleep.

A huge yawn overtook me, making me stumble forward out of the elevator. I gripped the doorknob for balance and shook it off. As I slid the key into the lock, the door flung open.

A worried Casey swept me into his arms. "Are you okay?"

"Besides you suffocating me, I think so. I'm exhausted."

He let go and held me at arm's length, looking me over.

"I'm fine." I yawned.

I kicked the door closed behind me and pushed him backward.

"Mind if I take over your couch for a while?" I slipped my shoes off.

"What happened?"

"We got him. Both of them."

"How did it go?"

I yawned again. "Can we talk about this when I wake up?"

"Oh . . . I'm sorry. No, you take my bed . . . "

I was too tired to argue. I padded to his bed and was asleep in seconds.

Four hours later, I rolled over and hit my arm on Casey's nightstand. *Ow.* My arm tingled.

Light streamed in the windows. I sat up straight. My mom probably had texted wanting to check in. I threw back the covers, trying to figure out where I'd left my phone. Red caught my eye toward the bottom of the bed, and I reached for it. There was nothing there. I blinked a few times to clear my vision. It was wet. Kneeling on the bed, I leaned closer.

Is that blood?

I inspected my legs and found a small gash bruised around the edges. And then I remembered the stabbing pain I'd felt when the idiot dropped me on the ground.

I pulled Casey's bed apart and checked all his sheets and blankets for any trace of blood. Luckily, it had only gotten on the sheets. I carried them with me out of Casey's room and into the hall, where I realized suddenly I still had no idea where his laundry room was.

I looked in his spare room and his hall bathroom and came up empty.

"Abby?" Casey said from the kitchen.

I walked into the kitchen, my arms loaded with his sheets. "Where's your laundry room?"

"Oh, you didn't have to do that."

"Actually, I did." I turned to show him the blood spot.

"What happened?" He took the sheets from me and dropped them to the floor.

I pulled up my pant leg.

"Oh my gosh, Abby, when did you do that?"

"Last night, I guess. I hit it, and it hurt, but I forgot about it."

He grabbed a rag and started cleaning it up for me. "Does it hurt?"

"A little."

"It really could use a stitch, but I have some glue in my first aid kit. I'll glue it for you, but it's going to sting."

I lay waist-up on the counter, waiting for him to come back with the glue. The cold granite made my skin prickle.

"Still tired?" he asked.

"Uh-huh."

He bent down behind me. His fingers found the cut and pulled it closed. I sucked in a breath as the glue seeped into the cut. He blew gently, helping the glue dry faster.

"Oh, shoot. I was looking for my phone. Do you know where it is? My mom's probably tried to get ahold of me."

"She did. I texted her back. She thought it was you. She thinks you're at work."

I sighed. "Good. Speaking of the coffee house, I think maybe it's time to quit."

*   *   *   *

Brad came to the coffee house late the next evening.

"Hey," I said. My brows furrowed.

Brad had never visited me by himself, ever.

"You got a minute?"

I nodded and slipped around the front of the counter.

"What's up?" I asked.

"We're surprising Casey with a trip to Las Vegas for his birthday. I wanted to let you know so you weren't worried. He won't know where we're going until we get there and . . ." He smirked. ". . . we're taking his phone."

Casey's birthday was less than a week away.

"Oh. That's going to be so much fun." I felt a pang of regret that I wasn't old enough to join them. "When are you leaving?"

"Now. The guys are in the car. Wish us luck!" Brad grinned. "Oh." He reached into his jacket and pulled out an envelope. "Edward asked me to give this to you."

"What is it?" I asked, feeling the thickness between my fingers.

"Payment. See ya."

I watched him leave. *I guess I'm spending the weekend training.*

I peeked inside the envelope as I headed into the back room to put it in my bag and stopped dead in my tracks.

Oh my gosh.

The stack of twenty-dollar bills made my mouth go dry.

I shoved it in my bag and decided now was the time. I grabbed a piece of paper off the printer and started writing my resignation.

*   *   *   *

My phone rang, rousing me from a deep sleep. For a moment, I thought I'd dreamed it, but then the ringing continued. I grabbed my phone off the nightstand and glanced at the clock.

Three a.m.

I groaned.

"Hello?" I mumbled into the phone.

"Abby!" someone yelled into my ear. I yanked it away, wincing. I glanced at the screen.

"Casey?"

"Hey! What are you doing?" His happy voice carried through the phone, loud and clear from two inches away.

I sighed.

"I'm sleeping." I sat back against my elbows. "Did you need something?"

"No. Jus-st wa-nted to say hi!" he slurred. I could hear the guys in the background trying to take the phone from him.

"Okay, then. I hope you have a great birthday. Have fun. I'll talk to you later, okay?"

There was a *click* on the other end, and I assumed the guys won. I tossed the phone back to the nightstand, lay back down, and fell fast asleep.

In the darkness, my heart drummed in my chest, pumping loudly in my ears. I was cornered. An echo bounced back at me—the room must be huge—yet I felt as if the walls were closing in on me.

I shook my head, trying to recall what led me here, but everything jumbled together. This was wrong. I was alone and afraid, and I needed to get out. I shouldn't be here.

Then, as if waking up, everything started to clear. This was a dream.

I looked at the walls around me. A window wasn't far away. My feet refused to move. Move, *I urged myself. And then, all at once, one foot after the other, I walked until I stood in front of the window. I kept my hands clear of the break in a single pane and peered out.*

A creak sounded behind me. Light engulfed the other half of the room, revealing nothing but empty space. I swiveled around on my heel to face the light, my back to the window. A figure stood in the doorway gazing in. I shrank back until I slammed against a wall.

My eyes shot open. I stumbled, then froze. Eyeing my surroundings, I knew something wasn't right.

Where am I?

As my vision cleared, I could see my bedroom door was closed, and I wasn't inside. My own name stared back at me from my door. Light streamed through the windows, casting a shadow of the staircase on the wall. I rushed to go back inside my room before my mom—or worse, George—caught me. I was too rattled to try to make something up. I shut my door behind me and locked it. What had happened?

My arm throbbed. Did I run into something? Yawning, I glanced at the clock. Up earlier than I needed to be. *Great.*

After school, I showed up at Lucian's, ready for whatever he wanted to throw at me despite the bags that hung under my eyes.

I was exhausted after Casey's middle-of-the-night call and my unplanned trip to the hallway. I hadn't spoken to Casey since. By my figuring, he probably wasn't feeling so hot today.

I walked right into Lucian's house—something that had more or less become expected. I no longer felt strange doing it. His house felt like a second home.

"What'll it be today? Kickboxing? Swimming? Weight lifting?" I asked as I strolled into the room.

Lucian shook his head. "Time for the next step." He rolled out a large blue page and looked up at me. His proud smile vanished. "You look like hell."

"Good to see you too." I rolled my eyes.

"I'm sorry, but geez."

"Yeah, yeah, I get it. What's all this? Are those blueprints?" I asked.

"Look at you being all smart."

I lightly kicked the back of his knee, making it give out. His body jolted to one side. He gave me his best side-eye.

"These are the blueprints for the warehouse."

My eyebrows raised. "How'd you get your hands on those?"

"Do you even have to ask?"

I ignored him. "What are we going to do with them?"

"Seriously? Are you new here? You're going to memorize them. You have to know this building well. As well as your own house. Maybe even better."

I dropped myself into a chair and looked it over. There was so much to them, including pipes and electrical diagrams, that it was hard to see what was what.

Lucian grabbed two more.

"First floor. Second floor. Roof." He pointed to each roll. "I've got a meeting. Go over those, and I'll be back in an hour or so."

As soon as the door shut, I grabbed the first one, threw a floor pillow down, and spread out in front of the back door. Nobody said I couldn't at least enjoy my study session.

I went over the three large sheets that looked more like a series of mazes. Using my finger, I traced my way through the building over and over.

My eyes felt like they were crossing. I tried to focus on the twists and turns, but when everything began to run together, I quit. I needed a break. Leaning back, I rested my head on the door frame and watched the waves come in.

The next thing I knew, Lucian was shaking me. "Abby! Wake up."

Momentarily, the sun blinded me.

"Eww." I wiped away the drool on my arm.

Lucian grimaced. "Tell me about it."

"Shut up!"

"Learn much that way?"

"Everything started blurring together. I was just trying to take a break, not fall asleep."

He shook his head and put his hand out. "Give 'em."

I rolled them up and handed them over, then slouched back into the door frame to wake up.

"Ready?" he asked. He was already dressed in basketball shorts and a tank top.

Did he expect me to just jump up?

I groaned. "Five more minutes?"

"Not a chance." He grabbed my hand and hoisted me up, slid open the door, and stepped outside.

I followed him out. My tired body dragged more than usual. Lucian slowed his pace over and over until he was jogging beside me, keeping my pace.

"What's up with you today?"

"I'm tired."

"I gathered."

"Well, Casey and the guys went to Las Vegas for his twenty-first birthday, and I'm guessing he had a bit too much to drink. He called me in the middle of the night."

Lucian laughed.

"Well, yeah, it was a little funny except the being woken up part. When I went back to sleep, I had my dream. I moved again, in real life. I woke up in the hallway outside my bedroom door."

He raised his eyebrows. "I see." He paused. "Was there anything new?"

I stopped jogging. "I'm sorry, I didn't really take the time to think about that when I was freaking out about being outside of my bedroom." I ground my teeth together.

"Abby, relax. I was just asking. Besides, people sleepwalk all the time. It's probably one of the most normal things going on with you right now."

Ugh! I dropped into the sand. I hated that he was probably right. Maybe I was making too big of a deal out of it. Lots of people sleepwalk. Totally normal.

"Maybe you're right."

Except it didn't feel normal waking up that way.

He stared down at me. His ever-present grin was gone, replaced by a seriousness I only saw when Edward was around.

He sat beside me, watching the waves, and let the silence drag on.

"Do you think you'll always be a Protector?" I asked.

He gave me a strange look. "That's an odd question."

"Why?"

"What else would I do?"

"I don't know."

He blew out a breath. "Some Protectors like to retire, settle down, have a family, but for me . . ." He paused. "I don't know what I'd do with myself. Helping people is all I know."

I nodded. How *did* one change something they'd always known?

We watched the waves for a long time before I stood up.

"We can keep going."

He shook his head. "We'll take today off. You should go home and sleep."

"Thanks."

As soon as I got home, I flopped onto my bed and fell asleep.

My phone buzzed in my hand, still on silent from school, startling me awake.

I groaned. "Not . . . again . . . "

The phone continued buzzing.

"Hello?"

"Hey," Casey's voice came through the speaker.

"Hey," I said, my voice cracking.

"Did I wake you?"

"Yeah. I was taking a nap." I yawned and glanced at the clock. Seven p.m.

"I thought you'd be just getting home from training," he said. A question hung on his words.

"We called it a day early. I wasn't in it. Didn't get enough sleep."

Casey fell silent. The phone crackled. "That was because of me, wasn't it?"

"Partly."

"I'm sorry. The guys said I called you . . . I don't remember . . . anything." His voice was just above a whisper. He sighed into the phone. "I'm never drinking again."

"It's fine. If it makes you feel any better, it sounded like you were having fun."

"I hope so. I've been in bed all day."

"Sorry." I didn't know what to say. My brain wasn't fully awake. "Are you okay?"

"Yeah, fine."

"Are you sure? You aren't mad at me, are you?"

"No, of course not. I had my dream again last night. I'm just exhausted."

He hesitated. "Should I come home?'

"What? No! Why? There's nothing you can do."

"Are you sure?"

"Yes! Have fun! I hope you have an awesome birthday, and maybe you can try to   remember some of it." I teased. "Oh, and I have some news."

"Oh?"

"I put in my notice at work."

"Wow. That's big."

"I know! I got my pay for the last assignment from Brad when he came to tell me he was taking you, and it just felt right."

"Well, I'm happy for you—maybe only for the selfish reason that I'll get to see you more often."

I giggled. "I'm excited for that, too."

"Good. We'll have to celebrate." He sighed. "I should go. I love you."

"I love you, too."

"Bye."

I ended the call. *I can't wait until he gets back.*

*   *   *   *

The next day, I arrived at Lucian's ready to train.

"Lucian?"

No answer.

The house was silent, but the back door was wide open, the curtains blowing in the breeze. My worries faded. He was probably just outside. *Stupid training making me paranoid.*

I stepped outside, and there was Lucian standing over a grid of rope and string. It looked like some sort of a maze.

"What on earth are you doing?" I asked.

"Making a warehouse."

"What?"

He looked at me. "You fell asleep looking at the blueprints, so we're going to try it a different way. How much of this looks familiar?"

I looked over what he was doing. "Ah . . . no?"

He gave me a dirty look.

"Some," I said, biting my lip.

He cocked his head. "I hope more than *some* looks familiar."

"It's different seeing it like this."

"Then I guess it's a good thing we're doing this. This will be a lot more like what it will feel like in person." He stood up and brushed off his clothes. "I think that's it." He looked over his work and nodded, then knelt once more to tie one more string.

"Start at the door." He pointed to the opening closest to me.

I slipped off my shoes, stepped in, and started to walk around. I felt silly walking through a maze that only rose a foot off the sand.

Lucian pointed to the furthest large room on the left. "That's where I would estimate your dream takes place based on where the window faces."

"Okay."

I took my time getting a feel for each of the doorways. Some stopped short. "Is this a closet?" I asked.

"Yeah. There are three."

He sat down and gave me a few more minutes before he pulled out a handkerchief, resting it on his knee.

"Let me know when you're ready for a test."

I took a few more minutes using my feet to feel my way along, just in case.

"All right."

Lucian stood up and tied the blindfold over my eyes, blocking out any light. He grabbed my shoulders. "Go to the room where your dream takes place."

I took a deep breath and started walking, lifting my foot to feel the barriers. On a turn, my ankle caught the rope, and down I went face-first into the sand. I spit, trying to get the granules out of my mouth. Ripping off the blindfold, I turned to Lucian, who was on his back laughing.

"This is not funny!!"

"You didn't just watch it happen. It was funny. Very funny."

"Well, I don't think I can do this. It's too hard."

"Just stop trying to walk through walls."

The way his lips turned upward made me want to smack him. I glared at him. I threw the blindfold at him and lifted myself from the sand.

"Come here. Try again."

I crossed my arms and made my way over to him. He twirled his finger in the air, telling me to turn around. He tied the blindfold on once more.

I started walking again, more slowly this time.

"Use the rope to guide you. I know it's low, but in the real building you'll be able to use the walls. Figure out the doorways, where the openings are. Find the one room you know you actually go inside."

After a long time, I felt like I'd finally made it to the room we assumed the dream took place.

"Am I there?" I asked.

"You got it."

"Yes! I think I've got it down."

"Let's try this. Go into the first room."

It took me a few minutes to find my way but not nearly as long as it had taken me to find the dream room.

"Okay, this is it right?"

"Yep. Now spin around ten times. Then find your way to the dream room again, and then your way out."

It was a lot harder after being spun. I felt more disoriented than ever. I bobbled a few times, almost losing my balance. I could only imagine what I looked like stumbling around inside a makeshift maze of string.

"This is hard." I pressed my hands to the sides of my head.

"Yeah, but imagine if you got hit in the head while inside. It can make you dizzy and disoriented. You'll be glad you did this if that happens. We have no idea what you'll be walking into, so we have to plan for everything."

After I found my way again, he asked me to run through a few more scenarios, showing me exits and escape strategies until the sun set and we could barely see the neon string.

I felt a lot more confident that I would know the building well when the time came. Butterflies still flitted about in my stomach when I thought about it.

Casey cleared his throat on the porch.

"Casey!" Jumping over the rope barriers, I ran to him and jumped into his arms. "You're back!"

He chuckled. "You didn't miss me or anything, did you?" His rough voice tickled my ear.

"What are you guys working on? This looks . . . interesting."

"It's a mockup of the warehouse," Lucian said. "I think she's just about got it."

"Good." Casey nodded. "Are you still working?"

"Nah, we're finished. You can go. Have fun."

I grinned. "Bye Lucian! Thank you!"

I couldn't wait to spend time with Casey.

"How was your trip?" I asked.

"Exhausting . . . and . . ." His whole body shuddered. ". . . enlightening."

"Oh yeah?"

"You don't have plans already for my birthday, do you?"

"Maybe . . ." I grinned. "Why?"

"Do me a favor?"

"What?"

"Forget about my birthday. I've had enough birthday fun—and drinks—to last a year."

"That bad?"

"Let's just say, I won't be drinking again for a *long* time, and immortals recover from alcohol faster than normal."

I grimaced for him. It made me feel more confident that my plans would be just what he needed.

*   *   *   *

Two days later, I showed up at Casey's apartment after school. I knocked on his door and waited, bouncing from one foot to the other.

"Happy birthday!" I shouted when the door opened.

Casey wore sweats and a t-shirt, and his hair was undone and disheveled. I frowned.

"Are you okay?"

He put his arm around my waist and pulled me in. "I'm fine. Just still recovering from this weekend. Shouldn't you be with Lucian?"

"Nope. I have today off. It's your birthday."

"I thought I told you to forget about my birthday?" He smirked.

"And you thought I'd actually listen?" I shook my head. "*Tsk tsk*. You don't know me very well."

He kissed me. "It's a good thing you're cute."

"Come on—we have to go."

"Go where?"

"You'll see," I said in a sing-song voice.

I drove so it would be a surprise where we were going. When I pulled up in front of the massage place, a small smile formed on his face.

"Massages? That's brilliant. How do you do that?"

"Do what?" I asked.

"Know just the right thing to do."

I looped my arm in his as we walked inside.

Casey was called back first, followed shortly by me. The masseuse led me into a room and left me to undress. The room was darkened, lit only enough to allow me to not bump into things.

When the masseuse returned, she began at my shoulders and worked her way to my feet. My achy muscles relaxed more than they had in months.

An hour seemed to pass in the blink of an eye. I found myself wishing I'd sprung for longer.

Casey was waiting in the lobby when I walked out. He looked relaxed enough to fall asleep where he sat.

He held my hand as we walked to the car, lifting it to his lips. "This is the perfect way to spend my birthday. Thank you."

My cheeks heated. "Maybe I just did it for my own selfish reasons—that massage was very relaxing, you know."

He shook his head, chuckling.

He opened the car door for me but stopped me from getting in. He gave me a quick peck on the lips, then nodded toward the car.

After our massages, we got a small ice cream cake and some take-out and went back to Casey's to eat while we watched a movie. All my treat, of course.

I snuggled against him when we finished eating, fighting to stay awake before I finally gave up.

"I should get home. I can't keep my eyes open watching this anymore. That massage really relaxed me."

"Do you want me to take you?" Casey asked.

"No, I'll be fine."

"All right." He walked me to the door, holding my hand. "This was the perfect way to spend my birthday. Thank you."

He opened the door, and we ambled toward the elevator. "I should walk you down."

"No, no. I'll be fine. Go to bed."

He kissed me goodbye and watched me get into the elevator.

"Happy birthday!" I said just as the elevator doors closed.

I yawned as I made my way through the parking garage. I slapped my cheeks and sat behind the wheel, trying to wake myself.

Throwing the car in reverse, I checked my mirrors. The split-second glance in the rearview made me gasp. Someone was standing behind my car, silhouetted in the darkness. My heart rate spiked.

I initiated my gift, locking the doors. I double-checked them just to be sure it had worked before spinning around in my seat. The figure was gone. I searched around the entire car without finding anything out of place.

Now wide awake, I pressed the gas pedal. I couldn't get out of there fast enough. My eyes watched the rearview far more than normal. As I turned into the street, bright lights filled the mirror. Panic pressed against my chest. The lights were all too familiar.

I turned toward my house, and the bright lights followed closely. I checked my side mirrors. Street lights lit up the side of the SUV. The all-black vehicle sent me spiraling into a flashback. My heart raced.

I reached for my phone. When I should have turned, I kept going. The SUV followed.

Pick up. Pick up.

I felt sick to my stomach.

"Hello?" Casey mumbled into the phone.

"Casey . . ." I check my mirror for the hundredth time. "I think I'm being followed."

His voice tightened. "Where are you?"

I looked around. "I'm almost to my school."

"You've passed your house then?"

"Yeah."

"Good."

"Casey, what should I do?"

"Calm down. It's okay. First tell me why you think you're being followed."

"When I left the parking garage, I swear I saw someone in my rearview mirror. But when I looked again, nobody was there. So I got out of there as fast as I could."

"Why didn't you call me? I should have walked you down." He sounded breathless now, as if he was walking fast. "Are they still following?"

"Yeah."

"What happened next?"

"I don't know. When I looked behind me, they were just there."

"Okay, I need you to turn soon. Where you won't isolate yourself."

"Okay, I'm almost to a light."

I turned, and when the headlights followed, I wanted to cry. "They followed."

"It's okay. Keep going. I'm coming. What streets did you just pass?"

I glanced for what seemed like the thousandth time in my mirror just as the headlights made a sudden turn. They bounced around the corner behind me, and I breathed a sigh of relief.

Thank god.

"Abby?"

"They turned . . . " I said, sheepish to admit I was wrong. I felt so foolish. Fabricating something out of nothing. "Casey . . . I'm sorry. I shouldn't have gotten you out of bed."

"Abby, it's fine. I'll turn back and meet you at your house."

"Okay."

Casey stood leaning on his car when I pulled into the driveway in sweats and a t-shirt.

I felt so silly as I made my way over to him.

He engulfed me in his arms.

"You're quivering," he whispered in my ear.

I buried my face in his chest. "I feel so stupid. I'm sorry."

"Always trust your gut. That's all you did. More times than not, it'll be right. So what if it wasn't this time? I'm just glad you're okay and it was a false alarm." He yawned.

I kissed his cheek. "Go home. Go to bed. I shouldn't have gotten you up. It's your birthday." I pushed away from him.

"Are you kidding? Getting to see you again is a great way to end my birthday."

I narrowed my eyes at him. "I just left."

"Yep, and I missed you already."

I shook my head. "You're crazy."

He pulled me into his arms. "About you." He kissed me hard on the lips and grinned.

"Now, into the house," he said. "I can't leave until you're inside."

*   *   *   *

Today, I decided, I'd show Lucian my gift. For once, I didn't feel like I was failing them. I did this all on my own. It felt good.

He opened the door as I walked up.

This will be fun.

"Hey," I said.

"Hey."

I walked inside behind him and focused on the door. It shut without a finger grazing it.

Lucian didn't notice. I giggled.

"We're going to do things a little differently today," he said.

He headed toward the back door. Just as he reached for the handle, it slid open. My hand rose to my mouth to cover my grin and stifle my laughter. He stepped through and sat down, completely unphased, like a door opening by itself was normal.

I dropped my hand, still grinning as I stepped outside.

"I thought you could tell me what you feel most confident with and what you think you need more work on."

"Okay. Well, I'm not very strong yet. I could probably use more weight training."

I slid a chair out without touching it and sat down.

"I agree."

It was getting harder to look at him with a straight face. "I think my sparring is fairly good. I'm confident I could take someone down."

Lucian smiled but waited for me to continue.

"And running . . . uh . . . I think I'm pretty good there."

"Nice try. Endurance can always get better. Running stays."

I crossed my legs and gripped my knee with both hands.

Let's see if he can get this.

I stared at the pillow sitting next to him. It lifted off the couch and smacked him upside the head.

"What the . . . " He looked down at the pillow lying next to him. A grin crept up on his shocked face. "Did you do that?"

I nodded, my lips curling.

"That's amazing. Do it again."

I focused on the chair next to me at the table and pushed it in. He sat forward, an excited look in his eye.

"You know what this means, right?"

I gave him a puzzled look.

"It means you're going to be pretty unstoppable for a mortal."

I liked the sound of that.

CHAPTER FOURTEEN

The end of the school year was nearing. In the midst of finals, the senior class—myself included—was gearing up for graduation. Despite my crazy schedule, I'd managed to get all of my credits in line to graduate a whole year early like I'd hoped—as long as all my finals went well.

Plans for prom were circulating. As I sat back listening to everyone at our lunch table, I couldn't help but get excited for them. Though I hadn't decided if *I* wanted to go yet—and I'd soon be out of time. Dancing seemed a bit silly as I prepared for what lay ahead. But the Christmas dance had been so fun, so I was on the fence. And my eighteenth birthday was the day after prom.

"Ryan asked me last week," Bailey gushed. "Came out of my house and my entire yard had been filled with heart signs. One of them was enormous and said *'Prom?'* It was amazing."

"That's so sweet!" Alexis said. "I've had a few people ask."

"Of course you have." Breanne rolled her eyes.

"But I haven't answered anyone yet."

"Are you going to?" Bailey asked.

Alexis shrugged.

"Did you do anything special to answer Ryan, Bailey?" I pulled myself from my silence.

"Not yet. But I'm going to tomorrow." She beamed. "I'm going to get a dozen donuts and write *'YES'* across the three in the center and give them to him tomorrow before first hour."

"Oooh, yum." Breanne licked her lips.

I smiled listening to Bailey's excitement. I wanted to be excited about prom, but my reservations kept dragging me down. I couldn't even imagine going.

Maybe that was part of the problem.

*　　　*　　　*　　　*

Sunday rolled around, and—for once—it was a rare day off training. I planned to do nothing. Absolutely nothing.

Casey and Lucian had a meeting with Edward tonight. I never asked what it was about, mostly because I knew it was about me. My training was almost complete, something that both excited and terrified me.

"Hey honey," Mom said, leaning into the room. "No plans tonight?"

"You're looking at them."

She raised her eyebrows.

"What?" I asked.

"Well, you've just been going nonstop. It's strange to see you lying there staring at the ceiling."

"Relaxing," I said.

"I see."

She came in and sat down next to me on the bed.

"Have you decided if you're going to prom yet?" she asked. "You're running out of time to get a dress."

"I know. They stop selling tickets in a few days."

"Does Casey not want to go? Is that why you're torn?"

"No, actually the opposite. He really wants to go."

"Then you should go."

I glared at her.

She held up her arms in surrender. "Or don't. Just let me know when you decide. I'd love to go shopping for a dress with you."

"Okay."

She walked out of my room, leaving me wondering what I should do.

Would I regret not going?

Probably not.

*　　　*　　　*　　　*

Early that evening, the doorbell rang. I looked up from my homework. My heart beat faster, and my nerves flared. Being home alone always made me leery of answering the door. It had blown up in my face on more than one occasion.

I made my way to the door and peeked through the peephole. My hand shook as I rested it on the knob. A man I didn't know stood there holding a package.

It's just a delivery. I opened the door.

He didn't look like the standard delivery man. He was dressed in a suit rather than a uniform and drove a black sedan rather than a large truck.

"Abby Martin?" he asked.

"Yes?"

"I have a package for you."

For me?

He handed me the large gift package and was gone. I shut the door with my foot and tried to see who it could be from, but there was no return address. In fact, there were no addresses anywhere, not even mine. The black satin box looked more like a clothing box. Lifting the lid, I saw an envelope resting on delicate white tissue paper.

I opened the envelope and found Casey's handwriting on the note. My heart fluttered.

It would do me great pleasure if you would accompany me to prom.
Casey

I slid the note under the lid and took a deep breath. Running my finger along the thin paper, I lifted it ever so slowly.

Under the first layer lay a thin silver chain. A single charm glided down it, etched with one word: *'Strength.'* A smile rose on my face. It wasn't fancy or sophisticated. It was me.

I pushed the rest of the paper aside and found a sapphire floor-length dress that sparkled just right in the light. I held it up to myself. It was beautiful. Inside the box, something else caught my eye. Two tickets to prom.

Dropping everything but the gown, I raced upstairs to try it on. When I stood in front of the full-length mirror, I knew what my answer was.

Yes. 100% yes. It's perfect. I'm going to PROM!

My mom's voice broke me from my thoughts. "Abby? Are you home?"

"Up here," I called.

I could hear her climbing the stairs and rushed meet her. Once she stepped onto the landing, her jaw dropped.

"Oh my gosh, Abby, you look stunning!"

"Isn't it gorgeous?"

"Does this mean you're going to prom?"

I nodded.

She reached out and felt the fabric. "Where did you get it? We have to shop there more."

"Casey bought it."

Her eyes found mine, and her eyebrows creased. "What do you mean?"

I went downstairs, Mom trailing behind me. I picked up the note and handed it to her.

A huge smile spread across her lips. "That's so romantic. I'm impressed. You better go see that boy!"

"You're right," I raced upstairs.

I'd spent weeks debating whether or not to go to prom, and in one gesture, he had me all in. Not even just *all in*—he had me hands-down, no contest, excited for prom. I couldn't wait.

It wasn't until I pulled my car into the parking garage that I realized he wasn't home. I knew that. He was meeting with Edward.

Dang it.

Then an idea came to me. He'd gone through a lot to surprise me—I should surprise him, too. I dug through my purse and found the key he'd given me.

"Hello?" I called into the apartment, just to make sure he wasn't there. My own voice echoed back at me.

I shut the door and locked it, hoping he wouldn't be home for a while. I searched his kitchen drawers for anything I could use. In the third drawer, I found a package of markers, a pad of paper, and scissors.

I dropped everything on the coffee table and got to work. I tore out five pieces of paper and cut them all in half. I started small since I had no idea how much time I had. I drew the word *'Yes'* in bubbly handwriting and decorated each page before I took all ten pieces to his bedroom. I spread three on his bed and scattered the rest on the floor. Then I was back at the coffee table making more. By the time I finished, there were *'yes'* papers scattered from the front door, around the living room, and down a trail leading to each of the rooms.

Last, I wrote him a letter.

Casey,

I would love to accompany you to prom. You are amazing. You keep me on my toes, never ceasing to surprise me in all the best ways. Thank you.

I love you.

Love,

Abby

I left the note on his pillow. After I cleaned up the supplies, I took one last look at my handiwork and left the apartment. My stomach lurched with excitement. I couldn't wait until he got home and found it.

I rushed out of his apartment and down to my car, hoping to avoid running into him on the way out. My anticipation of his call grew with each passing moment.

At home, I held my phone, waiting. But his call never came. I fell asleep holding my phone and woke the next morning when I rolled over onto it, the hard case pressed into my cheek.

Rubbing my hand across my face, I checked the clock on my nightstand. *Shoot! I'm late.* I jumped up, got dressed, and hurried out the door.

It wasn't until the bell rang for lunch that I took the time to check my phone for the first time that day. Three missed calls and eight text messages. All from Casey.

My stomach dropped. In my haste to get to school, I'd forgotten all about his amazing gift and my response in his apartment. I held off going into the cafeteria to get food and called him back first without reading any of his texts. It only rang once before his panicked voice answered.

"Hello?"

"Hey!" I said.

"Are you okay?"

"I'm fine . . . why?"

"I've been calling you. You haven't answered . . . my apartment was broken into last night."

"What?"

"You were here last night, weren't you?"

"Ah . . . yeah."

"Everything was fine?"

"Of course. I would have called you right away if it wasn't."

"You didn't see anyone when you left right?"

I thought back to when I'd left. I was so excited that I'd rushed out of there, but I couldn't recall seeing anyone.

"I don't remember anyone."

"What time did you leave?"

I tried to think back to the time I'd gotten home, but I blanked. I couldn't be exact.

"Uh . . . I'm not sure. Maybe around 8:00 or 8:30?"

"I didn't get home until 10:30. It had to have happened in between."

I'd barely missed whoever did it. I felt sick.

"Did they take anything?"

"No. They just trashed the place." There was anger in his voice.

"I wish I could come to you right now . . . "

"No, no. There's nothing here but a mess. You need to be in school."

"I'll come straight there from school."

"Okay. I'll see you later."

"Bye," I said.

It was hard to get through the rest of the day knowing what Casey must be going through.

Over and over in my head, I thought of leaving his apartment. *Did I see anyone?*

I hated that I couldn't picture leaving. It was all a blur.

When the final bell of the day rang, I booked it out of class, almost crashing right into Bailey.

"Oops. Sorry."

"Hey," Bailey said.

"Oh, Bailey. I didn't realize it was you."

"Distracted much?"

"You could say that," I said.

"Are you okay?"

"What? Oh, of course. Just have somewhere to be. Sorry. I'll see you later."

"Bye," she said as I bolted.

I didn't glance back at her as I hurried away, but I imagined she was probably watching me, confused.

The team stood in front of the elevator when the doors opened on Casey's floor.

"Hey," I said. "How is he?"

"Mad." Luke chewed his lip.

"I'm glad you're here," Brad said. "He needs you right now."

I nodded. Ferdinand gave me a quick side hug, and they stepped into the elevator.

Casey's door wasn't closed all the way, and as I got closer, I realized it was because it couldn't be closed. Someone had busted the hinges, and it hung crooked. I pressed it open a little further and squeezed through the gap.

"Casey?" I called.

"In here."

As I stepped in, my jaw dropped. There was glass everywhere. Every dish was thrown on the floor, the cabinets empty. Pictures and anything on the wall hurled to the ground. Even his coffee table was shattered. I hated to think what the rest of the apartment looked like. Casey was near the windows sweeping up glass.

I went straight over to him, picking my way through the debris, and wrapped my arms around him. He dropped the broom and embraced me with everything he had. His body shook. He buried his face in my shoulder. Only then did I realize he was crying. He clung to me until his body relaxed. He took a deep breath and wiped his face on his sleeve before he pulled away.

"Do they know who did it?"

He shook his head. "The surveillance video shows you leaving, and then the video cuts out until I get home."

"And I did lock the door, right?" I asked.

Casey leaned back and gave me a weird look. "Yes. This isn't your fault."

I nodded. I was sure I had, but a speck of doubt had come riding in when I couldn't mentally retrace my steps.

Casey picked up the broom again and began sweeping. I went to the kitchen and started picking up the big pieces of glass.

"You don't have to do that," he said.

I glared at him. "Of course I'm helping."

For a long time, we worked, silent. He didn't need to carry a conversation.

Soon, the living room and kitchen started looking better. Glass no longer littered the floor. Under the pieces of glass, I'd found a few of my *'yes'* notes.

Tears filled my eyes as I thought about what he should have come home to. I wondered if he even saw them. I refused to ask now—it would ruin it all. I hated what these people did.

I sighed and moved on to vacuuming the couch that was dotted with shards of glass. The front door creaked open.

Brad peeked in, carrying a toolbox. "How's it going in here?"

"It's getting better," I said.

Casey grunted.

Brad lifted his eyebrows and smiled at me. "Want to give me a hand, Case'?"

Brad hammered the pins out from the door hinges, and he and Casey lifted the door away from the opening and rested it against the wall. Brad set to work removing the hinges and installing new ones. Then, as if he'd been hiding it, he went around the corner and slid a new door into view.

"How's this, Case'?" He knocked on it a couple times. "Steel."

For the first time that day, I saw Casey crack a smile. However fleeting, it was good to see.

Casey and Brad worked together getting the door on the new hinges. I headed down the hallway with the broom in hand. There was glass all down the hall, so I set to work cleaning it up. The front door shut just as I finished the last pile of glass. I glanced around the corner as Casey and Brad stepped back to inspect their handiwork. I dumped the glass into the trash and joined them.

"I think this will be a lot harder to get open," Brad said.

"I hope so. I'm still not even sure how they managed to bust it open this time."

I picked up the broom, walked into his apartment, and set off down the hall.

"I'm going to start in the bedrooms, okay?" I called behind me.

"*No!*" Both Casey and Brad yelled at the same time.

I spun around, stunned. Both looked alarmed.

"Why?"

"Nothing. It's just . . ." Casey trailed off.

"It's just a really big mess."

I looked around. The whole apartment was a big mess.

"What aren't you telling me?" I asked.

They both looked as if they didn't know what to say. I wasn't going to stand there and watch them fumble around. I turned and marched down the hallway. Their loud feet chasing after me made me break out in a run. I threw open Casey's bedroom door. Almost instantly, I regretted it.

His room was in shambles. All the drawers to his dresser were pulled out and the contents dumped on the floor.

But what brought me to my knees were the words *'Abby's dog'* in bright red letters on the biggest wall.

They'd done this to get back at me. This was all because of me. Again.

"Abby, it's not a big deal." Casey lifted me back to my feet and held me up until I supported myself.

"This is never going to stop following me, is it?" I looked at Brad, but he gazed at the ground. I hadn't expected Eli to still hold sway on my life, but even now that I'd moved on, his goons still wanted to get back at me. I should have guessed there would be backlash. He'd been a celebrity in that circle. There were bound to be a few people still ticked off.

"Of course it will. That's why you're helping Edward. Remember? This is what you're fighting to put an end to."

I nodded, thinking about everything I did with Lucian to get ready to fight these types of rogue Protectors. "Do you have paint?" I asked.

"Uh . . ." Casey turned to Brad.

"Yeah. When I got the door, I got paint, too."

"Where is it?" I asked.

Brad pointed toward the front of the apartment. I walked past them and found the paint and supplies Brad had bought and set to work.

"Can we help?" Brad asked.

"No."

I had to do this. These words wouldn't be here if it weren't for me. Casey and Brad seemed to understand and moved furniture out of the way, laid plastic beneath, and set up a ladder nearby for when I needed it.

Casey clasped his hand over mine. "I can do this. It's not a big deal."

"No."

Casey nodded. "Let us know if you need anything." He kissed my forehead before they left me alone.

An hour and a half—and multiple coats of paint—later, there was no trace that the words were ever there.

I cleaned up the room and put all the furniture back myself, leaving a small gap so it didn't touch the wall, and then I made Casey's bed. The note I'd written was lying under the bed. I set it on his pillow. At least he'd have something nice to look at before he went to bed that night. Perhaps it'd be the first time he even saw it. I didn't know.

I cleaned the rest of the room and left all his clothes nicely folded on the bed. I had no idea which drawers he wanted his things in.
Good enough.

I stood back and looked at his room. It wasn't the same, but it was close.

There was a small knock on the door, and Brad appeared. "How's it . . . wow!"

I wrung my hands, nervous. "You think?"

"This looks better than the rest of the place." He looked over at me, and his face softened. "Are you okay?"

"Yeah." For once, I meant it. There was a problem, but I'd fixed it—part of it—and that felt good.

Brad put his arm around my shoulders. "Casey will be fine if you're worried about him. Worse things have happened to him. To both of you."

I didn't want to think about those things.

"Are you hungry?" he asked.

"Yeah. What time is it, anyway?"

"Eight."

I sighed.

"Casey ordered pizza. Should be here in a couple minutes. You should get cleaned up."

I looked down at the paint splattered on my arms and hands. "Yeah, I will."

He nudged me toward the door and followed me to the kitchen. There was a card table and chairs set up in the living room. The rest of the apartment was looking so much better—the floors clear, any trace of broken things gone.

As soon as I sat down at the table, the doorbell rang. Both Casey and Brad stood, on alert. Casey opened the door, and Brad sat down once the smell of pizza wafted through the room. My mouth watered, and my stomach rumbled.

It was a quiet meal. None of us had much to say. And when I went home that night, I couldn't sleep well. I tossed and turned all night. But when I woke the next morning, there was a text from Casey.

Thanks for all your help yesterday, especially in my room. I love you, and I can't wait to take you to prom.

His message left me grinning from ear to ear. In all the chaos, neither of us had said anything about prom. I was relieved he found my note. I peeked at the dress hanging in my closet, and excited flutters consumed me.

*　　*　　*　　*

The next morning, I got to school extra early, hoping to run into Bailey. In my haste to get to Casey, I'd blown her off. I felt terrible.

I walked the halls without luck. It wasn't until I headed to first hour that I saw her across the hall.

"Bailey!" I called.

She turned toward me, and her face lit up. She made her way over to me through the people that crowded the hall.

"Hey, Abby," she said.

"I wanted to apologize for running off yesterday. I was in a hurry to get to Casey. His apartment was broken into."

"That's terrible!"

"I know. He seemed upset on the phone. . . so I was just worried about him."

"Don't worry about it. I figured you just had somewhere to be. I wasn't offended or anything. It takes a lot to offend me." She smiled and linked her arm with mine. "Should we get to class?"

I nodded. "Probably."

"So, did they take anything?" she asked.

"No. That's the weird part. They just massively trashed the place. Broken glass everywhere."

Bailey made a face. "Poor Casey."

"I know."

I didn't tell her about his bedroom. I didn't tell her it was my fault.

"I'd be so scared to go to his apartment. What if they come back?"

I looked over my shoulder. His apartment wasn't the only place they might be. A shiver ran down my spine.

CHAPTER FIFTEEN

Only two weeks had passed since Casey's apartment had been ransacked, but it seemed to be the furthest thing from his mind. Especially today.

Prom was in two hours, and I thought he might just be more excited for it than I was. I sat in front of the mirror as my mom put the finishing touches on my hair. She placed two more bobby pins, spritzed it with hairspray, and stood back to inspect me.

"You look beautiful."

"Thanks, Mom."

"Go get your dress on! He's going to be here soon!"

Once I was fully dressed, Mom took me outside to snap a few pictures. I posed in front of the house, smiling for photo after photo. Until a black limousine pulled up in front of the house and Casey stepped out. My jaw dropped.

"What?" he asked.

"You didn't have to do that!" I said.

"It wouldn't be prom if I didn't!"

"Smile," Mom said as George stood back, watching with a grin. She took a picture of us standing in front of the limo.

"You guys look great," George said.

I gave him a half smile. Things had been hot and cold between us ever since his confession. Tonight didn't change that.

Mom and George watched us get into the limo and drive away. She was beaming, and, in a way, I think she was living a little through me.

"Where are we going?"

"Not telling." He closed his mouth tight, pressing his lips into a thin line. He wasn't going to budge.

When the limo pulled into the drive-thru at a fast food place, I about died laughing.

"Really?"

"Yes, what better way could we use a limo?" He laughed.

We hit three more drive-thrus' before we headed to prom. My stomach hurt in only the best way, both from laughing and from eating far too much junk food and ice cream.

The limo pulled up in front of prom, and the driver came to hold the door for us. I looped my arm in Casey's, and we walked inside. Lights flashed and music blared. The crowd already pulsed with the beat. I flashed back to dancing with Drake at the club and cringed. I didn't have time to try to forget it when Bailey bounded up to us.

"Oh, Abby, I'm so glad you came!! That dress . . . oh my god! Where did you get it?" she squealed.

"I didn't. He did." I hooked my thumb at Casey.

"Ooh. You're going to have to tell me your secrets . . . later! Right now, we have to dance!" She threaded her arm through Ryan's, pulling him and us onto the dance floor. I couldn't resist Bailey's cheerful disposition. She made things ten times more fun.

When a slow song came on, I snuggled up to Casey.

"Thanks for nudging me to come tonight. I'm having so much fun, and I'd have missed it all if it weren't for you."

"I'm glad. The truth is, I wanted you to go for my own selfish reasons."

"Oh? Why?"

"I never went to my prom."

"Really?" I asked.

He nodded.

"I'd just found out I was a Protector . . . " His voice faded away.

"Oh." This was the first time he'd ever talked about finding out. I'd never thought to ask before now. I wanted to ask a hundred questions, but I stopped myself. There was a reason he hadn't told me much of it yet. I ran my hand along the fold of his tux jacket.

He sighed. "I didn't handle it well. I'm not proud to say that I took off. I hated the idea. It was going to change everything." His head drooped. "About a month later, Cade found me. He taught me that being a Protector was a gift rather than a burden."

I smiled and rested my head on his chest.

"Anyway, I missed prom when I was away, so this gave me the chance to go that I cost myself."

"I'm glad. This has been an amazing night. You've made it perfect."

He squeezed me tighter. We spent the rest of the night dancing, and when it was time to leave, the limo was waiting at the curb.

"Ready?" Casey asked.

"Yep."

He helped me into the limo and climbed in behind me. I snuggled up to him on the huge back seat.

"So, did you have a good night?" he asked.

As the limo pulled out of the parking lot, it drove in the opposite direction of my house.

"Yeah . . . the best . . . "

I watched the scenery, waiting to turn back at some point, but we kept getting further and further from my house.

"Uh . . . where are we going?" I asked

Casey shrugged, but a smirk bloomed on his face.

"What do you have up your sleeve, Mister?"

He lifted his arm and looked up his jacket sleeve, then mimed as if he was dumping it out. I shook my head.

"I get it. You're not telling."

He grinned. "You're catching on."

After a while, the limo pulled into a parking lot at an enormous resort. I turned to Casey, my eyebrows quirking. "What are we doing here?"

He grinned and pointed to the door the driver was opening for us.

Casey guided me inside and to the counter.

"Checking in for Casey Jeffries."

"For two rooms, sir?"

"That's correct."

He paid, and the receptionist handed him two keys. She signaled a bellhop, who came over with a cart already loaded with bags.

"Hey, that's my bag," I said, looking at Casey in surprise. "How did you do this?"

"Planning. And, of course, a little help from your mom." He used the key and opened the first room. "Oh, and . . ."

"Happy birthday Abby!" Bailey yelled.

"Bailey," Casey said with a grin.

Bailey threw her arms around my neck as Casey set my bag in the room.

"This place is AH-mazing. I could just live here," she said.

"It sure looks like it." I turned back to Casey. I was in awe at his ability to pull off such extravagant gestures.

"I'll let you get settled and changed. We're meeting at the pool"—he checked his watch—"in ten minutes."

I jogged over to him, my dress hugging my legs.

"Thank you," I whispered in his ear. "You are more than I could have ever asked for." I lifted myself on tiptoe and gave him a tight squeeze.

"You deserve it," he whispered back. "I'll be in the room next door if you need anything."

I stepped back and watched him shut the door, and then whipped around to face Bailey. "How long has he had this planned?"

"Well, a few weeks. At least that's when he told me about it."

"Oh my gosh, I can't believe he did all this."

"You only turn eighteen once." Bailey shrugged.

I grinned. "It's true." I grabbed my phone and texted my mom. *Thanks Mom! Best birthday EVER!*

Bailey and I took out the bobby pins holding our hair in place. I threw mine up in a messy bun and pulled on my swimsuit.

"Ready?" Bailey asked.

"One sec!" I threw a t-shirt over my suit for the walk down. "Now I am."

Down at the pool, we walked through the gate, and the whole team was already there.

"Guys!" I yelled.

Ferdinand, Luke, and Brad ran over and picked me up.

"Happy birthday to you"—they bounced me up and down—"happy birthday to you, happy birthday dear Abby, happy birthday to you!"

Then without warning, I was airborne. They threw me into the pool and dove in after me. Casey and Bailey laughed and jumped in behind us.

I spotted a basketball across the pool and swam to it.

"Who's up for a game?" I held the ball up in the air.

I didn't even see him coming. Ferdinand snatched the ball from my hands and slam dunked it.

"Me," he said.

"Ooh, me too!" Bailey called.

We teamed up three against three, but halfway into the game only the guys had scored.

"This is so hard!" I said. "I'm too short. I can't even make a basket *without* anyone guarding the hoop! I give up."

"Me too." Bailey pointed toward the hot tub. "I want to go over there."

I grinned. "I'm with you on that one." I turned to Casey. "You coming?"

"I will in a bit. I'm going to finish out the game."

I nodded and followed Bailey to the hot tub. We slowly entered the steaming water, letting our bodies acclimate to the heat. Goosebumps prickled my skin. I sucked in a breath as I eased my body in deeper. We watched the guys play, and one thing was certain—it was a lot more fun watching than playing.

"I wish Ryan could have come," Bailey said.

"He wasn't able to?"

She shook her head. "He isn't eighteen yet. His parents didn't think it was a good idea."

"Oh."

"But . . . I think it's a little better having lots of eye candy."

My mouth dropped. "Bailey!"

"What? You know you've looked."

I didn't answer, but I couldn't wipe the guilty grin off my face.

"See!" She pointed at me.

"All right. Fine." I grinned.

Ferdinand and Brad won the game, no doubt due to Ferdinand's height.

The boys began to meander their way toward the hot tub, except for Brad, who walked away to make a phone call—most likely to his girlfriend.

Casey's hand on my shoulder tore my eyes away from Brad.

"You okay?" he asked.

"Oh yeah, fine. I just zoned out for a second."

"Tired?" he asked.

"Yeah."

He glanced at his watch and smiled. "Well, it's midnight. You're officially eighteen. I can walk you back to your room so you can go to bed if you want, or . . . "

He glanced up. I followed his eyes to Brad, who now held a tray of cupcakes. My mouth watered. Before I could answer, they all started singing "Happy Birthday" all over again. All eyes were on me, and I blushed.

As I stood up from blowing out the candles, Luke rushed forward, pushing the tray up into my face. Frosting covered half my face. I grabbed the closest cupcake and ran after him, forgetting all about the slippery concrete. My foot lost traction, and down I went, both legs in the air. My hip slammed into the pool deck. At first, I lay there as the pain set in. The stars sparkled in the sky above me. I seethed through my teeth, breathing through the pain.

Footsteps sounded all around me as everyone ran over to see if I was okay. My eyes locked on Luke. I grabbed his hand and shoved the cupcake—which I'd somehow managed to save in my ungraceful fall—into his face in one last-ditch effort to get him back.

"Ow," I whined. "You made me fall."

He helped me up and wiped his face. "We're even," he said.

I shook my head. "No way."

There were no cuts, but it was tender to the touch. The bruise I was sure to have would be a doozy.

"And that's my cue to go to bed. I'm beat," Bailey said.

Ferdinand jumped up. "Let me walk you."

She smiled. "Such a gentleman. Happy birthday, Abby."

"Thanks. I'll see you in the morning."

Casey and I went for a walk after Bailey went back to the room. It was quiet around the resort, like we were the only ones there. Casey found a small round chaise overlooking a fountain on the pond. I snuggled against him.

"How's your leg?"

"It hurts." I frowned. "I need some of Cade's magic cream."

A rumbled sounded in his chest as he chuckled.

"Thank you for today," I said. "It was one of the best days I've had in a long time."

"Then my task is complete."

I felt myself drifting to sleep as we lay there looking out at the water. The falling water relaxed me, like a distant lullaby.

"Hey, am I that boring?" Casey teased, poking me in the side.

"I'm sorry," I mumbled. "I'm so exhausted."

"Let's get you to your room."

"Yes, please."

Casey swooped me up in his arms and carried me to my room despite my protests. He pressed his lips to my cheek as he set me down.

"Happy birthday, Abby. You're the best thing that's happened to me, and I can't wait to do more things like this for you."

I slipped into the room, changed, and collapsed into the empty bed opposite Bailey's. The darkness in the room made it easy to fall right to sleep.

Distant, repetitive knocking woke me from a deep sleep. It took me a moment to remember where I was. My eyes squinted against the light that peeked through the curtains. Bailey still slept in the next bed.

The knocking sounded again. I groaned, rolled out of bed, and threw open the door without checking who it was. In hindsight, I realized that was dumb, but the smell of food made me forget all about my momentary lapse in judgment.

A waiter with a cart stood outside. His head was down, making it impossible to see his face around the bill of his hat. The two silver domes captivated me. Food. My stomach groaned.

"Breakfast," he said. His voice sounded strange, but I brushed it off.

I rubbed my eyes.

"Oh, come in, come in," I said, yawing. I stepped back to usher him inside.

He walked in and pushed the cart to the center of the room. He lifted the silver lids, exposing giant plates of blueberry pancakes.

Then he turned to leave the room, and I followed behind him, walking him to the door.

Out of nowhere, he spun around and caught me by the nose with his outstretched elbow. I fell back into the wall, blinded with pain. He advanced closer, backing me solidly against the wall. *Don't wait for him to make the first move.*

I swung my arm forward, the palm of my hand barely missing his nose as he dodged to the side. He reached forward to grab my arm as I brought my leg up and kicked him in the side of the knee. I felt a crunch under my foot, and he went down. I gave him one last swift kick where it counted and dodged around him, out the door. My fists pounded on Casey's door so hard I was sure I would wake the whole floor.

Ferdinand ripped open the door. His hair was disheveled in a way I'd never seen before, and his groggy face looked alarmed. Casey collided with him while trying to pull on some jeans.

"A man," I panted, pointing toward my room.

They flew past me into my room. I stood, rooted in their doorway, catching my breath.

"Brad?" Their voices carried into the hall.

My mouth dropped.

Brad stood hunched over between Ferdinand and Casey. His arm was curled around Casey's neck while his other hand pressed against his groin.

The hat that once obscured his face lay discarded on the floor.

"What the hell is going on?" Ferdinand asked.

"Test," Brad groaned.

I slapped Brad across the face, brushed past him, and sat down to eat. My toe collided with the edge of Bailey's bed.

"What's going on? "Bailey asked. She sounded half asleep as she sat up.

I wondered how she could have slept through all the noise, and then she pulled ear plugs from her ears. I rolled my eyes.

"The boys brought us breakfast. They're leaving to get dressed."

I didn't glance in their direction again, and I heard the door close moments later.

Steam could be surging from my ears I was so mad. When was Edward going to stop? I understood his desire to test me, I did. But on my birthday? And after I'd already done a mission? I'd thought we were past this.

The silverware clinked against the plate when I used more force than needed to pick up the soft pancake. I took a deep breath.

This will not ruin my day. This will not ruin my day.

"Abby? Is that blood?"

"Wha-?"

I lifted my hand to feel below my still-stinging nose. Blood covered my first two fingers.

"Ugh! Must be a bloody nose." I jumped up to wipe it.

The jerk gave me a bloody nose.

I glanced in the mirror—aside from the blood, you wouldn't even be able to tell there was a problem.

Bailey went to work after breakfast, but not before she handed me a wrapped box holding a cute new outfit.

"I thought you might need something new to wear for your birthday."

I looked in the mirror and decided that this was the perfect outfit. She knew me well.

The rest of my birthday was spent with Casey, Mom, and George. Between meals out and presents, I felt spoiled beyond anything I'd ever imagined.

At the end of the day, Casey took me outside where he handed me a small box.

"Casey." I stared at him. "You've already done so much. You didn't have to get me anything."

He pursed his lips, cocked his head to the side, and pushed the box into my hand.

When I lifted the lid, a silver bracelet with a swirled design etched in it shifted inside the box. A charm with the same wording as the necklace: *'Strength.'*

"It matches . . ." I paused, holding the necklace in my hand. "Casey, it's beautiful."

He lifted it from the box and placed it around my wrist.

"Even in the thick of things, you can see them and be reminded you that you can do this. I wanted to give you strength."

I grabbed him by his collar, pulled him in, and kissed him, hard. Then I winced when my nose pressed against his cheek.

"Ow."

Casey dropped his hands from my waist, looking alarmed.

"My nose," I groaned. "Brad . . ."

"I'm sorry," he said.

I waved my hand in his direction. The only thing that lifted the momentary rush of pain was pressure from my hand.

"Brad told me he was the last one," Casey said.

"Really?" I asked, peeking around my hand. "Did he say why Edward even needed to test me again after I'd already proven myself?"

He nodded, his mouth set in a line. "Edward wanted to be sure you still had your guard up."

I shook my head.

"You did fine. Don't worry about it."

Quiet lingered for a long time between us, the night sounds fell all around, and the sky darkened to black.

As my birthday came to an end, I felt optimistic about what the future would hold.

CHAPTER SIXTEEN

Hours and hours went into my training. Even after my success with the small tests and my first 'assignment', I began to wonder if I could pull this off in the long run.

Casey, on the other hand, was very encouraging. He told me often how impressed he was with my skill. Something I didn't take lightly—it was a big compliment coming from a Protector.

I walked into Casey's apartment, my anxiety through the roof. *This is it.*

This was the big one. I breathed in deep, calming myself.

Lucian, Casey, and Edward—the three guys who'd kept me busy for months now—sat in a huddle in the living room. Their heads lifted as I came into the room, and silence fell between them.

"Hi." I hesitated, feeling nervous.

Casey waved me over to sit next to him.

"Hello Abby," Edward said.

Lucian winked.

Edward waited until I settled in. Casey weaved his fingers in mine. Then, without wasting time on chit-chat, Edward jumped right in.

"This is the beginning. You'll need to be prepared for anything. On alert at all times."

I nodded.

"I'll be assigning a Protector to you as soon as I leave here. He will somehow insert himself into your life tomorrow, and shortly after, he will introduce himself. Be prepared. Don't let your guard down."

Butterflies flapped in my stomach. My Protector. He would be assigned to protect me just as Eli had been assigned to me. This time, I knew what was going on behind the scenes, but he didn't know that. To him, I was just another case. One more person to protect. This would, once again, put my acting—or rather, lying—skills to the test.

"I put in your file that you enjoying hanging out at the coffee house. You'll need to go there at least once a day and hang out for a couple hours. Bring a book, drink some coffee, this part should be easy. This will give him ample opportunities to see you."

"Okay."

Edward looked at Casey. "You will have to stay away from Abby starting as soon as she leaves today."

Casey nodded without showing emotion.

This shouldn't have surprised me, but I wasn't prepared for it.

I would have to cut all contact with Casey and the team until my mission was over. It made perfect sense. I bit my lip, trying to mask my sadness, a trick Lucian had taught me. For once, I felt like I'd succeeded at shielding my emotions, but on the inside, I thought I was going to lose it. I breathed in and out.

"How long do you want me to be under?" I asked.

Edward leaned back in his seat. I could see the wheels turning in his head. He seemed to be trying to decide what to tell me.

"The truth would be great," I said.

Both Lucian and Casey's heads whipped in my direction, their eyes bugging out.

I crossed my arms, waiting.

Bit by bit, a grin formed on Edward's face. "A few weeks at the least."

My jaw set. *A few weeks.* I wanted to scream. "I'll be right back," I said, excusing myself.

I rushed to the bathroom, the heat from my face spreading down my neck. I threw the door closed behind me. Glancing in the mirror, I was embarrassed to see the redness in my face. My eyes pooled with tears.

None of my training had prepared me for being completely cut off from my support. How could I do this without them?

A soft knock sounded on the door. "Abby?" Casey called.

I wiped away the tears and pinched my cheeks, trying to will away any appearance of distress. When that didn't work, I splashed water on my face.

He knocked again. "Can I come in?"

I unlocked the door with water still dripping off my face.

He took one look at me and bent down to get a towel from under the cabinet. He held out the small towel to me, but when I didn't take it, he gently patted my face and chin dry.

"What's wrong?" he asked.

"I'm an idiot."

"I disagree. Why do you say that?"

"I didn't even think about having to stop talking to you. It never even crossed my mind. But it should have. It's obvious."

Casey grinned. "I'm going to miss you, too."

"This isn't funny. Why are you smiling?" I demanded.

"You're upset because you'll miss me."

I pushed him away and snatched the towel from his hand. I finished blotting away the water.

"I love you," he said.

I froze. "What?"

He gripped my hands and turned me toward him. His green eyes stared into mine, and the world stopped. "Abby, you challenge me. You excite me. You make me happier than I've ever been. I love you so much more than I ever thought possible."

I felt the passion behind his words with every fiber in my body. It took my breath away. "I love you, too."

*　　*　　*　　*

I pulled up in front of the coffee house, just as I used to almost every day before I quit. I felt as if I were embarking on a new journey. Today marked the start of my first real mission. One that would last more time than I'd realized.

I unbuckled my seatbelt and made my way inside. Someone new stood at the counter.

"Hi! What can I get you?" he asked.

"Uh, a black-and-white mocha, please. Iced."

"Name?"

"Abby."

He rang me up and went over to the espresso bar to make it.

I felt like a stranger in a place I'd worked for months. It was a strange feeling.

When he handed me my drink, I headed outside, thankful that the evening temperature had cooled to a mere 100 degrees—much better than the midday heat of 115. Still, I wasn't sure how long I'd be able to sit in the heat even with my ice-cold drink before I'd have to retreat inside or leave.

For a little while, I sat, just relaxing and enjoying the fact that I had nothing pressing to do but sit and wait for my Protector to present himself—or herself. There weren't many people at the coffee house today. Once in a while, someone would walk by or go inside. For the most part, I watched the cars drive by.

I picked up my book and lost myself in its pages.

"Excuse me?"

I turned, my mouth open, and looked up into his brown eyes. "Uh . . . what's up?"

"What's that you're drinking?"

I picked up my cup without thinking about it. My fingers came off a bit sticky from a small amount of misplaced chocolate drizzled down the side. "Oh, it's a black-and-white mocha."

"Thanks. I never know what to order at these places, and that looks good." He turned to walk away but stopped. "I'm Jay, by the way." He waited, holding the door handle.

"Abby." I smiled.

He gave a single nod and went inside. I watched him walk to the counter. Then I went back to reading.

Before long, I finished the last of my coffee. I stood up and stretched. Gathering my things, I picked up my cup. My hand found the sticky spot again. *Ugh.* I headed back inside to toss it out and to get a napkin to clean off my hands.

He came up behind me. I sidled back against the front counter. *A little too close there, buddy.*

"Sorry, I'm not trying to follow you." He reached for a napkin. "I spilled."

I smiled and felt silly for being on edge. He walked back to a table inside without another word.

Darn Edward for making me more paranoid. *'Never let your guard down.'* I rolled my eyes.

Jay nodded to me as I walked out the door. I dropped my head and went straight to my car. Behind the wheel, a thought struck me: Jay was my Protector. It had to be him.

I watched the door, waiting to see if he would leave too, now that I had. Sure enough, moments later Jay emerged, glanced around, and left in a silver car at the far end of the shopping complex.

The first thing I wanted to do was call Casey, but I stopped myself. *No contact.* We couldn't chance it. Edward wasn't wrong, but it sucked not being able to talk to Casey. He was my rock.

At home, it felt strange to have free time. Without training, work, and Casey, I had loads of it. I didn't know what to do with myself.

Flipping through the channels got old, so I went into the kitchen. I found my mom finishing the dishes. I stood there, flooded with memories. My new life often took me away from her—not that she wasn't busy with George, but I felt responsible.

"Hey," I said.

"Oh, hi honey."

I sat at the counter and watched her.

"No Casey tonight?" she asked while she dried her hands.

I shook my head. "He's busy. Want to go out? Just you and me?"

"Sure! Let me go change."

We got to a fancy Italian restaurant less than an hour later. It was packed, but they were able to get us in right away. We were lost in conversation when someone caught my eye. I stared like a child seeing something for the first time. No matter how much I stared, it didn't change who I saw sitting there. Three tables over sat Jay.

I knew this was part of the drill. Protectors had to keep a close eye on their assignment to assure their protection well before they immersed themselves into their new role. Usually the assignment didn't notice since they were still perfect strangers. Once again, one more reason I was ahead of most. I knew I was being followed.

It unsettled me. This Protector could be a criminal, and here he was following me around, getting to know my schedule, and learning all there was to know about me while my mom sat across from me. What was this guy capable of?

"So, honey, what do you want to do for graduation? Do you want to have a party?"

Her question struck a chord. "No, let's just do something on our own. Go to dinner or something." I would never be able to explain why Casey wasn't at my graduation party. Under any other circumstances, nothing would have kept him away.

She beamed at me. "Okay. We can do that. Are you sure?"

"Of course."

"I'm so proud of you. I can't believe you're graduating a year early!"

I smiled and looked around. I never knew how to respond to compliments, even coming from my mom.

"It's not that big of a deal."

"Oh honey, it really is. You should be proud of yourself."

"It's not like I'm going straight to college. Don't forget, I'm taking the year off. Hopefully to travel some."

"I know, I know. Which is why I got you this." Mom pulled out an envelope with my name on it and pushed it toward me.

I eyed her. Sliding my finger through the flap, I tore it open. Inside was a one-way plane voucher.

"What?" I said in shock.

"I'm so proud of you for working so hard and graduating early. You said you wanted to travel, so I'm giving you at least the means of getting where you want to go."

"Oh my gosh, Mom! Thank you!"

"You're welcome, honey. I can't wait to see where life takes you." She reached across the table, a tear in her eye.

"Mom, you're going to make me cry."

"I'm sorry." She sniffled. "No crying. I'll stop."

"I'm going to run to the bathroom."

She nodded, wiping her eyes.

I couldn't believe it—a plane ticket for anywhere I wanted to go. Best graduation gift ever.

Before I left the restroom, I washed my hands and fixed my hair. I pushed through the door and paused just for a second when someone ran into me.

"I'm so sorry! I wasn't looking where I was . . ."

I looked up into a familiar face.

"Hey, it's you," Jay said.

"Oh, hi," I said. I smiled.

"It's good to see you. I'll let you get back to . . . whoever you're with." He chuckled as he stumbled over the words.

Mom had already paid the check by the time I returned. "Ready?" she asked.

"Yep."

"I have an idea."

"What?" I asked.

"Let's go shopping." She was so giddy I couldn't help but giggle at her enthusiasm "You're going to need a new outfit for graduation! Three days!"

*   *   *   *

It's funny, I always pictured my graduation intermingling with plans for college—dorm rooms and class schedules and choosing a major. Now that it was here, it seemed ironic that college had hardly crossed my mind.

As I slipped into my robe and thought of all the other graduates with these plans, I felt jealous, just for a moment. Their life was figured out—organized. Mine was being juggled like a game of chance.

My hand shook as I zipped the front and looked in the mirror. I couldn't believe I was in my cap and gown. I felt jittery as I imagined the moment I'd walk across the stage and accept my diploma. This was really happening. Finally. I was graduating.

"Abby? Are you ready? We're going to be late!" Mom called up the stairs.

"Coming!"

I stepped outside and headed to the car where my mom was waiting with her camera.

"You look beautiful," she said.

"Thanks, Mom."

"Okay, go stand over there." She pointed toward the tree.

In front of the house, we took a few pictures, complete with one of Mom, Dad, and me taken by George, before we headed to the football field at the school. A new wave of nerves hit my stomach when I saw the field all set up with hundreds of chairs, lights blazing down on them.

"Should I save a seat for Casey?" Mom asked.

"Oh . . . no, he had to go out of town. His grandma's sick," I said.

"Oh really? That's too bad."

"Yeah, I'm not even sure when he'll be back. It sounds like she might not make it."

They dropped me off at the entrance for the graduates and left to find a parking spot.

"Good luck, honey," Dad called out the window.

I grinned to myself.

I found my place between the two seniors whose names came before and after mine and sat down on the edge of my seat. My stomach flipped and flopped with anticipation.

The chairs filled in around me, and before long, the ceremony began under the bright lights of the football field. Speaker after speaker stood at the podium and gave their speeches before they finally started calling names to receive diplomas.

When the moment came for my name to be called, a wave of nausea overcame me. As soon as I stood, it dissipated into silence. Everything blurred together, and the lights blinded me as I marched across the stage. I looked into the stands as I flipped my tassel to the other side. I couldn't make out anyone, but I knew my crowd was up there, somewhere. Casey, too. Even though we hadn't spoken, he'd told me he would be there, no matter what. I smiled up at them, wherever they were, and descended the stairs, taking extra care not to miss a step and fall on my face.

It was over. I sighed. High school done.

CHAPTER SEVENTEEN

Three more days passed before I saw Jay again. I was beginning to wonder if the plan had changed and nobody contacted me. It was hard not to be frustrated things weren't moving along faster. Of course, the only reason I could contact anyone was if I completed my mission or needed help. Though Edward had assured me someone would be watching, and, for once, I didn't doubt him.

Late in the afternoon, the door chimed at the coffee house. Peeking around my book, I watched Jay walk in. My old co-worker took his order. I continued watching out of the corner of my eye while I pretended to continue reading. I spotted his eyes wandering in my directions.

I decided I'd have a little fun knowing he'd be trying to insert himself in my life—and the only way that could happen was if he talked to me. I collected my things when his back was turned and headed to the restroom.

I chuckled to myself as I checked my hair in the mirror, imagining him sitting down with his drink wondering where I'd gone. Knowing a little about what the future held made it easier to be more carefree—at least in this moment.

As I left the restroom, I spotted Jay sipping his drink at a corner table opposite the one I'd been sitting at. I made my way around the perimeter and sat at the table furthest from him, grinning to myself. I opened my book and got back to reading.

Only a few minutes had passed when he stepped over and cleared his throat.

"We meet again."

"Oh, I guess so."

"Abby, right?" he asked.

"That's right."

His bright smile lit up his face. He held up his drink. "You got me hooked."

"I'm glad you liked it."

He turned, looking over his shoulder, and then back at me.

"This might be a bit forward, but do you have plans right now?" he asked.

This was it.

"Um . . . you're right. That is really forward."

"May I?" he asked, pointing to the chair across from me.

I stared into his eyes, pausing briefly to make him squirm, then I nodded.

"I like to think that fate has a hand in these things. Running into you two times here and once at the restaurant." He grinned. "I don't believe that's a coincidence. And then there's this." He pointed at his drink. "We have something in common."

"It appears we do. But I don't even know how old you are."

"I'm nineteen. Does that settle it?"

I pressed my finger to my chin, considering. I was enjoying this.

"I don't know." I grinned. "Like what?"

"Dinner, maybe?"

"Uh . . . sure."

"Great. Should we go now?"

"After I finish this chapter."

Dimples bloomed on his face as he tried not to smile. He crossed his arms and sat back in his seat. Waiting.

I lifted my book from the table, holding it in front of my face to block my smug grin. I couldn't concentrate on the book. I flipped the pages after I skimmed the words until I came to the next chapter. I closed it and set it on the table. "Done."

He hopped up and was at the door so quickly I wondered if he was worried I'd change my mind.

A little too eager there, buddy.

He made his way to the same silver car I'd seen him drive away in a week ago. For once, a Protector didn't open my door for me. Jay stayed on his side of the car while I got in. It was a put-off at first, but I recalled a time not so long ago, before Protectors, where nobody opened doors for me and that was normal. I pushed my annoyance away.

I slid into the seat and shoved my apron into my purse. Being in a stranger's car wasn't something I was used to, and it felt awkward. I didn't know what to say or how to sit. I crossed and uncrossed my legs before finally finding a comfortable position.

"Hungry?" he asked.

I shrugged. He kept driving.

"Do you live around here?"

"Yeah, about five minutes away," I said, pointing in the direction of my house.

He nodded.

As the car fell silent, I bit my lip and watched where we were going. When he pulled into an ice rink, my jaw dropped.

"Ice skating?"

"Uh-huh."

"I thought we were getting dinner?"

"You didn't seem hungry. I thought we could skate until you were. We could get dinner instead?"

"Oh no, this is great. I love ice skating, but I bet I'm going to fall on my butt."

"You're on! I bet you'll stay on your feet and show me up!"

I grinned. "Loser buys ice cream."

Jay held out his hand. I shook it, and we headed inside.

He'd even thought to bring a jacket for me. Not something I carried with me when it was so hot out.

We hit the ice, and in the first five minutes, we both tumbled to the ice . . . more than once, in my case. I even pulled him down with me.

"I've got to get the hang of this!" I said, laughing off my fall. "I'm not sure how much more my butt can take!"

"I only fell twice, and I don't think my butt could take it again," he said, holding his rear.

I knew better—he probably wouldn't even remember he'd fallen by the time he got home tonight. I, on the other hand, would probably be sore for a week.

By the end of the night, we were graceful and gliding around the rink without much effort. We even dared to goof around, mimicking things we saw other skaters do. Jay went big for his next trick and failed miserably. His feet tumbled over each other, making him look a little like a fawn walking on the ice. He landed on his hip and slid five feet away.

I bent over laughing, "*What* was that?"

"That was *supposed* to be a figure skating turn."

I laughed so hard that I bent over and crouched down to keep from toppling over. Heat spread through my cheeks when he looked up at me. I stood upright and backed away.

When the DJ ended the music and the lights came up, we coasted to the exit and sat down to remove our skates.

"That was so much fun! And I was right," I gloated. "You owe me ice cream."

"Yeah, you were pretty terrible at first."

"Hey!"

He threw his arm around me and pulled me into his side. "I'm just kidding . . . sort of."

I shoved him away. "Rude!"

He grabbed my skates and brought them back to the counter. I watched him walk away with a pang of guilt. This felt all too real. Like a real date. I felt guilty for enjoying myself while I still had Casey out there somewhere, probably worrying. I couldn't fault Jay, though, he seemed like a great guy pulling out all the stops making the night fun. I felt zero pressure to carry a conversation until the ice was broken—or maybe just my tailbone.

"Should we get dinner or just skip to dessert?" he asked.

I thought for a second. "Dessert."

His smile reached his eyes. "You read my mind. Up for a walk?"

"Sure."

He stuck his elbow out, and I looped my arm in his.

The warm air surrounded us, and I could feel my cold hands thawing out right away. The clear night gave us a full view of the stars shining. It made our walk to get ice cream that much more beautiful.

After picking out vanilla ice cream with chocolate-covered peanuts, we sat down and ate. It tasted so good. I dribbled it on my arm on accident. With a snort, I jumped up and rushed to the counter to ask for napkins. The girl at the counter gave me a quick look and reached under the counter. She placed a small pile of napkins in my hand using her full hand. She left her hand on the top for longer than I expected.

When I looked up at her to find out why, her eyes penetrated mine like she was trying to tell me something. Then she looked back down at the napkins and lifted her hand before going back to work as if nothing had happened. I inspected the top napkin. The word *'bathroom'* was written very small in the corner. I grabbed it and balled it up in my fist.

"On second thought, I'm going to run to the restroom. I don't want my arm to be sticky. Be right back."

He nodded and continued eating.

My heart pumped as I pushed open the door. I didn't see anyone at first, but as I walked in, I could see that someone was in the last stall with the door open. Not just anyone—judging by the boots, it was a man. In the women's restroom, that could only mean they were there to meet me.

I hesitated. I should have run away, but something told me that this guy was on my side. Or maybe I just hoped so.

It hadn't been a full week since I'd cut all contact, yet it felt much longer.

I inched closer, and my hands shook. A head popped around the corner, making me jump. Ferdinand's large stature loomed in the stall.

He grabbed my arm, pulled me inside, and locked the door.

"What are you doing here?" I whispered.

"Watching," he said.

I gave him a huge hug, letting myself hold on a little longer as his arms enclosed me like a cocoon. The familiarity made me relax. "I've missed you guys so much, but this is going to blow my cover."

He waved my objection away. "No, no. It's fine."

"What do you need? I have to get back."

"Are you okay?"

"I'm fine."

His face changed.

"What?"

"Your arm was wrapped around his. I just . . . wanted to make sure . . .you were okay."

I put my hand on his arm. "I know. This is me undercover."

"I don't like it."

"I am missing Casey more than you even know. Trust me, I know what I'm doing. "

He crossed his arms. "You're sure?"

I nodded. "Of course. Besides, you should be used to this. You know that being a Protector sometimes means getting . . . close."

He shook his head. "Never watched it from the outside with someone. It's different. You'll let us know if things aren't good, right? You don't have to do this if you're uncomfortable . . ."

I nodded again. "Trust me. I'll be fine."

He hesitated but then unlocked the stall and pushed me out.

"Tell Casey I'll be back in no time," I whispered. And then I slipped out of the bathroom.

I felt the sting in my eyes as the door shut behind me. Tonight had been so fun that I'd almost forgotten what I was here for. Almost forgotten I hadn't spoken to Casey in days. Almost.

Plastering a smile on my face, I came around the corner. As soon as I sat down, I shoved a huge bite of ice cream in my mouth, taking a moment to collect myself before I had to speak.

"How was yours?" I asked when I noticed his was gone and he was just watching me eat.

"Good," he said with a grin. "Everything okay?"

"Of course!" I said a little too quickly and with too much enthusiasm. I bit my lip.

His eyebrows rose. "Ah. Okay then."

The air around us seemed to freeze in that awkward moment. I didn't know what to say to make it better, so I hastily shoved the last of my ice cream in my mouth and rushed to toss it in the trash. As I headed back, fighting a brain freeze, an arm caught me around the small of my back. I jumped sideways and swung around to see a surprised Jay.

"I'm sorry!" I said, feeling sheepish.

"Are you sure everything is alright?"

I brushed the hair out of my face and took a deep breath. "I'm fine. Just a little jumpy, I guess."

He nodded. "I'll bring you back to your car," he said, his voice smooth as silk. He held out his hand, gesturing for me to go ahead of him.

The car was silent for the first few miles. I turned to look at him.

"I'm really sorry," I said.

"For what?"

"This . . . hasn't ended well." I fidgeted with my purse strap.

He reached over and put his hand on top of mine.

"I don't know what you're talking about. If there's something you want to talk about, I'm here, though. I know we don't really know each other well yet, but I'm a good listener."

I glanced out the window. "I'll remember that. Are you from here?"

"Nope. Moved here a year ago. You?"

"Same."

"Really?"

I turned toward him and smiled.

"Where are you from?" he asked.

"California."

"Hence the surfing." He chuckled.

"Yep."

"What about you? Where are you from?"

"Oh, nowhere in particular. Here and there."

It seemed strange that he wouldn't have any specific place he called home. Knowing he was a Protector, I understood why, but most people wouldn't.

"Military?" I asked.

"Oh, no, nothing like that. We just moved around a lot when I was little."

"I see."

He pulled into a spot next to my car. Any other time, it would have seemed like a coincidence.

He jumped out and ran around the car, opening my door just as I finished collecting my things.

"I had so much fun tonight," I said.

"I'm glad. I did too." He paused. "I'd love to take you out again."

"That would be nice."

"How about tomorrow?"

I giggled. "Won't you get sick of seeing me?"

"Never." He smirked and handed me his phone. "Your number?"

For just a second, I hesitated, my thumbs hovering over his screen. Then I pressed my new number into his phone and handed it back to him.

"Thanks." He reached out for me, giving me a tight squeeze. He leaned over as he pulled away, and his lips brushed my cheek. He stepped back and watched me get in my car and pull away.

During my drive home, a wave of emotions hit me from worry to guilt. The next time had to be better, didn't it? And maybe I wouldn't have any unexpected visitors to throw me off.

I wondered what Jay must think of me. I must have looked like some nerve-stricken crazy girl.

At home, I grabbed my personal phone and sent a group text to the team and Casey.

Please no contact. It makes my job harder. I miss you guys. —Abbs
As soon as it sent, I deleted it from my phone, just in case.

Casey

Four days. That's how long it'd been since I'd spoken to Abby. It seemed much longer. It killed me not to see how she was doing. The highly secretive rotating schedule of surveillance excluded me.

"It's for your own good." Edward had said.

I shook my head. I didn't even want to think about what he meant by that.

At least they got to see her. To see that she was okay. They tried to keep me updated the best they could, but their 'she's fine' wasn't cutting it. They didn't know her like I did. How could they even know if she was fine?

I snatched my phone from my pocket the second I felt it's telltale vibration.

Please no contact. It makes my job harder. I miss you guys. — Abbs

The message struck a nerve. I was being kept in the dark about the one person who meant everything to me.

It took only a moment for my phone to ring. Ferdinand. My anger boiled.

"What happened?" I barked into the phone.

"Casey, I'm sorry. I know I broke protocol, but I was careful. I promise."

"Why?" I demanded. "What happened?"

Ferdinand hesitated. It wasn't like him. I didn't have the patience for it.

"Just say it!" I shouted.

"She was on a date." He paused. "I know I shouldn't have. He was getting too close to her, putting his arm around her. I had to make sure she was still okay. I'm sorry."

My stomach sagged like I'd swallowed a bowling ball. I couldn't speak. There were no words. I knew the job. I knew the reason she was playing along. But hearing it sent me into a whirlwind of emotions I hadn't expected. It was like a sucker punch to the gut.

"She's okay, Casey. She really is."

"How did you contact her?"

"I met her in the bathroom. He doesn't have a clue."

"You're positive?"

"Positive. And Casey?"

"What?"

"She wanted me to tell you she'll be back in no time."

Knowing the words came from her eased my tension and brought a smile to my face. Fake dating or not, she was still thinking of me. And that made this easier . . . somehow.

CHAPTER EIGHTEEN

Jay stood outside the theater waiting for me. I watched him for a moment before I got out of my car. On the surface, he didn't seem bad. And maybe he wasn't. That was my job, to figure out the truth.

Today was our second date. I didn't want to admit it, I was excited. The last date, despite its awkward ending, was the most fun I'd had in a while. Not training. Just living.

I sighed and stepped out of my car.

His face lit up as I approached, and I felt a pang of guilt for deceiving him.

"Hey there, beautiful."

"Hey," I said.

"Have you recovered from skating yet?" he asked after he paid for our tickets.

I rubbed my backside. "Not quite."

"Then I guess it's good the seats are padded."

He put his arm around my waist. I stiffened. He gave me a strange look.

"Are you okay?" he asked.

"Yeah. I'm fine, sorry." I moved closer to him, trying to show him it was fine.

He guided us into the theater and pointed to two seats in the middle. "How about those?"

I nodded and followed him up. He left right away to get popcorn, leaving me to save our seats.

I needed to stop being so jumpy, or he'd think there was something wrong with me. Maybe there was.

I adjusted how my purse sat on the armrest and fixed my hair. Then a thought crossed my mind: Was one of my team watching me right now? Were they watching me fix my hair for another guy?

I peeked around the chairs, but I didn't recognize anyone. I crossed my hands in my lap to keep myself from fixing myself more, just in case.

Jay returned and handed me a soda and held the popcorn between us.

Partway through the movie, Jay put the popcorn on the floor and lifted the armrest. He put his arm around me. Instinctively, I sank into his side, leaning into him. His masculine cologne held a hint of ginger that I liked.

He rested his mouth on the top of my head. It wasn't quite a kiss yet still held some promise of one. It was a sweet gesture without pushing too much.

When the credits rolled, I found myself wondering how the movie had ended. My distracted thoughts lingered elsewhere. I followed Jay to the end of our row where he stopped and reached out for me to take his hand.

"So, what did you think?" he asked.

"Oh, I liked it."

"I didn't expect that end at all. Did you?"

"Uh. Nope. Never saw that coming." I felt guilty for not having a clue what he was talking about.

"Are you hungry?" he asked.

Glancing at the empty popcorn container, I shook my head.

He laughed. "Me either. You up for a walk?"

"Sure."

We moseyed along the shops of the outdoor mall.

"So, what do you do for work?" I asked.

"I'm an assistant."

"Oh? What type of things do you do?"" I asked.

"The usual. Run errands, make appointments, get lunch."

"Sounds . . . fun."

He laughed. "Loads." He paused. "What do you do? Are you a spy? Or a secret agent?"

I laughed, but on the inside it was a little too dead-on, and I stumbled to find words. "I worked as a waitress for a little while. But my ex worked there, so I needed a change when we broke up."

"Oh? I gather it wasn't a good break-up?"

"Ah . . . you could say that."

"What happened?" he asked.

"I'd rather not talk about it."

"I get it." He let silence fall between us for just a moment. "Have there been many boyfriends in your life?"

I decided to leave Casey out of it. "Nope. Eli was really the only one." I cringed. Should I have said his name?

"Eli, huh?"

I felt nauseated. Maybe I shouldn't have said his name. He probably knew all about Eli. Most Protector's did.

"What about you, lots of girlfriends?"

"A few, nobody serious though."

I nodded. An awkward pause followed. I blurted out the first thing that came to mind. "What's the craziest thing you've ever done?" It was random, but in the end, it was something that I should know. After all, it might get me closer to knowing something—anything—dark about him.

He stopped and looked at me like he was trying to figure out why I'd asked.

"Is that a weird question?" I asked.

He smiled and started walking again. "No. Uh, let's see. The craziest?"

I nodded, grinning.

"Skydiving or maybe cliff jumping."

"You've been skydiving? Yikes. No way you'd catch me doing that!" I shook my head.

"It's a blast. You really should try it someday. I'm going to go again."

"I'll stay on the ground, thank you!"

He chuckled. "Okay, you can watch me land. What about you?"

"Me? Nothing." The countless crazy things of the last year flooded through my mind. What could I tell him? He certainly wouldn't accept *nothing* as an answer.

"Oh, come on. There's got to be something."

"Uh . . . maybe surfing?" I pressed my finger to my lips.

"Oh, man. There's nothing else? We're going to have to fix that! You need to get out more."

"I don't know about that."

"We'll see." He winked at me.

At the end of the shops, we turned back, and he walked me to my car.

"Thank you for tonight."

"You're welcome." His handsome face grew more enticing when he grinned.

I bit my lip and opened my car door. Tossing my purse into the passenger seat, I turned back to him.

He reached for my belt loops and pulled me toward him. I knew what was coming, and my stomach lurched. It felt like he was moving in slow motion. His mouth moved closer and closer to mine. At the last second, I turned my head, and he kissed my cheek.

I grimaced.

I gave him a quick hug and climbed in my car. I couldn't even look him in the face. My car roared to life, and I pulled out of the lot as quickly as I could, leaving him standing there looking surprised.

That awkward moment ran through my head over and over again the rest of the night. I felt horrible. I wanted to call him to apologize, but how could I when the mere thought of bringing it up made my mouth go dry?

Was I doing this right? It didn't feel like it. What kind of information was I even supposed to get? This wasn't as easy as the bar. Not even close. I couldn't outright ask him about things I wasn't even supposed to know about. And so far nothing he'd done was out of the ordinary. Not even the craziest thing he'd done. People go skydiving and cliff jumping every day. Next time, I'd find out more, I hoped.

The next day, I sat down at a table by the window and sipped my latte, ignoring the book I'd brought. Jay walked in.

"Hey Abby," he said. His low voice hit me right in the gut.

"Hey," I said, wiping foam from my lip.

"I was hoping I'd find you here. Can I sit down?"

I nodded.

"I wanted to talk to you . . . in person." He paused. "I wanted to . . . uh . . . apologize. I'm sorry if I rushed things . . . you know. . . last night."

"Oh, don't worry about it. I'm sorry too." I stopped there. Exactly what was I sorry for? Nothing sounded right in my head. Mainly I was sorry for making him feel embarrassed.

"You have nothing to be sorry for. I hope I didn't ruin things . . ." He let his words hang in the air.

"No. Of course not."

He smiled. Behind that smile, I knew he held the answers to all our questions. Somewhere in there was a criminal—or maybe not.

"Can I make it up to you? Take you out tonight? Dinner?" he asked.

"I'd like that."

He stood to leave, and I stood up as well. He leaned down and hugged me goodbye. I thought he was going to say something, and I turned my head just in time for his lips to meet mine. He pulled back so fast I wasn't even sure it had happened.

"Sorry," he said, his head down, eyes not meeting mine. "I was just going to kiss your cheek."

My eyes widened in surprise.

I took a deep breath and centered myself. *This is an act. That's all this is.*

I lifted his chin with my finger. Rising on tiptoe, I pressed my lips to his for the briefest of seconds. Then I turned and walked out the front door, my book and latte in my hand. I could feel his eyes on my back as I walked away.

I giggled to myself. Nothing like keeping a guy wanting more.

CHAPTER NINETEEN

At dusk, I stepped to the curb to wait for Jay. This was the first time I'd let him pick me up at home. The last thing I wanted to do was fend off questions from my mom about where Casey was and if something had happened with us. The truth was that I didn't know where Casey was, and it killed me every day I didn't speak to him.

"Hey," Jay said as I got into the car. His long brown hair was combed straight back.

"Hi," I said.

He pulled away from the curb, and then his phone rang. He checked the screen and then turned to me as if he was debating if he should answer it.

"Get it, it's okay."

He pulled over and put it to his ear. I turned away in an attempt to give him the small amount of privacy I could.

A few *yes's* and *no's* later, he set the phone in his lap.

"Sorry about that."

"Everything okay?" I asked.

"Problem at work." He paused like he was trying to decide what to do.

"If you need to cancel, that's all right," I offered.

I wondered if this had something to do with real Protector business, or the rogue Protectors.

"No, absolutely not." He turned to me. "Would it be okay if we made a pit stop?"

"Sure."

"It won't be long. I promise."

I questioned if I'd made the wrong choice when I realized where we were headed. I'd never thought he would take me here. It hadn't even crossed my mind.

As he pulled into the area that brought us to the elders' warehouse, I held my breath. Which building would he go to? Then he drove past the elders' compound, and I began to worry. He pulled up right across from the dragon symbol.

I wrung my hands.

"Is this where you work? I thought you were an assistant." My nerves were rattling me to my core, and it took everything in me not to let my voice shake.

"Yeah, my boss owns this place." He pointed toward the building from my dream, and I grimaced. *Of course it is.*

Not even two weeks had passed since I'd gone undercover, and I'd already made my way to the one place I'd thought about for months. Maybe getting to the bottom of all of this wouldn't take as long as Edward thought.

He parked next to a door, shut the car off, and got out.

I folded my hands in my lap.

"I'm really sorry about this. I shouldn't be long." And then he was gone.

Was this it? Was this the moment that led up to my dream? Sitting here wasn't good. I was sure of that.

I held my phone, waiting. I fought with myself. I should be out partying with my friends—only two weeks had passed since graduation. I shouldn't be worried about Protector business. Yet, somehow these gifts were thrust upon me.

Across the lot, I spotted a man getting out of an all-black SUV that looked familiar. As the man drew nearer, his face made my jaw drop. He was even more familiar than his car. This was the man who had followed me for weeks. The one who'd kept me on edge, who'd teamed up with Eli to corner me and try to kill me. The elders never figured out who he was, but there he was, headed straight for me.

I slouched down and hid my face as he passed.

He glanced around as he slinked toward the door. Then he disappeared inside.

There was no doubt in my mind—this was it. It felt wrong. So utterly wrong.

I typed a quick text and sent it to both Lucian and Casey.

I think something's wrong.

Grabbing what I might need from my purse, I shoved everything in my pockets and slipped out of the car—but not before I grabbed the car keys. He wasn't going to get away that easily if I had anything to do with it.

Casey

A pool hall—that's what the guys suggested. Looking at the place, I couldn't see why anyone would want to come here. Darkness filled all the corners. I searched the room until I found them racking up a new game two tables away.

My phone chimed.

One glance at the screen, and my stomach twisted into a knot.

I think something's wrong.

For a split second, I looked at the guys.

Fear sparked inside me. I gave a quick whistle and jerked my head toward the door.

Time seemed to stop. The guys looked at each other, and like a gun had gone off, we bolted through the door, knocking down chairs as we went.

Abby

My nerves threatened to choke me as I grasped the door handle. Thanks to Lucian's 3D mockup on the beach, I wasn't walking in blind. I knew this place with my eyes closed. Hopefully it would prove useful. He'd told me I needed to know my way in the dark just as well in the light.

Leaning against the frame, I took a deep breath. Once I entered, there was no turning back. I held my breath and slipped inside. Only a single bulb lit the hallway. A shiver ran down my spine. Closing my eyes, I shook it off.

I felt sick.

I can do this.

As I moved away from the door, it was hard to see. I slowed my pace to a crawl and pressed my back against the nearest wall. Voices came from ahead. I squinted against the darkness in search of eyes that might be trained on me.

Satisfied I was alone, I padded on as quietly as possible until I came to a door. The voices inside grew louder. The door was open only a crack, just enough for me to peek inside. Jay and three others were in view, facing someone I couldn't see. It sounded like there were more people within, just out of view.

"Where is she?" a man demanded.

"In the car." Jay's voice shook.

"You shouldn't have brought her here," a man to Jay's right said. He turned ever so slightly, and the light caught his face. It was the man from the SUV.

I covered my mouth with my hand, trying to mask my erratic breathing.

"We were going on a date. You're the one who called me here. What did you want me to do? Cancel? And make her more suspicious *after* I've already picked her up?"

"Enough. What's done is done. What has she told you?" someone asked.

They were talking about me. Someone moved across the room, and I jumped back, worried they might see me. I waited a few seconds and moved forward again.

"Nothing. She hasn't even let on she knows who we are."

The guy slammed his fist on the table. "What is taking you so long?"

"I don't want to spook her. All that would do is get Edward looking over my shoulder to make sure I'm doing my job. Is that what you want?"

"May as well just take care of her now. No sense in wasting any more time."

Jay dropped his head. "But what if she's not working with him? Eli only suspected Edward wanted her, but it all could have been nothing. We've all seen how much he hated Edward."

"I want to know what she knows. I want to know who she is and why she's been hanging out with all the big names," said a man who sounded as if he was in charge.

Everyone quieted when he spoke, but I couldn't see him. "Find out what all these big-wig *Protectors*"—he said the word as if it made him want to vomit—"are doing with her. Edward, Lucian, that boyfriend."

"I'm don't think they're still together," Jay mumbled, his voice barely audible.

"What?"

"I-I don't think they're still together."

"Why?" the boss asked.

"I've been taking her on dates . . . I've kissed her. I just . . . I don't think . . . they're still together."

"Maybe his apartment was enough to make him walk away," SUV guy said with a laugh. "She's far too much work. Anyone can see that. She's not even immortal."

"She's not too much work," Jay said.

"You falling for this girl?" SUV guy spat.

Jay turned and stared down SUV guy like he wanted to say more.

"Enough. You have until the end of the night, then we kill her. We need to finish what Eli started, before she gets any deeper into finding out what we're doing."

"Fine . . ." Jay said, the anger in his voice boiling. He turned to leave but then stopped. "Unless she's not involved, right?"

Jay was on my side? He seemed good—even in a room full of so much hatred. Yet somehow he'd wound up involved with them in the first place, so he couldn't be that good. Could he?

A few laughs echoed around the room.

"Sure. If she hasn't been sent in as a spy, I'll spare her . . ." He cackled. "Maybe."

I had to get out of here. I stepped back, but my shoe caught a crack in the concrete floor. I stumbled into the wall. I bit my lip to stop myself from crying out.

It wasn't enough. My back thudded against the wall.

Everyone fell silent.

"What was that?" the formal man asked, his voice quieter than earlier.

I ran. Ran as fast as I could down the corridor toward the room from my dream.

Casey

"We'll take mine," Brad yelled.

We jumped in his truck, and it roared onto the road. I punched a few buttons on my phone and pinpointed her exact location.

"It's the warehouse," I said under my breath.

One flash of the screen, and Brad's jaw tightened. He pressed the accelerator further to the floor.

"Who's supposed to be watching?"

Nobody spoke. They didn't know. My teeth ground together.

His truck seemed to fly down the road, yet nothing could get us there fast enough. In minutes, the truck whipped into the driveway, and I hit the pavement before the car stopped rolling. My knee gave out as I landed. I winced for a second and kept running. The rest of the team wasn't far behind. Our footsteps echoed on the pavement.

We bolted through the door blind, something we didn't often do. We knew the building from the blueprints, of course, but we had no idea what could be happening inside.

I squinted in the dark hallway. As if they knew we were coming, the door opened and out rushed multiple men. My eyes focused on one thing. Guns. They were armed.

"Hey! What do you think you're doing?" the first yelled.

I lunged, not giving them the chance to use their weapons. Behind me, the guys were already on my heels. More men pushed their way into view.

A loud explosion rocked the small hallway, and, for just a second, everything moved in slow motion. Pain ripped through my shoulder. I gulped back my shock. I stumbled backward, and when another explosion rang out, pain tore through my abdomen.

"Abby . . ." I gurgled.

My vision blurred. Ferdinand collided with the shooter, and the gun went off once more. I hit the floor, and everything went black.

Abby

A door behind me squeaked. I grabbed the handle and closed my eyes. *Should I change the plan?*

I wanted to flee from this place. To run right back out the front door and never look back. Instead, I pushed on. The door opened just enough for me to enter. I froze on the other side, realizing I didn't know what I was walking into. The huge room was dark except for the small window. I stopped to listen, my heartbeat in my ears. Aside from that, I heard nothing. And then footsteps and shouts filled the hallway just on the other side of the door.

What happened next, I didn't know, but when gunshots rang out I cowered. Sliding my back against the wall, inching my way further into the large room, I made my way to the window just to be sure the emblem was present as I remembered.

There it was.

I shrank back into the shadows against the wall, my breathing heavy. *Now what?*

Once again, my dream brought me somewhere people were after me. Once again, I didn't have a way out. It wasn't supposed to happen this way. This time, I was trained. This time I went into this knowing what I was getting myself into, and still here I stood unsure of what to do next, with only seconds before they found me. I listened for any sound, but it went dead silent. Where were they? What was happening?

All of the sudden, a hand closed over my mouth, and I was in someone's clutches. I yanked and pulled, but their grip only tightened. I tried to scream. They dragged me backward, deeper into the shadows.

"Stop . . . fighting . . . me," the man grunted.

He sounded vaguely familiar, but I couldn't place it.

I felt weak in the knees unable to move as I flashed back to another time. The sounds of a train filled my ears so loudly I could hear nothing else until I was jolted back to reality.

"Abby!" The man shook me back and forth.

He spun me around. In the dark, I couldn't see his face, but his breath was hot. I tried to back away, though he still grasped my arms, not giving me an inch.

I started to yank myself away again.

"Stop fighting me, Abby!" His voice was so commanding it made me quiver.

"Then let me go!" I shrieked, but his hand clamped over my mouth again.

"I'm helping you! Would you just stop? And be quiet! They'll hear us!"

Every part of me resisted, and every nerve in my body told me this was wrong, but the familiarity in his voice made me falter.

In my split-second hesitation, his head fell back, allowing the light to catch his face just enough. *George?*

"What are you doing here?" I hissed.

"Come on. We have to get out of here." He started to walk in the other direction, but I stood rooted, refusing to move.

"Wait, I can't. I have a mission."

"Did you hear that? That's a gun! There is no mission anymore. You have been compromised. They know who you are. They're going to kill you!"

"They were talking about me."

"Abby, we have to leave. Now."

"But—"

"There's nothing you can do. There's no time."

He leaned over and looked out the window, searching for something. I wished I knew what.

The door burst open—not at all like it had in my dream. Two men stood in the doorway. The first held a gun up toward us.

"Stop right there!" the gunman shouted. He took a step closer.

"We have to go now! Come on!" George shouted.

"I wouldn't do that, Abby," the gunman warned.

He knew my name. I took one step away, and the gun fired. The flash stole my attention as my hands went up around my head. The crack of impact behind me drew my attention back to the gunman.

A warning shot.

I made my decision, focusing on the gun. It flew from his hand and landed ten feet from him. Stunned, he stared from me to the gun. His face contorted, and he lunged toward the gun.

George grabbed my wrist and pulled me to the other end of the room to a door I hadn't seen in my dreams. One Lucian had never mentioned.

At the last second, I focused once again on the gun and threw it ten feet further away from the gunman just before his fingers could brush it. We were through the door and running up a staircase before I could even ask where we were going. I followed, hoping I was doing the right thing.

George opened the door at the top, and we were hit with a gush of air that almost knocked me back down. I stumbled forward, trying to regain my balance.

The whip of the helicopter blades made it impossible to hear anything else. George grabbed my hand and pulled me toward the open door, ducking until we climbed inside.

"Quick, give me your phone," George yelled.

"My phone? Why?" I clutched it to my chest. It was my one lifeline to everyone I knew and loved.

"It can be traced. You can't bring it."

I glanced down my very first phone, it's pink body illuminated by the screen as a tear rolled down my face. Then I handed it over.

Carefully he removed the memory card, then the battery. "I'm sorry." He set it on the ground and smashed it under his boot.

"I assume you want this one, too," I said, handing over the phone Edward had given me.

George's brow furrowed for a second, and then he grabbed it and smashed it.

"Go! Go!" He shouted as he buckled me in first and then himself.

As we rose, I found myself looking back down at the building as the door on the roof flew open once more and three men rushed out. I couldn't see their faces from our altitude, though I wished I could.

George threw on a headset and passed one to me. The noise level cut down, and I heard George's voice loud and clear.

"Are you okay?" he asked.

I nodded. "We have to call Casey and Lucian. Let them know I got out."

George shook his head.

"What? They're probably already down there. I texted them."

"We can't tell them anything." George shook his head. "He can't know."

"Why? He has to know!"

"These guys are going to come looking for you. They know everything about you. The first person they'll go to is him. Keeping him in the dark is the best thing we can do for him."

"If it isn't safe for me, it isn't for him either. They'll hurt him!"

"Abby, he can handle himself."

Of course he can. He's immortal.

"But he's going to think . . ." I couldn't even say the words.

George's face took on a grim hue.

"What about Mom? And Dad?"

"I haven't figured that part out yet."

"Then I can't go. They'll be worried. Turn around." I began to panic that I'd messed everything up by going with him.

Oh my gosh. What am I going to do?

"Please. You have to turn around!" My breathing became erratic.

"Abby! Calm down. You're going to hyperventilate."

I put my head between my knees and tried to take deep breaths.

"Where are we going?" I asked, angling my mouth toward the microphone just in case my voice was too quiet.

He turned to me with sympathy in his eyes. "You have to go away."

"You said that, but what do you mean? Where?"

"I have a safe house for you."

A safe house. Like I was in some movie running from criminals. I couldn't believe this was even reality.

George started talking to the pilots, his words a blur among the whip of the blades as I tried to grasp reality. It couldn't be real. It had to be a dream. A dream I wished I could wake up from and find myself warm in my own bed. For once, I prayed for one of my awful nightmares. I pinched myself, though nothing changed.

George's hand landed gently on my back, coaxing me to calm down.

I sat up, tears streaming down my face. "How am I supposed to just leave them?"

He shook his head. "I don't know."

"Edward never said anything like this could happen. I was only supposed to help. Tell him who the bad guys were, and they would go in and get them. That's it. They weren't supposed to know anything about me. What did I do?" I asked as tears filled my eyes. "This wasn't supposed to happen."

"Nobody was prepared for this. Nobody could have known."

I turned away from George. I hated this. My heart hurt. I leaned my head against the window.

What have I done?

A while later, we landed, and George ushered me onto a plane. It was a small, luxurious aircraft that I could see celebrities flying on. Under different circumstances, I might have been excited. But the padded white leather seats made me feel confined.

"Where are we going?" I asked. My voice, monotone and dry, didn't sound like my own.

"Florida." He smirked. "Someone told me it's going to make you happy."

The corner of my mouth twitched upward. The plane accelerated down the runway before we lifted into the air.

A short time later, after the fading adrenaline left me feeling weak, I fell asleep, not waking until the plane jostled me as we landed. My hand slipped from under my chin, and my head hit the window.

"Oww," I grumbled, rubbing away the ache in my groggy haze.

As my mind came to, my anxiety returned, bringing with it all of my fears.

George guided me off the plane and into a black car where someone I didn't know drove us away from the airport. The car merged onto a freeway. Palm trees lit up by streetlights lined the roads, swaying in the wind. Traffic was light, and I imagined most people were home with their families. Where I should be.

We sat silent in the back seat for a while.

"Are you going to hate me forever?" George asked.

"I don't hate you."

"I'd hate me."

"It isn't your fault. It's mine," I said.

"Don't blame yourself."

"I should have never agreed to this. Casey was right."

"Sir, we have arrived," the driver said.

The car rolled to a stop in front of a house. I couldn't see much in the darkness, but as I stepped out of the car, the sound of crashing waves welcomed me.

"Will this be suitable?" George asked. A small smile showed on his face.

I let his question hang. I suspected Edward was really trying to make this up to me.

George took the time to show me around. Then he stood at the kitchen counter as if he was waiting for something.

I settled myself in one of the dining room chairs and brought my knees to my chest. Deep down, I knew what was coming. He was going to leave me here. Alone.

"Now what?" I asked.

"I need you to write a letter to your mom."

I nodded. This was the one thing that put me at ease. I could tell her. In my words, and then I'd pray she understood in the only way she could.

"You can't tell her why you left . . ."

"I know."

"Or where you are."

"I'd have to know where I was to be able to tell her that, wouldn't I?"

"I'll give you a few minutes."

He left the room, and I could hear the echo of him talking on the phone down the hall.

    Mom,

        I know this may seem sudden, but I need some time to clear my head now that I've graduated. I used the ticket you bought me to travel for a while. I can't wait to see the world!

        I don't know when I'll be back, but I'll write when I can. Please tell Dad I love him and that I'm sorry I didn't call.

        I miss you already.

                I love you,

                    Abby

Tears fell as I signed my name and thought of her reading it. I folded it and pushed it away. *There. I did it.*

I turned away. I couldn't look at it a second longer.

"I'm done," I called out.

Moments later, George returned and picked up the letter. He fiddled with it in his hands like he didn't want to say something.

"Spit it out," I said.

"Before I go, can I ask you something?"

I looked up from the table. "What?"

"How long have you had that gift?"

I smiled. "Not long."

He nodded. "I need to go."

He was setting me out on my own for the first time in my life. I used to think about this day and envision it so much differently. My mom should be here for my first send-off. *How can I do this without my mom?*

"Are you going to be okay?" he asked.

I laughed. "Does it even matter?"

"It does."

"Well then, no," I said, jutting out my bottom lip and crossing my arms.

He shook his head. "You'll be fine. I really have to go. I'm already going to be late."

There was a loud knock at the back door. I jumped.

George smiled. "That's my cue." And then he was gone.

Casey

Why is my mouth so dry?

I rolled over. Pain filled my whole side.

"You'll be better off just lying still."

My eyes opened, squinting against the light. Cade stood over me.

"What . . ." I croaked, the dryness sealing my throat.

"Here." Cade held out a glass of water with a straw in it.

I started to sit up, and he stopped me. He lowered the glass so I could drink without moving.

"What happened?"

Cade's face changed. He looked down at the floor.

Then it all came rushing back to me. Abby's text. Men with guns.

"I was shot."

Cade nodded.

I shot upright, ignoring the pain. "Abby. Where's Abby?"

"Whoa." Cade sank into the bed next to me.

"Cade. Where's Abby?"

Cade looked into my eyes. I could see it in his face, the sudden paleness. The same fearful look he always gave me as a kid when he didn't want to say something.

I started to swing my legs to the other side of the bed.

"Case, 'stop. I'll tell you. The truth is, I don't know where she is."

"What?"

"After you got shot, it was utter chaos."

"Wait, how do you know?"

He looked me in the eyes once more.

"It was my turn to watch. I didn't realize anything was happening . . . until I saw you four running inside." He looked down. "I'm sorry. I should have known."

"What happened?" I demanded.

"After you were shot, it was chaos. The team had to get you out of there." He looked down again. "I told them I'd go after her. I got my butt handed to me." He shook his head. "I didn't think I'd ever get to her, but then Ferdinand and Luke came back. But by the time we got through them all, she was gone."

"What? What do you mean *gone*?"

"We broke through them and raced after her, but she was in a helicopter already flying away."

"Who took her?"

Cade shook his head. "We don't know."

I fell back against the pillow. I'd failed her. My ultimate fear from the moment she'd said *yes*. She was gone. I had to do something.

"I have to call Edward. He's got to know something."

Cade shook his head again. "He doesn't."

"Well, maybe he's learned something since you talked to him." I pushed myself toward the edge of the bed. Pain radiated through my abdomen and shoulder. Cade came around the bed as I stood, just in time to catch me when my leg gave out.

"You were shot in the leg, too," he said.

I dropped onto the bed, frustrated. Cade crossed the room and handed me a set of crutches. "I'm not sure how much these will help with your shoulder."

I stood, favoring the bad leg, and used the crutches to see how I did. The pain was bad but not unbearable.

"Where's my phone?"

"Broken."

I grumbled. "What if she's tried to call?"

"Edward is in the living room with the team."

My eyes narrowed. "Then why didn't you say that sooner?"

Cade shrugged. "Didn't want you to hurt yourself trying to get out of here when there's nothing you can do anyway."

If I weren't in so much pain, I'd have punched him in the gut. I hobbled toward the closed door the best I could, stopping when I reached it. "Can you at least open that for me?"

Cade stepped forward, opened the door, and let me pass. He was so exasperating.

Voices floated down the hallway.

It took longer than I would have liked to even make it to the kitchen. The room stilled as I came into view. I gripped the counter and breathed through the pain before continuing to where they were seated. They watched me struggle to the couch and waited for me to get settled. I dropped the crutches to the floor.

"What do we know?" I asked, cutting straight to the chase.

Luke, Ferdinand, and Brad all stared at the floor, unable to make eye contact.

"Nothing," Edward said.

"How can that be? We had one person watching her every move. Four people went in after her. And still we know absolutely nothing?"

"Nothing went like we could have predicted," Ferdinand said.

"Nothing ever goes as we predict!"

"Casey, that helicopter came out of nowhere. Somehow, they grabbed her and ran. The helicopter landed for only a few seconds. Only long enough for them to board before it lifted again. It's like they planned this from the start."

"Where's Jay?" I demanded.

"In custody. We only managed to apprehend him and one other man."

"Have they said anything?" I asked.

Edward shook his head. "Both deny any connection to a helicopter. And Casey"—he paused—"they've said that their plan was never to extract her. It was to kill her."

Kill my Abby. For what? Of course, she should never have gotten tangled up with Edward in the first place, but in all that she had been through, she never hurt anyone. It made me sick to my stomach.

"What about Abby's mom? And dad? Where do they think she is?"

The team looked at Edward, as if they'd never even thought to wonder about her folks.

"George gave her mother a letter explaining that she needed time by herself."

"Did she believe it?"

"I'm uncertain. George is handling that front."

"And why is that exactly?" Brad asked. His confusion was evident.

Edward looked at me and then Brad. "I would have thought this would have been shared amongst you."

"It wasn't my place." I looked down at my hands folded in my lap.

Edward nodded. "George is a retired Protector."

"What? How is that possible?"

The looks of disbelief on their faces didn't surprise me.

"It's what George wanted when he retired. And yes, it is possible, though not easy to accomplish. Given all that George did during his service, he earned it. All of that is beside the point. Right now George is our best asset at keeping this whole issue under wraps."

"Maybe that's exactly what we don't need. Maybe we need this all out in the open," I spat.

"You can't mean that," Luke said.

"Why? Everything that matters to me is gone."

"If this got out, it would be the end of what we do. Think of all the deaths that would cause."

Everyone started talking at once.

Edward held up his hands, silencing the room. "Right now, Casey needs time to heal and come to terms with what has happened. We will get her back. I promise you that."

$$*\qquad*\qquad*\qquad*$$

The next day I was back on my feet. Twenty-four hours. That's how long it took for my injuries to heal. Never had it taken so long, and I hoped it never would again. The nausea, on the other hand, refused to dissipate. It settled in the pit of my stomach. The more time that passed since Abby went missing, the worse it became.

Cade had been there throughout, making sure I had everything I needed and keeping me company. If I hadn't been in so much turmoil worrying about Abby, I might have enjoyed it.

None of us really slept. I knew the team was doing everything they could to chase down any shred of hope. So far, nothing had been helpful. I worried more and more as time went on that they wouldn't be able to keep up this pace much longer, and we weren't getting any closer to finding her.

Since I was finally back to normal, Cade left to go meet up with Edward for the latest briefing. The moment he left, I knew there was one thing I needed to do. One thing that hadn't left my mind the entire time I'd been laid up.

I drove straight to the warehouse. The team had gone through it to find evidence that would help, but nothing had presented itself. I didn't really think I'd find anything, but I had to look the place over. It was the last place she was seen.

It didn't surprise me that the parking lot was empty when I pulled in. I let myself into the warehouse and immediately had to plug my nose to block out the smell of stale blood. My blood. And maybe a few others. I couldn't really be sure.

I sidestepped around the red-stained concrete.

The first room was empty aside from a desk and chair in the center, and an old, worn leather couch. All the drawers of the desk were open and empty. I moved on through the whole building and to the roof.

I should have been there sooner.

On my way back through the warehouse, a menacing voice called out to me from the first room. I froze.

Someone's here?

"Who's there?"

I braced myself, ready to fight, and pushed open the door once more. There was nobody in the room.

A deep chuckle rumbled from a large intercom-type speaker in the center of the ceiling. Next to it, a small light blinked. A surveillance camera. I should have known.

"Were you expecting someone to be there?"

"Who are you?"

"Oh, let's not worry about that. I do believe there is something you can help me with."

"What?"

"Tell me where Abby is."

"How would I know? You took her!" I shouted.

Anger laced his voice. "You're hiding her. Don't take me for a fool."

"I'm going to find her. You'd do well to understand I'd do anything for her."

The deep laugh vibrated the speakers again. "Oh, I'm counting on it. But just know, I won't stop looking for her either. She's cost me far too many men. May the better man win. Goodbye, Casey. It was awfully nice chatting with you." He paused. "Oh, one other thing—I do hope you were able to replace everything in that pretty little apartment of yours."

Then the speaker went silent.

Anger filled me. "Damn," I yelled, swinging my hand out, slamming a drawer on the desk. I kicked open the door and stormed out of the building.

I had to find her, one way or another. I pulled my phone from my pocket and shut it off. I gave it one last look before I dropped it to the ground and smashed it to pieces.

Cade

"Pick up, pick up . . ." I urged, calling Casey for the thousandth time since he'd dropped off the face of the earth.

He'd left without telling anyone where he was going and hadn't been heard from since.

Love could make someone do crazy things. With Abby missing, there wasn't much he wouldn't do to get her back.

"Don't do anything stupid!" I yelled at the phone when he didn't answer again.

I paced his apartment, unable to bring myself to leave in case he happened to come home.

My faith in that diminished every day.

Where are you, man?

I called Brad again.

"Hello?"

"Has anyone heard from him?" I asked.

"No. I don't like this. It's not like him."

I couldn't hear this. I knew exactly what my brother was like, and as much as I hated to admit it, it *was* just like him. The side of him nobody had seen in a very long time.

"Call me if anyone hears from him."

"I will."

I tossed my phone across the table. It slid off to the floor.

"Damn it, Case'! What are you doing?"

Feeling the frustration rise up inside me, I shoved my hands into my hair, ready to pull it all out.

Why did I leave? I saw how anxious he was. The desperation. And I just left him alone. It felt like history replaying itself, yet this time the stakes were far higher. He wasn't an upset teenager running away from his problems anymore. If I knew him, he was running straight into the lion's den . . . alone.

Casey

Months of pounding the pavement and shaking down every lowlife hangout I knew of—and a few I found after making some useless ingrates talk—and I'd only learned one thing: nobody had Abby.

This was the last stop. The only lead I had left. Every other rock was overturned.

As the sun peaked on the horizon, I knew there was only one other explanation to her disappearance.

I threw the car in reverse.

Indignation and resentment festered deep within me. I should have seen this for what it was.

My car had hardly stopped moving when I threw it in park. It was hard to restrain myself as I marched up to the door of the house. *He's just a pawn,* I tried to tell myself. *Edward's pawn.*

My fist pounded on the door over and over, long after I meant to stop. I stumbled when it swung open and my fist connected with nothing.

"Casey?" Lucian turned his head to the side. "Is that you?"

I fought the urge to punch him in his sleepy face. "Who else would it be?" I snarled.

"Your hair . . . beard. Everyone's been worried about you."

"Where is she?" I ground my teeth together.

"Abby? We haven't found her."

I shook my head, reached into the back of my pants, and pulled out the gun. I held it up, not trusting myself to point it directly at him. I needed him to tell me where she was.

"Don't make me use this. It won't kill you, but it sure as hell hurts."

"Whoa, Casey. What are you doing?"

"I've spent months searching every criminal hellhole I could find. I've been punched, jumped, and shot. And gave quite a few the same treatment. Nobody has her. Now, I'm not going to ask again."

"Calm down, come inside and we'll talk."

I turned the gun and aimed for his abdomen. Lucian turned and walked into the house. I kicked the door closed behind me.

Abby

Months of living alone had given me too much time to consider my next move once this was all over. Would I go to college? Would I stay in Florida? Or go back to Arizona? To California?

The only thing I was positive about—I couldn't wait to get back to my life. To Casey. Even with the beach out my back door, I wasn't happy. Casey wasn't here. My mom wasn't here. I couldn't even call my dad.

In all my time here, Edward had called only once on my second day to apologize. Then, like clockwork, a box of chocolate showed up on my doorstep every week. The exquisite box and expensive chocolates could only be from him. Maybe it was his way of making it up to me. I couldn't be sure, but they tasted really good.

George, on the other hand, made sure to call me weekly. He assured me during our calls that the time would come, and this would all be over. As the months passed, I doubted it more and more. Just give it another week, he'd say. I think he was just trying to give me hope when there was so little to be hopeful for. I yearned to talk to my mom. It just wasn't possible. She couldn't know where I was.

Every day, the same knock sounded on the back door. Without looking, I always knew who it was. The one person who was seeing me through my time here. My only shred of sanity.

Lucian.

Even Willow, his girlfriend, had no idea where I was, making me the biggest secret both of us kept from the most important people in our lives. The guilt of that betrayal hung heavy on my shoulders. If only I'd said no to Edward, I wouldn't have gotten us all in this mess. I could almost hear Casey's voice as he said, *'Told you so.'*

Lucian stocked my fridge with food, kept me company, and, of course, continued my training, keeping me in shape just in case I needed to defend myself. *'You never know,'* he would say.

I didn't argue. What else did I have to do?

231

Some nights I made him dinner, and I often wondered what he told Willow on those nights, but most of the time I ate alone in front of the TV. Sometimes the TV was just a reminder of what I was missing.

Casey. My heart ached thinking of him. I missed him so much. So many nights I wished I could call him just to hear his voice, to tell him I was okay, but I knew that could be dangerous. I wondered often what he must be thinking. George said he hadn't given up hope that I'd come back, but as far as he knew, the bad Protectors took me and I hadn't been seen since. I cringed thinking about what that must feel like.

I poured cereal for breakfast and, as expected, the knock sounded on the door. I cinched my robe a bit tighter out of habit.

"Hey Lucian," I called as the door slid open behind me.

There was a pause.

"A-bby," said a muted voice strangled with emotion.

I froze. Then I turned around slowly.

I dropped the spoon. It clattered to the floor.

Despite the dirty, overgrown hair and long beard, there was no mistaking who stood there, staring at me with those striking green eyes.

"*Casey?*"

CHAPTER TWENTY

Edward showed up at the house within the hour to apologize to Casey for keeping him in the dark. I don't think he expected Casey to request retirement on the spot. I know I didn't.

Based on his list of demands, he'd put a lot of thought into this, though he had to wait for the official hearing with all of the elders for approval. The biggest request of them all was that he wanted to have the option of coming back, so if—someday down the road—he wanted his Protector life back, he could. This seemed to make Edward happy, so I was sure they'd grant it. And I had a big inkling it wouldn't be long before he was back at it. It was in his blood. But I knew just as well as he that he needed a good long break.

Edward surprised us both by gifting me the house—for once, the idea of living there didn't seem so gloomy. He even planned to continue a more-than-generous salary for the rest of my life even though I could never work undercover again even if I wanted to. That ship had sailed long before anyone even realized my cover was blown. I wouldn't have to work another day in my life.

We watched Edward leave that day, and it seemed like life was finally falling into place just the way it should.

We spent the night together cuddled up on the porch, talking until the stars faded into the brightening morning sky.

Casey and I even talked about the idea of going back to school. It was exciting to consider all the possibilities our lives could hold. But one thing I was sure of—I wanted to help people. That was the whole reason I'd jumped in with Edward in the first place. Just because that hadn't panned out didn't mean I was going to give up on that dream.

Today, I'd face my mom for the first time in months since I'd vanished to travel the world—
or so she thought. Part of me was dreading the conversation, yet the rest of me was just barely able to contain my excitement.

Casey dropped me off in front of my mom's.

"I'll see you tomorrow night?" he asked.

I nodded, gave him a quick peck, and shut the door. I hated being apart from him already, but he had his own business to handle here, and my main focus was on my mom.

Somehow, I had to let Mom, Dad, and George know I'd found my place in this world. In Florida.

I took a deep breath and opened the front door. "Hello?"

"Abby?" George rounded the corner first. He swung around nervously toward the stairs. "What are you doing here?"

"Casey found me. He made the rounds with all of the enemies, mine or otherwise, over the last couple months, and I don't think they'll be coming back to settle any debts." I grinned.

He squeezed me. "You have no idea how happy that makes me. Your mom . . . she's been worried sick."

"Where is she?" I asked.

"Upstairs."

I took a deep breath, and up I went.

Rounding the corner into my mom's room, I almost collided with her.

"Abby!"

As I stumbled back from running into her, she reached forward and pulled me against her in the biggest hug she'd ever given me.

"I can't believe you're finally here." She clung to me. "I've missed you so much."

"I've missed you too." I breathed in the smell of her shampoo.

She pulled away and smacked me on the arm over and over. "Don't you ever do that to me again!"

I giggled. "Okay . . . okay," I said, barely able to get the words out.

*   *   *   *

The next day, my mom and I were hanging out in my bedroom getting everything ready for me to leave again.

"I hate that I'm losing you again. Are you sure about this?" Mom handed me the last of the clothes laid out on my bed.

"You aren't losing me. You're going to love it there. It's gorgeous."

She sat down on the bed, a pout on her face. "I knew this was coming eventually. But I'm not ready. Having you gone the last few months has been so hard."

"I'll call all the time," I said.

"Promise?"

"I promise."

She looked me in the eyes like she wasn't sure she believed me.

"I will!"

"Good." She fiddled with my bedspread. "What did your dad think?"

"You mean after he stopped yelling at me for disappearing? He didn't seem to have an opinion. I think he was in shock."

Mom rolled her eyes. "That sounds about right. I'm feeling a bit of that myself."

"Me too."

"What else are you bringing?" she asked.

I grabbed my laptop and zipped up the duffel. "That's it. I'm leaving the rest for when I come visit. No extra room for you," I teased.

She held up her hands. "Got it!"

I slung the bag over my shoulder.

"Do you really have to leave already?"

I glanced at my clock. "Yeah, my ride to the airport should be here already."

Ferdinand pulled up in a truck as soon as I opened the front door.

I gave my mom a big hug. "Bye."

She didn't let go when I tried to pull back.

"Ah . . . Mom . . ."

She gave me one last squeeze. "Fine. I love you. Be safe."

"I will. I love you too."

I waved as I hopped in the truck.

The best of all was that I could go back to visit my mom whenever I wanted since Lucian let me keep his key. I had my very own portal to her right down the beach.

"Headed back already?" Lucian asked when I knocked on his door in Arizona.

"Yep, this is the last of it." I showed him the large duffel.

"Here, let me take that." He grabbed it, heaving it off my shoulder.

I led the way out the back door, but when I stepped out onto the deck, my mouth dropped open.

A rose-petal path on the beach was outlined in candles, enough to light the way.

I turned back to Lucian.

"Go on. I'll bring this by tomorrow." He dropped the bag just inside the back door.

I grinned and made my way down the path. My stomach tickled with anticipation.

Halfway there, a single small sand dollar lay in the path. I smiled to myself, thinking of its significance. A milestone in my life. I stooped down and picked it up, letting it lay in the palm of my hand. My hands shook.

I could see Casey, his face clean shaven, standing in the distance, barefoot in shorts and a tee. I took off running, throwing myself into his arms.

"This is beautiful," I said.

"Not as beautiful as you."

He kissed me before setting me back in the sand.

"Being away from you for these past few months has been torture. Having you back in my arms is the best gift anyone could ever give me. I never dreamed of anything other than being a Protector, until you. I could only hope to wake up next to your beauty for the rest of my life." He pulled back and dropped to his knee.

My hands covered my open mouth.

"Will you marry me?"

I didn't have to give it a second thought.

"*Yes!*"

To my readers,

Thank you for reading The Obscured series. I was sad to end this series, which is why it turned into four books instead of three that I meant it to be when I started. If you loved it, I would be honored if you took the time to review. I do read each and every one!

But what's next? I've already begun something new that I'm really excited about. I hope you will stick with me and keep an eye out for announcements, giveaways, and of course new releases.

Yours,
C. M. Boers
www.cmboers.com

Acknowledgements

I spent a long time writing this last book in the Obscured series. Not just because it was really hard to end Abby's story, but also due to personal circumstances that kept me away from my laptop. The one thing that kept me going when it got hard was my husband. Thank you for always reminding me why I should keep going.

For my friends, who always kept tabs on how I was doing in my writing journey and checking in on me when they knew I was struggling. It meant more than you know.
Thank you Kelli!

About the Author

Obscured was C. M.'s debut novel. What began as a way to spend her free time slowly transitioned into a passion for writing.

C. M. is a mother of three. She grew up in the sunshine state of Arizona with a love of reading and an ambition to write. But she never took her writing seriously until after the birth of her first child. After that she took up writing more seriously in her spare time and hasn't stopped since.